A Touch of Silk

By Caro Fraser

THE CAPER COURT SERIES

A Touch of Silk

CARO FRASER

Allison & Busby Limited
11 Wardour Mews
London W1F 8AN
allisonandbusby.com

First published in Great Britain by Allison & Busby in 2020.

A CIP catalogue record for this book is available from
the British Library.

First Edition

ISBN 978-0-7490-2582-3

Typeset in 11/16 pt Sabon LT Pro by
Allison & Busby Ltd

The paper used for this Allison & Busby publication
has been produced from trees that have been legally sourced
from well-managed and credibly certified forests.

Printed and bound by
CPI Group (UK) Ltd, Croydon, CR0 4YY

CHAPTER ONE

It was a raw, blustery Monday in late March, and a biting wind laden with bursts of icy rain whipped the bare branches of the trees in King's Bench Walk. Anthony Cross, a tall, dark-haired barrister in his mid-thirties, swung himself off his bicycle and eased it into the bike rack. As he did so, he caught sight of a familiar, silver-haired figure in a cashmere coat crossing the cobbles.

'Morning,' he called out.

Leo Davies smiled as he drew near, his heart lifting in genuine pleasure at the sight of the younger man. 'Good morning. How was the holiday?'

'Barbados was excellent, thanks. Bit of a pain coming back to this.'

He locked his bike and the two of them made their way together up King's Bench Walk to the chambers where they both worked. 5 Caper Court, one of the most renowned sets of commercial chambers in the Temple, was home to some forty or so barristers, whose interests were protected and careers guided under the benign supervision of Henry Dawes, the head clerk, and his deputy, Felicity Waller.

It was Felicity who greeted Leo and Anthony as they came into the clerks' room that morning. Buxom, cheerful, with dark curly hair and an irrepressible personality, her appearance was somewhat at odds with the dignity of her office. Instead of the customary black-and-white business attire of most of her colleagues, she dressed to suit her mood, expressed today in the form of a very short bright red skirt, black tights and knee-length boots, and a tight-fitting blue woollen jumper.

'Morning, Mr D,' she called out cheerily. He was her favourite amongst the tenants of 5 Caper Court. She thought of him as one of the few genuine people in chambers. He might be the most brilliant commercial QC in London, with a raft of well-heeled international clients and a reputation for being both formidable and charming. She liked the fact that, unlike most of his peers, Leo had come up the hard way, from working-class beginnings in a Welsh village, with none of the benefits of a public school education and the network of opportunity that went with it. He had also helped her weather a variety of storms in her life, both emotional and professional, and she had a bit of a crush on him – he might be nearer sixty than fifty, but with those eyes, and that beautiful silver hair, he was still a looker.

'Good morning, Felicity.'

'You know you've got a con with Bilboroughs soon?'

'I do indeed. I thought I'd be here half an hour ago. The traffic on the Embankment was hellish.'

6

'Maybe you should be like Mr Cross and get yourself a bike. You'd get around a lot quicker.'

'You're probably right,' said Leo, 'but I don't really want to come into chambers sweating, and then have to spend half an hour showering and changing. To say nothing of breathing in a load of particulates.'

At that moment a blonde woman in a black suit strode into the clerks' room, took her post from the pigeonhole and left without a glance or word of acknowledgement to the others.

'Who was that?' asked Anthony.

'Natalie King,' replied Henry. 'She joined us from 7 KBW while you were away.' Henry Dawes was in his late thirties, with a mournful demeanour that masked a light soul and a loving heart. He had long nursed a deep and abiding affection for Felicity, but an incipient romance between them a few years ago – which had withered and died on Felicity's part within a few months – had left a mark on their otherwise harmonious relationship.

'Oh yes – the Claire Underwood of the commercial world. Scary.' Anthony sighed as he unzipped his parka. 'I don't know who anyone is any more – hardly anyone comes into chambers, and everyone seems to get e-briefs. Give me a hard copy any day. The last time I was in court they spent fifteen minutes trying to locate a witness bundle that had simply disappeared from the system overnight.'

'Bit of an exaggeration to say no one comes in any more,' observed Leo. 'They have to, for all our endless committee meetings. We seem to be forming a new committee every week. The bloody things are so disruptive.'

'The younger element seem to like them,' observed Henry.

'The Hitler Youth lot, you mean – they just love structures and rules. Sometimes it feels like being run by a kind of junior thought police. Where's the individualism? The whole place is becoming so corporate.'

'You're such a rebel, Mr D.' Felicity smiled.

'As I'm constantly being reminded.'

Leo and Anthony left the clerks' room and went upstairs.

Leo paused on the landing outside his room. 'Speaking of meetings, the pupillage committee is meeting tomorrow – you're on that, aren't you?'

'Afraid so. I couldn't think of a decent excuse not to be.'

'Maybe you can give my candidate, Alistair Egan, a bit of a leg-up,' said Leo, as he keyed in his security code. 'He did a mini-pupillage with you, didn't he?'

'Yes. I liked him. Seemed very much on the ball.'

'He's remarkably promising. I want to make sure he gets an interview.' He gave Anthony a glance. 'Care to come in for a moment? I was instructed on a grounding case recently, and I could do with your views.'

Anthony followed Leo into his room, which was spotlessly tidy, free of the clutter of briefs and papers that usually littered the other tenants' rooms. Neat shelves containing legal casebooks lined one wall, and on the opposite wall hung a series of German expressionist woodcuts. The furniture consisted of nothing more than an extremely expensive and well-sprung Herman Miller office chair, a polished walnut desk, and a large circular conference table. The only items that gave any clue to the inner life of Leo Davies QC were two silver-framed photographs that stood on the desk – one of a pretty, smiling young woman, Leo's daughter from a fleeting relationship twenty-seven years previously, and the other of his twelve-year-old son, Oliver, the product of a short-lived marriage that had disintegrated over a decade ago. Leo and his ex-wife Rachel, a City solicitor, remained on amenable terms and shared the care of Oliver, but the relationship was strained by the fact that Rachel, even though she had remarried, still had strong feelings for her ex-husband – feelings of both love and animosity.

Anthony took a seat. Leo hung up his coat, extracted a bundle of papers from his briefcase, and fired up his laptop. He glanced at Anthony, taking in his easy, athletic posture and the holiday tan that enhanced his good looks, remembering the day he had first set foot in this room, raw, fresh-faced, barely more than a boy in his Marks & Spencer suit, eager to learn and please. Now, some fifteen years later, he was an assured, much-sought-after junior barrister with a reputation for speed and thoroughness, a healthy bank balance and discerning tastes for the finer things in life. Leo felt he had been responsible for a good part of Anthony's development. He liked to think his mentoring had been more than merely professional, that he had educated Anthony socially, artistically, intellectually – and sexually, too, on the basis that such beauty could not be allowed to go to waste. He felt no guilt about that. Leo was beyond guilt. He had always taken his pleasures where he found them, with men and women, being of the view that everyone's sexual sensibilities were simply there for the awakening. For Leo, his own personal pleasure had always been paramount, and if he was dimly aware that Anthony, in the wake of their occasional sexual encounters – and nothing had occurred for a long time now – felt any self-disgust or unhappiness, that had merely added a certain relish.

9

Leo's gaze shifted from Anthony to his laptop screen. 'Let me just bring up the instructions.'

While Leo scrolled through pages of documents, Anthony glanced at the photograph of Leo's daughter, Gabrielle, with a flicker of disquiet. It was in the past now, but he couldn't help thinking that the Fates that had brought her into his life had been particularly malicious. Had he known she was Leo's daughter, would he ever have slept with her? The whole thing was bizarrely confused. Until a few years ago Leo himself hadn't even known he had a daughter until, armed with background information from her mother, Gabrielle had tracked him down. Anthony couldn't help wondering now, looking back, if he had been attracted to her because she reminded him of Leo. But that romance was dead and done now, and probably just as well. A complex case had taken him to Singapore for months on end, and the thing had simply fizzled out – though he'd been surprised and mildly hurt by the speed with which her affection and enthusiasm had cooled. Leo had been ostensibly indifferent, but it was only when the Singapore case settled that Anthony realised that it had been Leo who had been largely instrumental in getting him instructed on it in the first place.

Leo, Leo. Anthony studied the older man as he gazed at the laptop screen, its faint light etching the sharpness of his cheekbones, and the wing-like darkness of eyebrows that contrasted with his thick silver hair. Those eyes, too – a piercing blue that could flash with inviting warmth or glacial coldness, depending on his mood. The charisma of the man was undeniable. In his early days at 5 Caper Court, when he was young and idealistic, Anthony's heart used to contract with pleasure at hearing Leo's voice, his laughter in the clerks' room, or the sound of his swift footstep on the stairs. The knowledge that at any moment he would see Leo, be able to talk to and listen to him, would set off shockwaves of excitement. At twenty-one, he had never met anyone so witty, so knowledgeable about life and all the fine things to be had from it, and at the same time so profoundly intelligent, so passionate about the law, and with such a razor-sharp intellect. That he and Leo came from similar backgrounds – families without much money, a grammar school and non-Oxbridge education – had made him feel they had a special bond. Infatuation, pure and simple. It was undeniably still there. But it had taken some time to find out just how coolly negligent Leo could be where people were concerned, how careless of their feelings. He remembered all too clearly the night their friendship had tipped into something else – something he still couldn't understand or properly acknowledge. So yes – just as well he and Gabrielle were no longer seeing one another.

'Here we go,' said Leo, leaning back in his chair. 'The *Alpha Six*, bulk carrier, loaded a cargo of fifty thousand tons of iron ore in Liberia, and grounded half a mile out of port. A constructive total loss. We're on for the charterers.'

'Don't tell me. The cargo shifted due to excessive moisture content, and the shipowners are saying the charterers falsified the cargo declaration?'

'How did you guess? Our P&I club has had surveyors running around out there for weeks. I know you had a similar case a few months ago, so I thought I'd pick your brain.'

11

Anthony raised an eyebrow. 'As cases go, isn't this rather below your pay grade?'

'The charterer is Montial. They used to put all their work Charles Brownwood's way, but he's moving to the bench, and they want someone new to instruct. If this one goes well it could open up a lucrative line of work.'

'Nice to have the world's largest commodities trader briefing you on a regular basis.'

'Quite. Also, this shipment was one of the first to come out of their new mining facility in Liberia. They want to be seen to be running a reliable operation, and this incident doesn't exactly promote that image.'

They discussed the case for fifteen minutes or so, then Anthony glanced at his watch. 'I'd best make tracks. I'm due in court in an hour.' As he rose to leave, he couldn't help asking, 'How's Gabrielle these days?'

'Fine, so far as I know. I hardly see her from one month to the next. She's got a new tenancy now in a criminal set in Bedford Row. Or maybe you already knew that.'

'Yes, I heard.' He'd never discussed with Leo his break-up with Gabrielle. What was there to say, in any event? 'Right, I'll get going. See you later.'

The door closed. Leo sat, reflecting. Anthony evidently still had feelings for Gabrielle. But it was for everyone's good that that relationship had come to an end. It hadn't been difficult to sow the seeds of its destruction, by dropping a mention to a friend of a friend of Gabrielle's the manufactured rumour that Anthony was conducting quite a steamy affair with one of the female partners in the Singapore law firm. As he'd anticipated, Gabrielle had picked it up and come to him with her concerns, and it had been the easiest thing in the world to tell her that, regretfully, he'd heard the same thing, at the same time advising her that rather than confronting Anthony with his behaviour, she'd be best off cutting her losses, retaining her dignity and cool, and letting the relationship peter out. Touching, he reflected, how readily his daughter had believed him. But he had acted out of her best interests. Given the history between himself and Anthony, any relationship between Anthony and his daughter had seemed positively unhealthy. There were plenty of other young men for her to fall in love with.

As he moved his laptop and papers over to the conference table for the meeting, his mobile phone rang. The sight of Sergei's name on the screen gave him one of those delicious, heart-stopping moments that didn't come often enough these days. He let the phone buzz for a moment, then answered it, keeping his tone casual.

'Sergei – it's been a while.'

'Hi, Leo.' The voice was warm, dark, Russian-accented. 'How are you?'

'I'm well – you?'

'Tired. Got in at seven this morning from New York.' His voice held a yawn. Leo imagined his lean dancer's body stretched out on some hotel bed. 'The company is in London for two weeks till the end of April. I thought maybe we could get together.'

Leo allowed a second's hesitation before responding. 'Listen, I'm just about to go into a meeting. How about if I call you later?'

'Yeah, sure.' Leo heard the shrug of disappointment in Sergei's voice. Perfect.

He ended the call. Nothing for six months – and Leo knew for a fact that the Barinov Ballet Company had had two tour dates in London in the past year – and suddenly he rang out of the blue wanting to meet up. As though he was the one who set the terms. Leo pondered for a moment, wondering how to play this. Not to call back, to let the fortnight pass without seeing Sergei and enjoying his beautiful body, would be cutting off his own nose to spite his face. It was just a question of making it clear who was in control. And that, of course, was part of the fun.

Shortly after six Leo drove back from chambers to his home in Chelsea. He had bought the handsome three-storey house in Gratton Crescent a few years ago. It was larger than he needed, but it gave Oliver his own bedroom and playroom, and Leo liked the well-proportioned rooms with their long windows, and the leafy peace of the large rear garden. He eased the Aston Martin into a parking bay and got out. The blustery weather earlier in the day had died away, and for the first time, the air held a mild note of spring. The clocks had gone forward the previous weekend, and the evening sky was still light. He went up the steps and unlocked the front door. The house was silent. As he took off his overcoat he noticed that the coatrack was laden with what seemed like a ridiculous number of Sarah's jackets and coats. Why couldn't she put stuff back in her wardrobe? It made the hallway look spectacularly messy. On impulse he gathered them from the hooks and carted them all upstairs, and dumped them in her bedroom. She'd left in a rush the day before, headed off on a spa break with some girlfriends, and the room was in its usual untidy state, with clothes over chairs, the curtains still drawn, and a scattering of make-up on her dressing table.

He gazed around the room in irritation. As an on-off girlfriend, he liked having Sarah around. She was a clever, stimulating girl, and extremely sexy. She understood him in ways that few other people did. But when, in a moment of unusual susceptibility, he had suggested she should move in with him, he hadn't realised that enforced companionship might rob their relationship of one of its most attractive aspects – unpredictability. True, she was volatile and impulsive, and hugely undomesticated, and led her own life much of the time. But she took for granted the rather messy space she now occupied in his life. Sexually she was too available. She had made him too available. He compensated for all of this by seeing other people on the side – being careful that she should never find out.

His mind moved to Sergei. It might be irksome that the touring life of a ballet dancer made it impossible to predict when an opportunity might arise to continue their clandestine affair, but surely that was the point? Therein lay the excitement, the challenge. He took his phone from his pocket and rang Sergei's number.

'Hi.' Sergei's tone was light, expectant. He sounded relieved to get Leo's call. Which was just the balance Leo wanted.

'Hi. Are you still tired, or did you manage to get some sleep?'

'A few hours. I'm feeling OK.'

'Good. I thought maybe you'd like to come round this evening. Have some dinner, maybe stay the night – unless you have rehearsals tomorrow?'

'We don't start rehearsing till Wednesday. Everyone's jet-lagged. Yeah, I'd like to come over. Give me an hour.'

Leo returned his phone to his pocket and went downstairs to the kitchen to put together some ingredients for dinner. Something light, perhaps, bearing in mind the pleasurable exertions that lay ahead.

CHAPTER TWO

The next morning Leo was up at eight. He showered, dressed, made coffee, and took some up to the bedroom where Sergei was drowsing amongst a tangle of sheets.

'Here you go. Something to perk you up.' Leo set the mug down next to the bed and went to fetch a tie from the closet.

Sergei sat up and reached out for the coffee, and Leo cast an appreciative glance at his lean, well-muscled body, the tapering waist and narrow hips. Dancers had such a beautiful blend of strength and grace. Last night had been a refreshing change from sexual domesticity with Sarah, which made it all the more irritating to think that he had to take steps to ensure she didn't find out. There would be hell to pay if she did. As long as she lived beneath his roof, he could do without domestic squabbles.

He finished knotting his tie and shrugged on his suit jacket. Sergei reached out a hand. 'Stay for half an hour?'

Leo gazed into Sergei's dark, liquid eyes and returned his smile. 'I'd love to, but I can't.'

Sergei pouted theatrically. The camp gesture irritated Leo, but he bent and kissed him, saying, 'Help yourself to breakfast. You know where everything is.'

Sergei yawned and lay back on the pillows. 'I'll call you before the company leaves London.'

The pupillage committee was meeting at ten that morning. It was composed mainly of younger members of chambers, but Leo still felt it his duty, as head of chambers, to attend, tedious though he found it. The job of the committee was to consider applications from candidates hopeful of securing a pupillage at 5 Caper Court, a much-sought-after, twelve-month opportunity to work on cases and learn from the best minds in chambers, and carrying with it the possibility of a permanent tenancy at the end.

Leo took a seat next to Anthony as the various committee members trickled into the meeting room. 'Tell me, how much do we award our pupils these days?' he murmured.

'It's gone up to seventy grand.'

'Good grief. And tax-free, too. Back in my day, unless your parents could afford to pay your way, you had to get by on what you could scrape together from scholarships and part-time work.'

'You have to admit it's made it less elitist.'

'You think so?' Leo glanced up in surprise as Natalie King took a seat at the end of the table. 'Why is she here?'

Anthony shrugged. 'Maybe she's keen to get involved in stuff.'

Leo regarded Natalie. She was dressed in an elegant and expensively cut black suit and a cream silk blouse, with minimal jewellery and make-up, and wore her blonde hair in a shoulder-length bob. Now in her mid-forties, she was still extremely attractive, in a somewhat chilly way. Had they had a thing together in their younger days? He wasn't entirely sure, but would be surprised if they hadn't. In his encounters with her on numerous cases over the years he had found her to be an intellectually daunting opponent, and a formidable advocate, and he had welcomed her arrival at 5 Caper Court. She would be an asset.

Lisa Blackmore, the chair of the committee, called the meeting to order. She was a diminutive thirty-year-old, with whom Leo had what could best be described as a somewhat prickly relationship. He admired her abilities as a lawyer, but was troubled by her lack of humour, and her beady-eyed tendency to focus on minor squabbles in chambers and turn them into major issues. She was one of a high-minded, up-and-coming cohort of younger tenants who regarded 5 Caper Court not as a loose, friendly association of individuals bound together by agreements that recognised their joint and several interests, but as a sleek, corporate vehicle that would propel their ambitious careers along prosperous and (of course) righteous paths. These younger tenants regarded Leo and others of his generation, with their relaxed and caustically incorrect attitudes to life and work, as dinosaurs, so much dead wood to be cleared out of their paths.

On Lisa's left sat Arun Sikand, 5 Caper Court's first Sikh tenant, and another young member of what Leo regarded as the militant tendency within chambers.

'Right, let's get down to business,' said Lisa. 'We have an unusual situation, in that one of the people to whom we offered a pupillage has dropped out. So we're only looking at a handful of potential interviewees – four or five at the outside, I'd have thought. Let's run through who we've got.'

They considered the merits of the various applicants for fifteen minutes or so, and just as Leo was about to mention his protégé, Alistair Egan, Natalie spoke up.

'There's a name I'd like to add to the list.' She slid a sheaf of papers over to Lisa. 'Sian Attwood. She's not a conventional candidate, but I think she's exceptionally strong. For the past four years she's been lecturing in law at Oriel College, but she decided she'd like to change tack and take up a career at the Bar. She was admitted last year. She has a starred double-first from Cambridge, she's won any number of scholarships, and last year she wrote an outstanding paper on dishonest assistance of a breach of trust after the exercise of a lien on sub-freights.'

Leo raised an eyebrow. 'A somewhat esoteric aspect of law.'

'She sounds interesting,' said Lisa, glancing through the papers and then passing them to Arun.

David Liphook, a stocky, middle-aged QC, and a long-standing friend of Leo's, spoke up. 'Don't you think academics tend to be – well, somewhat academic? Being a practitioner at the Commercial Bar, or in our chambers at any rate, requires a high degree of pragmatism.'

'That's something you can judge at interview,' said Natalie.

'Well, while we're at it,' said Leo, 'I have someone in mind as well. Alistair Egan. Some of you may remember

him. He's done a couple of mini-pupillages with us.'
There was a murmur of recognition. 'He may not have
a starred double-first from Cambridge, but he's shown
exceptional ability, and I for one would like to see him
given a chance with us.'

'What are his qualifications?' asked Natalie.

'A two-one from Newcastle. In history. He did a GDL
conversion.'

'Is that really the quality of candidate we're looking
for?' Natalie glanced around the table. 'I would have
thought an Oxbridge degree – a first, or a two-one at
least – must be a prerequisite?'

'Well, if it was, I for one wouldn't be here,' replied Leo.

'The Bar was a less competitive place back then,' said
Natalie. 'Surely nowadays we can afford the luxury of only
looking at those of the highest calibre.'

There was a brief, astonished silence. Leo smiled, and
cast his glance downwards.

For Anthony the insult was too blatant to ignore. 'It
seems to me you wouldn't recognise calibre if you fell
over it on the stairs,' he said to Natalie. She stared at him
coldly, and people shifted uneasily in their chairs. 'Perhaps
a few weeks in our company isn't long enough for you to
properly judge the contribution of your fellow tenants. We
don't just go by qualifications and pieces of paper. Talent
is everything. Which is why I vote to give Alistair Egan an
interview. He was very impressive in his short time here.'

'Hear, hear,' said David.

'I don't see why we shouldn't interview both,' said Lisa.

'I do,' said Natalie. 'I hesitate to make this personal, but
I think Leo may have a particular reason why he's putting

this young man's name forward.' She turned to Leo. 'Wasn't it because of some special relationship with you that he got his mini-pupillage here in the first place?'

Leo raised his eyes and met Natalie's frigid stare. 'That is an outrageous suggestion. And you have absolutely no justification for making it.'

'I think I have every justification. These may be enlightened times, but how can we turn a blind eye to the kind of romantic favouritism that has characterised your behaviour with junior members of the Bar over the years?'

'Look here, we've all taken an interest in and promoted talented youngsters,' interjected David, in an attempt to defuse the situation. 'That hardly amounts—'

Natalie didn't take her eyes off Leo. 'He's an extremely attractive young man, and I happen to know that you've spent an inordinate amount of time in his company.'

'Are you joking?' demanded Anthony.

Natalie shifted her gaze to him. 'You of all people should be able to spot the signs.'

There was an appalled silence.

'I think you should be very careful what you say,' said Leo.

Lisa Blackmore sat silently, glancing from Leo to Natalie as though weighing up the balance of power.

David murmured in a placatory manner, 'Please, I think we should calm down and try to look rationally—'

'If this committee interviews Sian Attwood without interviewing Alistair Egan, as head of chambers I will demand a full investigation into the frankly slanderous remarks made here today,' interrupted Leo.

Lisa glanced at Natalie. 'If you have nothing to substantiate your remarks, I think maybe you should withdraw them.'

Natalie shrugged. 'Very well. But you can't go on with this slapdash way of doing things. These chambers need to apply rigorous standards, and academically this young man sounds inadequate.'

'That, as you have pointed out,' replied Leo, 'is something you can judge at interview.'

David said quickly, 'Look here, since both candidates come on the personal recommendation of two senior members of chambers, I think we should add their names to the list.' There were hesitant murmurs of agreement. 'That gives us four candidates in all, I think?'

Lisa nodded. She wrote for a moment, and then read out the list of names. 'I'll notify the committee of the dates for interview in due course.' She looked up. 'I think that concludes the business of the meeting for the day. Thank you, everyone.'

Leo rose without a word, pushing back his chair, and left the room, followed by Anthony and David. The other committee members filed out, leaving just Natalie, Lisa and Arun.

'Do you know something no one else does?' Lisa asked Natalie.

'We all know Leo Davies' reputation. He has a history of promoting good-looking young men in whom he's taken – shall we call it, a close personal interest? Of course, it's not the kind of thing that is ever brought up—'

'You just did,' observed Arun.

Natalie gave him a cool glance. 'I would have thought you younger tenants would want to promote diversity within chambers. If you take on Leo Davies' protégé, you're just perpetuating the unreconstructed, stale male stereotype that does the image of the Bar no favours. At Caper Court we currently have thirty-two junior counsel, of whom just nine are women. Out of our ten QCs only two are women – myself and Ann Halliday. Someone like Sian Attwood is just what we need. We need to take steps to correct the gender and ethnic imbalance. We certainly don't need another of Leo's young male acolytes.'

'Well, we're interviewing them both,' said Lisa.

'More's the pity.' Natalie rose and left the committee room.

'That was unexpected,' remarked Leo as he and Anthony went upstairs.

'I'm surprised you're not angrier,' said Anthony. 'I'd be furious.' They reached the landing outside Leo's room, and after hesitating for a moment he asked, 'There's no truth in what she said, is there?'

'Of course not.'

'Then what is it she's got against you?'

'Maybe she made a pass at me once, and I wasn't in the mood. Who knows?'

'Not everything is about sex, you know.'

He gave Anthony a smile. 'I think you'll find it is.' He went into his room and closed the door.

As she pulled her car to a jerky stop in Gratton Crescent, Sarah Coleman was in a filthy mood. The country spa break that she and three friends had booked weeks ago had turned into a non-event. They had all set off after work in high spirits the previous evening, Sarah driving, but a pile-up on the M11 had caused an enormous traffic jam, and a journey that should have taken one hour turned into four. Then when they eventually reached the spa it turned out that Chloe, who had arranged the break, had made the prepaid booking for the week before in error. After a heated exchange over the spa's no-refund policy, they'd been forced to check into a nearby Travelodge. The drive back this morning had not been fun, with a lengthy squabble over whether or not they should all be forced to pay for Chloe's mistake.

She pulled down the sun visor and stared at her reflection in the mirror. She'd slept badly and she looked like shit. She sighed. She would be thirty-five soon, and it showed. She snapped the visor up and glanced towards the house, pondering her current domestic situation. When Leo had suggested last year that she should move in with him, she'd imagined it meant he had ideas of settling down. She'd be only too happy to marry him, to be kept in modest luxury and never have to work again. She'd had enough of slogging away in the City at her job as a senior legal in a shipping insurance firm. Marrying Leo would solve all her problems, and there was no reason why it shouldn't work. All good relationships were founded on mutual affection and respect, and they had enough of that. As for sex, it was as good now as it had been the first time, if not better. Her spine still tingled when she recalled the extraordinary and instant physical attraction between them on their first encounter years ago, at a dull academic summer garden party at some Oxford college. Ten minutes after meeting they'd left in Leo's car, headed for his country home and several hours of the most blissfully erotic sex. That afternoon had turned into a whole summer, an unspoken arrangement in which she looked after the house while he toiled in London, cooked and lazed around, and made herself generally available to Leo's whims and desires, with the occasional – and from Sarah's point of view, tiresome – participation of James, a local boy he'd picked up along the way. The trouble was, that summer had set the template for their relationship – sex without emotional commitment, friendship without loyalty. Besides their enduring mutual attraction, both physical and intellectual, they both possessed strong instincts for self-preservation, and over the years they had been kind and cruel to one another in equal measure, as circumstances required. And therein lay the fundamental flaw. That lack of trust was making it difficult for her to inch him towards marrying her.

She sat in the car for some minutes, weighing up strategies. It looked as though she was going to have to rewrite the rules of engagement, starting with her own behaviour. So far, she'd been careful to maintain the undemanding premise of their relationship, but perhaps now she needed to soften herself, be less emotionally casual, pay greater attention to domestic detail. Maybe she should cook more often in the evenings, even iron his shirts – he still paid three quid a time to have them laundered, which was fine by her, but these small things had a certain significance – steer him into going out together, try subtly to redirect their shared existence and shape it more in terms of a couple. It could be done. She had to give it a try, at any rate. Time was ticking on.

She got out of the car, fetched her overnight bag from the boot, and crossed the road to the house, filled with a new sense of purpose. She would have a long, hot shower, and then consider how best to effect the transformation of their relationship in slow, careful steps. Her well-worn fantasy – a wedding, beautiful babies (with their combined good looks, any offspring were bound to be beautiful), and the eventual prospect of becoming Lady Davies, when Leo was appointed a Supreme Court judge – suddenly had a fresher feel to it.

She went upstairs to her room and noticed that the door to Leo's bedroom was ajar and the room was in darkness. Not like him to leave the curtains drawn. He always, in what she thought was a schoolboyishly sweet way, left his bedroom in pristine condition before he went to work, curtains back, bed made, everything neat and tidy. Setting down her bag, she slipped into the room, went to the window, and drew back the heavy curtains. She turned, and was greeted by the sight of a well-honed male body sprawled naked on the bed, one that wasn't Leo's. Sergei roused himself sleepily, blinking against the light. For a long, wordless moment, he and Sarah stared at one another. Without any particular haste, Sergei drew the sheet up and frowned in puzzlement. Was she the housekeeper, or maybe the cleaner?

As she regarded the handsome stranger in Leo's bed, Sarah felt her fantasies slowly dissolving in the acid of cold reality. She'd spent these last months blithely thinking that Leo was exclusively hers. How could she possibly have imagined that his affairs were a thing of the past? This stranger was probably just one of any number of lovers he'd had since she'd moved in.

'Hi,' said Sergei, unsure of the etiquette for this situation. The girl, whoever she was, really didn't look too pleased to find him here. 'I'm Sergei.'

Sarah made no reply. She went to her room and shut the door. She sat down on the bed, only vaguely noticing the heap of coats and jackets, feeling numb, trying to process her thoughts and feelings. A few moments later she heard the Sergei person go downstairs. She listened to the sounds of him moving around in the kitchen in an unconcerned and unhurried way. Probably making himself breakfast. And why not? He had every right to be here. As much right as she did. They were both just Leo's playthings. Feelings of anger and humiliation swept through her. All these months she'd let herself be deceived. What a bloody fool she was. But she had only herself to blame. She'd always known the kind of person Leo was – unscrupulous, hedonistic, letting his desires dictate his behaviour. And their relationship had no rules. So she had no right to feel like a victim.

She sat thinking for a long while, until her anger had ebbed away and she was left facing the stark reality of her position. She couldn't stay. She couldn't delude herself any longer. He was never going to change, never going to marry her, or see her as the most important person in his life. The only individual of any importance to Leo was himself. She grabbed a few more clothes and added them to what was already in her overnight bag, together with an extra pair of shoes. She would stay at her father's flat in Westminster till she'd sorted herself out, turfed out the tenant she'd installed in her flat. Thank God she hadn't sold it. She would return tomorrow when Leo was at work and collect all the rest of her belongings. She felt a bleak flicker of satisfaction, thinking how startled he'd be to find her gone – gone without explanation. He might even be upset. Though that was probably too much to hope for.

When she went downstairs she found Sergei in the hallway, shrugging on his leather jacket. She glanced at him, thinking with detachment how extraordinarily good-looking he was, exactly Leo's type. They both went to open the front door at the same time, which caused momentary confusion.

'After you,' said Sarah, in a tone of mild irony.

'Please,' replied Sergei, opening the door with a courteous gesture, 'after *you*.'

She crossed the road to her car, slung her bag onto the passenger seat, and got in. Sergei stood on the steps, watching as she drove away, then thrust his hands into his pockets, glancing up and down the road as he waited for his Uber, shivering a little in the chilly spring air.

CHAPTER THREE

The following Saturday morning, Gabrielle called round while Leo was having breakfast. She was dressed in a crop top and leggings, and her dark blonde hair was pulled back in a scruffy ponytail. Her fine-boned face, much like Leo's, with the same thick, dark brows, was pink with exertion.

'Thought you might fancy joining me on my run,' she said, sinking onto a kitchen chair and depositing her phone and headphones on the table. She took a swig of Leo's orange juice.

'A kind thought, but I'm playing squash later – that's enough exercise for one day.' He glanced at her skimpy running gear. 'Aren't you freezing?'

'I warm up quickly. Besides, it's quite mild out there.'

'Have you had breakfast? I can offer you some rather fine toasted Waitrose sourdough.'

'Go on, then.' She went to the fridge and poured herself

a fresh glass of juice while Leo busied himself at the toaster. 'Who are you playing squash with?'

'Anthony.'

'How is he?'

To Leo, the fractional pause before she asked the question spoke volumes. Despite the fact the relationship was long over – and he assuaged his own guilt at the part he had played in that with the thought that it would have ended sooner or later, anyway – she evidently still cared about him.

'He's well. Just got back from a holiday in the Caribbean.' He brought the toast over. 'There you are. Help yourself to butter and marmalade.'

'Thanks.' Gabrielle reached for the butter. 'Did he go on his own?'

'No idea.'

Gabrielle took a bite of toast, then observed, 'It's very quiet round here. Where's Sarah?'

'She's gone.'

At first, when he'd come home to discover that Sarah had taken all her belongings and disappeared without a word, he'd been perplexed. But over drinks a couple of days later, Sergei had casually mentioned his encounter with her, and Leo had put two and two together. He had no intention of calling her, or apologising. She'd always known the deal. In a way he was sorry, but he knew himself well enough to accept that sooner or later his infidelities brought their own consequences. And that was fine with him. It made for a natural balance.

'You mean she's left?'

Leo nodded. Gabrielle sipped her juice. She'd never particularly liked Sarah. 'Did you have a fight?'

31

'Not as such. But I suspect she wants certain things I can't give her.'

'Which are?'

'I think like most women she's looking for some kind of long-term stability. And that, as you know, is not my speciality.'

'You think that's what most women want? Some bloke to look after them and provide for them? Honestly, Leo, you're an unreconstructed chauvinist. That's really not what women want, or need, from men any more.'

'Is that so?' He smiled and drained his coffee cup. 'I'm going for a shower. Enjoy your run. Lunch sometime soon?'

She nodded. 'I'll text you.'

He dropped a light kiss on her head and left the kitchen.

Gabrielle sat for a few minutes, finishing her toast and thinking about Anthony, and about the way their relationship had ended. Once upon a time she had genuinely believed it had potential. Then the rumour had reached her that he was having some kind of affair out in Singapore, and she'd stopped emailing him, taking the corresponding silence at his end as a sign of his guilt, and that things were over between them. He knew that she knew. It absolved him from doing anything more. They hadn't spoken since. But here Leo was, playing regular games of squash with him, carrying on their cosy friendship as though the way Anthony had treated her was of no consequence. It suddenly struck her, in a way that it hadn't before, that for Leo his relationship with Anthony was of paramount importance. Could this have had any bearing on her break-up with Anthony? She picked up her phone and headphones, and left the house to carry on with her run and think it through properly.

Leo and Anthony always played their games of squash at the RAC Club in the Mall. Despite being twenty years older, Leo generally gave Anthony a good run for his money, and today was no exception. They played three games, drawing two, with Leo winning the third by just two points.

'I'll have you next time,' said Anthony. 'How about a swim?'

They changed and made their way out to the swimming pool, an area of art deco opulence in Sicilian marble. In the mid-afternoon quiet the pool lay still and blue, reflecting the magnificence of the surrounding Doric columns and the high coved ceiling.

'I never get tired of how beautiful this place is,' remarked Leo. 'And it may say something about the chip on my shoulder, but it gives me immense satisfaction to know that the Oxford & Cambridge Club can't hold a candle to this.'

'Natalie really got to you the other day, didn't she?'

'All that bullshit about how only people with firsts from Oxbridge deserve a place in chambers. She claims to be a champion of diversity, and at the same time she wants the Bar to be populated with the academically elite. Something a tad hypocritical in that.'

They swam a few leisurely lengths, chatting, then went to shower and change.

'Do you have time for a drink?' asked Leo, as they got dried.

'Afraid not. Barry and I arranged to go and see Chay. He's not so good these days.'

Leo glanced at Anthony. 'Really? What's up?'

Anthony said nothing for a moment. He rubbed his hair dry and dropped the towel on the bench next to him. 'He has lung cancer. Stage four.'

'God, I'm sorry.' Leo knew Anthony's father, Chay. He was a renowned artist who, a few years previously, had established a museum and art gallery in an old brewery in Shoreditch, when the area was on the cusp of becoming fashionable, and Leo was one of the trustees of the museum. The news of his illness was a shock. He laid a hand on Anthony's shoulder, then slid his hand down the muscles of his arm and gripped his wrist in a sympathetic gesture.

Anthony felt warmth spread through his body. It was a long time since Leo had touched him. 'He hasn't told many people. I don't think he wants it known. I mean, he's having treatment, but – well, the success rate isn't good.'

'No, I know.' Leo took his hand away, and Anthony was filled with a sense of loss. Leo's mobile buzzed in his bag, and he fished for it, then walked to the other end of the changing room to take the call, shrugging on his shirt as he did so. Anthony watched him, letting the confusion of his feelings ebb away.

When the call was finished, they put their things together and left the club.

'Give your father my best,' said Leo, as they stood on the pavement.

'I will, thanks. Where are you headed?'

'To have a drink with Stephen Bishop, would you believe. That was him calling just now.' Stephen was a fellow QC at 5 Caper Court, of the same generation as Leo.

'Stephen? I didn't know you and he socialised much.'

'We don't, as a rule. He says he has something he needs to discuss with me. Maybe it's to do with chambers. He hasn't been in all week. He sounded a bit tense.'

'Well, have fun. I'll see you next week.'

Anthony cycled to his father's house in Shoreditch. It was a Georgian townhouse that had been lovingly restored, with certain eclectic modern twists, including a vast studio workshop in the basement. Anthony reckoned it had to be worth at least three million. It was a mystery and a marvel to him that his father had achieved the success he had. When he and his brother, Barry, were children, Chay had been a waster and scrounger with artistic pretensions, divorced from their mother, Judith, living in squats and dabbling in a number of creative mediums. His paintings had always seemed to Anthony to be without much distinction, abstract works that were no better or worse than similar offerings by other modern artists. But a few years ago, by being in the right place at the right time, and with the serendipity that favours the lucky few, Chay had begun to make a name for himself, and the peculiar momentum of the modern art market had propelled him to international fame. Anthony had never been able to work out whether the critical acclaim his father had received over the last few years was deserved or not. The art world was a mystery to him. The fact that he had never much liked his father hung on him these days like a guilty weight. He had always thought him vain and pretentious. It seemed unkind to feel that way about someone with cancer, but he remembered only too well what a drain he'd been on friends and family before his success, and how badly he'd treated their mother.

Anthony was surprised when a woman answered the door. She was tall and slender, with dark hair, large eyes in a small face, and was wearing a loose grey dress and chunky pieces of jewellery made out of dark stone. It took Anthony a few seconds to recognise her as Jocasta, Chay's girlfriend from the days when he was poor and struggling. The last Anthony had heard she'd been dumped along the way, together with Chay's socialist ideals and cheap clothes, the latter two replaced by a shiny new commercial pragmatism and designer outfits, and Jocasta by a series of more beautiful women. Yet here she was, sweet-faced and otherworldly as ever, her long hair now cropped in an elfin cut, beaming at him in delight. She was girlish still, but he estimated she must be in her mid-forties.

'Anthony! How lovely to see you.' She embraced him.

'Jocasta. It's been a while. How are you?'

'Oh, I'm wonderful, thanks. Come in.' She laid a gentle hand on his arm and drew him into the house. 'You've grown up since I last saw you. Sorry, that sounds like such an old-lady thing to say. Come down to the studio. Chay's working.'

'So, what are you up to these days?' asked Anthony. The last he recalled she'd been part of some artists' co-operative, weaving blankets.

'I have my own business, making hand-crafted textiles. Not a great living, but the important thing is to do what you love, don't you think?'

Anthony murmured in agreement. He followed her down broad, white concrete steps to Chay's basement workshop. It was a good fifty feet long, and the part that extended beyond the house was made entirely of glass, to allow natural light to the far end of the studio. The walls were lined with big open cupboards and shelves, stuffed with a chaotic mix of canvases and sketches and notebooks, and the middle of the room was taken up by two large central workstations littered with artist's debris. The area nearest the stairs contained a long sofa, a low table and a couple of armchairs, with a desk and files to one side serving as an office. Chay was at the far end of the studio, seated in front of a canvas, working to the sound of *Chromos* coming from wall-mounted speakers. Even from this distance Anthony could see how much weight he had lost. Always a thin man, he was now gaunt, the gaping spaces where his buttoned shirt hung on his emaciated frame making his neck and wrists look scrawny. The familiar grey-bristle halo of short-shaved hair was gone; his treatment had left him bald, and when he turned to look at Anthony his lack of eyebrows gave his face a startled expression. He laid down his brush and got up slowly.

Anthony walked to the end of the room and gave his father a hug. He did so lightly. Chay felt as if he might snap in two.

'Have a seat,' said Chay, sitting down again. Anthony pulled up a chair.

'Can I get you two a drink?' asked Jocasta, her smiling, enigmatic gaze shifting from father to son.

'Just tea for me, thanks,' replied Chay. He turned to Anthony. 'Something stronger for you?'

'Thanks – whatever you have is fine.'

When Jocasta had left, Anthony leant forward and touched his father's hand. Tactile gestures between them were rare.

'How are you doing?'

Chay gave a wan smile. He took off his tortoiseshell-framed glasses and rubbed his eyes. 'Surviving.'

'I didn't expect to find Jocasta here. She's a blast from the past.'

'She turned up on the doorstep a few weeks ago. She'd heard I was ill.' He replaced his glasses. 'Isn't that kind? I mean, years, and she turns up just to be with me. To help. She comes with me to my treatments, keeps me company, cooks me meals – not that I want to eat, particularly . . .' His voice trailed away, then he glanced up, his expression brightening as Jocasta returned with tea for Chay, and two vodka and tonics.

'The other one's for Barry,' she said as she set them down. 'He's just locking up his motorbike.'

A minute later Barry tramped downstairs and into the studio. He was dark, like his elder brother, but with straight hair, and a broader build. He was wearing skinny black jeans and a T-shirt bearing an image of the US with an arrow pointing to the UK, and the message 'I'm With Stupid'.

He chucked down his coat, bent down and gave Chay a hug, as gentle as Anthony's had been. Anthony noticed the way his father relaxed into Barry's embrace. They had always had an easier relationship. Despite the fact that Barry had never held down a decent job in his life, and was earning barely anything in his present job as a stand-up comedian, Chay had always bestowed on Barry an approval that never seemed to come Anthony's way. Chay's socialist and anti-capitalist credentials might be worn a little thin by his commercial success, but he wasn't going to endorse what

38

he saw as his eldest son's sell-out to the establishment, in becoming a barrister.

Jocasta observed them with a radiant smile. 'It's so wonderful to see the three of you together again after all this time. I'll leave you to talk.' And she floated off upstairs.

Barry pulled up a chair and sat down. 'So, Dad. How's the treatment going?'

'Where, more like,' murmured Chay. 'I have two more to go, and if the results are what I expect them to be, I'll pack the whole thing in.'

'Hey.' Barry took a long slug of his drink. 'Don't be defeatist.'

'I'm being realistic. What I have isn't survivable. And to be honest, I'd rather check out than go through any more treatment. Better the real thing than a living death.'

Barry and Anthony nodded. A gloomy silence fell. Barry got up and began to wander round the studio. He paused by the half-completed work on the easel. It was a portrait of Jocasta in muted pinks and greys. 'Nice.'

'You should do more portraits,' observed Anthony. He was pleased that his father was working again. He had done very little in the past few years, and interest in his paintings had been kept alive largely by retrospectives, and exhibitions of his work that had been acquired by galleries or private investors.

'You never really liked my abstract work, did you?' replied Chay.

'That wasn't what I meant.'

Barry continued his wandering tour of the studio. He pulled a folder from a shelf and opened it. It contained six charcoal drawings on cartridge paper, depictions of streets around Spitalfields.

'I like these,' said Barry. 'They're really great.'

Chay glanced over. 'Oh, those. I did them a few months ago. Don't care for them much. You can have them, if you like.'

'Really?'

'I might as well give stuff away now, to people who want it. They're yours.'

'Thanks.' Barry gazed at them admiringly for a moment, then returned them to the folder. 'I'll take them next time I'm over. I'm on the bike today.' He put the folder back on the shelf and sat down again.

The conversation limped along, Barry doing his best to keep it aloft with banter and jokes. Anthony admired him for that; he was too caught up in the potent sense of his father's depressed state, the muted terror of death, to offer any light-heartedness.

At last Chay said, 'Lads, I'm pretty tired. Thanks for coming, but I think I need to lie down.' He rose slowly, and walked the length of the room with his sons. When they reached the stairs he said, 'I won't come up with you. Ask Jocasta to come down, will you?'

They said their farewells, and went upstairs. Jocasta was coming down from the upper rooms, some laundry over her arm.

'We're just off,' said Barry. 'Dad's a bit whacked.'

'The treatment takes it out of him,' replied Jocasta. 'But he insists on carrying on working. I'm thinking of moving a bed down to the studio so that he doesn't have to keep going up and down stairs.'

So, thought Anthony, she was living here. 'I'll stop by next week,' he said. 'Probably one night after work.'

'If you could ring ahead just to make sure it's convenient?' She gave a smile, and picked up her mobile from the hall table. 'I'll give you my number.'

'I can call Dad,' replied Anthony.

There was a fractional hesitation. 'Take it, just in case.'

Outside on the pavement, as he was unchaining his bike, Anthony said to Barry, 'She's moved in and taken over.'

'Well, it's good, isn't it? That he's got someone living in, looking after him. It was a bit of a surprise, finding her here. I'd forgotten all about her.'

'Maybe one of us should have done something sooner. I didn't realise how frail he was getting.' He realised he hadn't seen his father for over a month. Easter and the Barbados holiday had intervened. He felt a tug of guilt, and something else – it irked him irrationally to find Jocasta in possession.

'How could either of us look after him?' Barry straddled his motorbike. 'We both work. Best we can do is step up the visits, try to keep him cheerful. Whole thing makes me feel so fucking helpless. Let me know when you're going round next week. I'll try to be there.' He fastened his helmet, revved the throttle, and roared off.

CHAPTER FOUR

Anthony cycled home to his flat in South Kensington, and parked his bike in the hallway. He had nothing planned for the evening, and was just debating what to do when his mobile beeped. He pulled it out and glanced at the WhatsApp message. It was from Gabrielle. 'Hi, how r u?' it said.

He felt his heart thumping as he texted back, 'Good, u?' He was astonished to hear from her. The chilly silence that had fallen between them since their relationship had ended had turned, in his mind, into a cold, unbridgeable chasm.

A few seconds later she replied. 'Want to meet up?'

He texted back immediately. 'Where?'

She named a pub in Notting Hill, and added, 'C u at 8.'

He clicked his phone off, feeling astonished and pleased, but confused, too. When she'd stopped replying to his emails when he'd been out in Singapore, he'd cast around for a reason. In the end he'd had to assume she'd lost interest, that for whatever reason, she no longer wanted the relationship to continue. It had been numbingly painful at the time. And wounding to his pride to have his messages left hanging in the air, unanswered. All he'd been able to do at the time was to match her silence, and spare himself further humiliation. And here she was, casually suggesting a drink, as though none of that had happened. But he would go. Of course he would go.

His phone buzzed with a call, startling him out of his thoughts.

'Hi, Ed.' His mind was still reeling slightly from the unexpected text exchange.

'Tony!' Edward's voice was a cheerful bellow. 'Just wondering what you're up to tonight? Hold on a sec—' He began to speak to some invisible third party 'No, no – two large G&Ts and a pint of Theakston's . . .' Anthony could hear the tumult of some pub or club in the background.

He and Edward, though unalike in every regard, had become friends years ago as pupils at 5 Caper Court, both fresh from Bar school. Edward, a cheerful, thickset young man with a thatch of fair hair, was the product of a wealthy family and a private education. Anthony, on the other hand, had gone to the local comprehensive, and had only managed to fund his way through Bar school on various hard-won scholarships and bursaries. As pupils they had been in competition for the one coveted vacancy in chambers. It had looked at the time as though Edward was bound to succeed, since he was the favoured nephew of the then head of chambers, and nepotism was still a powerful force, or had been then. But partly due to Edward's total lack of aptitude – he was affable, big-hearted, and not entirely brainless, but quite without Anthony's intellect and brilliance – and partly through Leo's support for Anthony, it was Anthony who had gained the tenancy. Not that Edward had much cared – being a barrister had been just one of many career possibilities open to him until such time as he came into his trust fund. That happy event had occurred three years ago, and Edward now did little more than enjoy life, look after his stocks and shares, and occasionally invest in various friends' start-ups. Despite the differences in their backgrounds, they were good friends, and Edward's rumbustious, sociable nature had often rescued Anthony from too much hard work and introspection.

Edward's voice came back. 'Sorry about that. Bloody noisy in here. We're just round the corner in the Anglesea Arms. Why don't you pop in?'

'Can't I'm afraid, Ed.'

'Don't tell me you're working on a case? You're always fucking working, Tony! Take some time off! It's Saturday!'

'I'm meeting someone.'

'Oh, what, a girl?'

'As it happens.'

'Ah, that's all right, then. Jolly good. That reminds me, have you booked your flights for the wedding? Hold on a sec—' His voice drifted away again. 'Don't you do contactless? Bloody hell. Here you go . . .' His voice returned. 'Annabel's insisting I double-check with everyone. I think she's worried that all the easyJet flights will get booked up and people won't come.'

'Yes, I booked ages ago.'

'God, never get married – planning a wedding's a full-time job, I can tell you.'

'How would you know? You've barely ever had one.'

'Ha fucking ha. Listen, I've got tickets for the England Wales game at Twickers on the second. You fancy coming?'

'Yeah, count me in.'

'Tickets weren't cheap – a hundred and twenty-five apiece.'

'No problem. I'll stick some money in your account.'

'Great. Anyway, let's meet up for a drink next week.'

'Let's do that.'

When the call ended, Anthony tapped into his mobile bank account and sent Edward money for the ticket, knowing he might forget if he didn't do it right away. He remembered the days when it had been a source of humiliation for him not to be able to afford the expensive treats that all well-heeled young people like Ed and his friends seemed to take for granted. Nowadays it was different. He thought nothing of dining at Le Gavroche, buying front row stalls theatre tickets, and throwing over a hundred quid at a rugby match. Those times when he'd searched under sofa cushions and in jeans and jacket pockets in the hopes of finding enough pound coins to finance an evening at the pub were the reason why he worked as hard as he did, never to have to endure that excruciating feeling of being poor, when everyone around him seemed to be rich. Maybe it was a little unhealthy, this constant need to prove himself materially, to gain acceptance and inclusion. But wasn't that what happiness was all about? Being able to afford the same things as everyone around you, to work hard and live comfortably? So why was he so often afflicted by the feeling that no matter how hard he worked, and how much he earned, it would never be quite enough? To escape these disquieting thoughts, he switched on the TV to catch up on the day's football, then went to make himself something to eat before going to meet Gabrielle.

* * *

Leo was bemused that Stephen Bishop had suggested meeting in a bar in Soho, instead of one of the handful of Mayfair clubs of which he was a member. Stephen, a portly QC in his early fifties, was a barrister very much of the conventional mould. He was a kindly and easy-going character with a steady, unremarkable commercial practice – the legal directories always referred to him as 'a safe pair of hands' – who wore old-fashioned pinstripe suits, and was a member of the Beefsteak and the Athenaeum. He and his wife, Charlotte, had been married for twenty-eight years, and had four grown-up children. Soho on a Saturday night was not where one would expect to find Stephen.

The bar, situated in a basement in Kingly Street, had a heavy retro forties theme, with wartime posters on the walls, period sofas and armchairs, and fringed lamps on the tables. Although it was early, the place was busy. Leo glanced around, but couldn't see Stephen. He was about to head to the bar when someone spoke his name. He turned and saw a woman seated in the corner next to the stairs. The muted light from the table lamp showed her to be plump, middle-aged, with short brown hair, pearls at her throat and ears, dressed in a paisley wrap-over dress and low-heeled shoes. On the table in front of her was what looked like a cup of tea. She had the look of a woman of the Tory shires, and seemed out of place amongst the shabby-chic youngsters drinking overpriced cocktails from jam jars and tin mugs. It took Leo several seconds to work out that it was Stephen. He walked over, dropped his sports bag, and sat down at the table, speechless.

'Thank you for coming,' said Stephen. His face, Leo could see, was carefully made up, with warm foundation, subtle dark-brown eyeshadow and mascara, and a plum-toned lipstick. Leo's first thought, as his shock subsided, was that Stephen's face, with its familiar expression of mild anxiety, looked genuinely and pleasantly feminine. He noticed, too, that instead of his customary square, black-rimmed glasses, he was wearing a pair with lighter frames, which softened his aspect.

'I think I'll have a drink,' said Leo. He indicated Stephen's teacup. 'That isn't tea, is it?'

'God, no. It's called a Bletchley, but basically it's just a whisky sour.'

A waiter came over and Leo ordered two more cocktails. 'Well,' he said, when the waiter had gone, 'talk to me.'

There was a long, embarrassed pause. Stephen looked down at the teacup in his hand. 'You're shocked, of course.' Leo was about to speak, but Stephen went on, 'This is who I want to be. Who I am.' He spoke firmly, but his expression when he looked up was apprehensive. 'It seemed to me that you'd be the best person in chambers to tell first.' His hand trembled a little as he lifted his drink. Leo noticed that his nails were painted to match his lipstick. 'You know, because of the bisexuality thing. I imagine you know what it's like to be judged. Or misjudged.'

Leo wasn't about to tell Stephen that he had long ceased to care what anyone in chambers thought about his sexual proclivities – if indeed he ever had. There had been times in his career when he'd been aware that scrutiny of his private life, particularly by influential conservative senior members of the judiciary, might be detrimental to his career, had it not been for his own strength of personality and ability to anticipate events, but he had never been afraid of who he

47

was. Stephen, however, was afraid. He could see that. And it was understandable.

'I'm not sure . . .' Leo hesitated, looking for the right words, 'I'm not sure my position is analogous. People see bisexuality as a cover for being gay, when actually it's about sex not mattering. Not to me, at any rate.' He paused again, trying to resolve his thoughts, to reconcile the Stephen he had always known with the person sitting before him. 'What you're doing is brave, but very different.' He gazed at his friend. 'I had no idea. Simply no idea. Do you want to tell me more?'

'It's been part of my life for about ten years now. Well, longer, probably. Charlotte's always known.' Leo thought of Stephen's wife, a formidably clever Treasury Counsel. It was difficult to imagine what she must have felt, what their life together had been like, all this time. 'It's just that I realised recently that it isn't enough to – well, it can't go on being something I do in secret. This is who I am. I have to be honest. To my family. To my colleagues. To the world.' He drew a deep breath. 'I can't pretend it's been easy with the children. But it's something they're going to have to learn to accept. As I told them, we're all adults.'

Again Leo hesitated. 'May I ask – do you intend to see this through all the way?'

'What do you mean?'

'Are you going to' – the waiter arrived with the drinks and set them down; Leo waited till he'd gone – 'transition completely? Have surgery, and so on?'

'I'm not sure. That's such a hard thing to contemplate. But I know – I think I've always known – that being masculine, expressing myself in that way, isn't right for me. This is who

I'm happiest being. Maybe this is just the first step.'

'To dress as . . . ?'

'As Stephanie.' He smoothed down the skirt of his dress. 'As I say, I wanted to let you know first, because you're an old friend, and because I thought you might be able to help me – advise me how to cope with the way you think others will react in chambers.'

Leo tried to think of any cross-dressing barristers he had come across, and failed. 'I can't deny it's going to be something of a surprise to everyone.' That, he thought, was an understatement. 'I'm not sure what you can do, apart from simply – well, do as you're doing this evening. Take the plunge. I mean, I don't think there should be problems. We have our diversity policy. People in chambers have known you for a long time. They're an accepting lot, and everyone likes you. I think it will be fine.'

'Still, I wondered if, as head of chambers, you could tell everyone. Prepare them.' Stephen leant to pick up his fresh drink and Leo saw, in the lamplight, the faint shadow of beard beneath the heavy foundation. He felt a sudden sense of dislocation. Everything – the bar with its ironic wartime echoes, Stephen's big, male hand with its painted nails, reaching for the silly china teacup – seemed a parody of reality. And yet it was reality. When he came across trans people in his social life, he never gave them a second thought. But there was the world, and then there was 5 Caper Court. Chambers had always been a place apart, reassuring in its immutability, its conventionality, and now all that was going to change. He had known Stephen for decades, had always regarded him in a fixed light, and this sudden alteration, an alteration that managed to be both crude yet subtle, confused Leo. He felt like a child, perplexed by some grown-up truth that had only just been revealed to him. He picked up his drink, knocking it back in two swallows, and put the cup back in its saucer.

'It's a nice dress.' He felt he had to say something reassuring about Stephen's new appearance.

'Thank you.' Stephen glanced down at it. 'Frankly, I think it's terribly boring. If I thought I could get away with wearing fishnet stockings, long black gloves, and high heels, I'd be much happier.' Leo pushed away this mildly disturbing vision. 'But one has to think about work, obviously.'

'Yes, so – what about clients?'

'I have a lot of letter-writing to do. I imagine it will be a sort of rolling-out process.' Leo realised that Stephanie's voice was just a shade lighter than Stephen's. Was that unconscious, he wondered, or deliberate? 'It's ongoing cases that are going to be the hardest. For instance, I've got a Court of Appeal hearing coming up – Kabushi Shipping, damages for breach of settlement.'

Leo nodded. 'David's on the other side, isn't he? Arguments about service of claims out of the jurisdiction, as I recall.'

Stephen nodded. 'That's the one. I'm anxious, obviously. All this might not go down terribly well with the clients. Japanese corporate culture, and all that.'

'No.'

'But I guess I'll just have to weather that storm, if and when it comes.' He sighed, and Leo noticed for the first time the swell of bosom beneath the bodice of the wrap-over dress. Padding, he presumed. It was grotesque, yet at the same time profoundly touching. An overwhelming surge of sympathy for his old friend suddenly caught his throat, so that for a few seconds he couldn't speak. The courage it had taken to do this. And the courage it would take in the months to come, to maintain a successful legal practice and live an endurable life.

He found his voice. 'Listen, why don't we have one more drink here, then go and have dinner?'

Stephen looked at him anxiously. 'You don't mind being seen with me?'

Leo thought back to the time years ago, when he and Stephen had both applied to take silk. He had succeeded, and Stephen had failed. How crestfallen Stephen had been. It had taken all Leo's powers of persuasion to convince him to try again. He could read the same self-doubt in him now.

'Stop thinking that way. I'm your friend. I'm proud of you for being brave and honest. I'm going to support you in this. And that starts this evening. Come on, let's get another drink and think about where to go.'

'And that's why you stopped answering my emails? Just because of some rumour?'

Anthony and Gabrielle were in a noisy Notting Hill pub, and conversation so far was tentative and difficult.

'It was more than that. I asked Leo about it, and he said he'd heard you were having an affair with one of the partners out in Singapore as well.'

'Double hearsay?'

Gabrielle smiled and tucked a strand of dark blonde hair behind one ear. She stared down into her drink for a few seconds. 'We had a long talk about it. I can't remember everything he said, but he gave me the definite impression that he knew more than he was letting on, that he was trying to spare my feelings. Anyway, by the end he'd convinced me that I'd be better off just ending things with you.'

'Silver-tongued Leo,' murmured Anthony. There was a moment's silence. 'I wasn't, you know. Having an affair. With anyone.'

She sighed and lifted her gaze to meet his. 'So where did Leo get his information?'

'He never had any. He just wanted to split us up. And you know why.'

She rested her chin on her hand. 'It never really bothered me, you know, whatever went on between you two.'

'No, but it bothers him.' A burst of noisy laughter from the next table drowned out his words.

Gabrielle craned her neck forward. 'What?'

Anthony raised his voice. 'I said—' He stopped, shook his head, and leant in closer. 'Look, it doesn't matter. I just want you to say you believe me.' He put his hand out, covering hers. 'Do you?'

She looked at him for a long moment, then impulsively leant forward and kissed him. 'Yes.'

He smiled. 'This place is awful. What do you say we go back to mine?'

She returned the smile. 'Sounds like a plan.'

CHAPTER FIVE

Several days later Anthony was sitting in Court 27 in the Rolls Building in Fetter Lane, trying to focus on his opponent's long-winded arguments in the matter of *Contira Bulk Trade v Armada Shipping*. He glanced up at Mrs Justice Steele, whose expression betrayed a certain weary exasperation – 4.35 p.m. on a rainy Friday was no time to be testing the judge's patience.

Mrs Justice Steele raised her gaze from the bundle of papers before her. 'Mr Abbott, it has already been established that the leakage of oil into a permanent ballast tank renders that tank potentially dangerous. Can you tell the court what precisely the point is that you're trying to make? Briefly, if you don't mind.'

'My Lady' – Anthony hid a smirk as Colin Hopkins, the barrister on the other side, did his usual unconscious little knee-bend; a very nice guy, Colin, but his overly obsequious manner tended to irritate judges – 'forgive me if I seem to be labouring the point. What I'm trying to suggest is that a crack between a cargo tank and a permanent ballast tank does not necessarily cause a vessel to be unseaworthy, in the sense that this word is used in the Norwegian Marine Insurance Plan, section forty-five.'

Mrs Justice Steele sighed. 'At last.' She glanced at the clock. 'I suggest we leave it here for today and resume on Monday at ten. You can elaborate on that argument then, Mr Hopkins.'

After a discussion of minor housekeeping issues, papers were shuffled and laptops closed, and the court rose for the day. Anthony spoke briefly to his solicitor, then changed out of his robes and made his way back to Caper Court for the meeting that Leo had called for five o'clock.

Leo had summoned Henry to his room to discuss the situation regarding Stephen. Henry, proud helmsman of the chambers vessel that he had for twenty years steered through seas smooth and rough, was used to coping with the vagaries and eccentricities of the individuals under his care, and received the news with his usual unflappability, merely pursing his lips and remarking, 'I can't say it won't present a few headaches. But we've coped with worse, sir. It's not like the quality of his work is going to change, is it? He's very dependable, is Mr Bishop.'

'That's Ms Bishop from now on, Henry. Something you'll need to drum into the rest of the clerks. And it will be Stephanie, not Stephen.' Leo glanced at his watch. 'I've called an informal meeting to give people the heads-up. That's in a few minutes. Then I'll be sending out an email later to everyone in chambers.' He rose and put on his jacket. 'As you say, Henry, it's bound to cause certain problems for you and the other clerks, as the public face of chambers, dealing with solicitors and so on. But I trust you to manage it all with your usual brilliance.'

Henry gave a rueful smile. 'Kind of you, sir.'

'Right, now to break the news to the unsuspecting hordes.'

There was some minor grumbling about the timing of the meeting from those members of chambers keen to get away for the weekend, but Leo was quick to reassure them that he wouldn't keep them long.

'I've called this meeting merely to make a brief announcement. I'm making it on behalf of Stephen Bishop, whom I saw last weekend.' Leo paused. 'As you all know, Stephen took some extended time off over Easter, and before he returns on Monday he wants everyone to be prepared for certain changes.' Leo paused. 'Put quite simply, he's decided that he's going to abandon his male identity, and to identify and express himself as a woman. That's how you'll be seeing him around chambers, and from now on he would like to be known as Stephanie.' People's faces were blank and unreadable, but he could sense their shock. 'Diversity is something the Bar is trying hard to embrace, and in these chambers we pride ourselves on our collegiate spirit. So I'm sure that, as her friends and colleagues, you will all give Stephanie your full support and understanding in her brave initiative.' Leo had decided to keep it simple and straightforward, making sure he got the pronouns right, moving tactfully from Stephen to Stephanie. He went on, 'And Stephanie also asked me to say this – she understands that it's going to be odd for most of you, and a not entirely easy adjustment, so she doesn't mind if people get pronouns or her name wrong at first. Rest easy on that score. And she very much wants people, if they have questions, to speak to her personally.'

He glanced around, waiting for the atmosphere to settle as people absorbed everything they had heard. He could sense, beneath the surprise, a general air of sympathy, but this was suddenly dispelled by an icy enquiry from Natalie.

'Is that the sole purpose of this meeting? I understood chambers meetings were only convened when there was a matter of constitutional or financial importance to discuss. I don't see how this qualifies.'

Leo suppressed a sigh. 'I did stress this was an informal meeting. And I might point out that no chambers issues are being decided here. I'm doing this out of courtesy – to you, as much as to Stephanie. It seemed to me that something as sensitive as this, involving a colleague, should be conveyed personally. That said, I will of course be issuing a formal announcement via email after this meeting so that everyone in chambers is made fully aware of the situation.' Natalie raised an eyebrow, but said nothing. 'OK, that's about it. Thank you for coming. Have a good weekend.'

People spoke not a word as they got to their feet and left. Leo was well aware that the conjecture and astonished debate would be saved for the pub or the wine bar. There would be plenty of it, he knew. As he returned to his room, Anthony and David Liphook caught up with him. 'Have you got a minute?' asked Anthony.

Leo regarded them both. 'I take it you want the complete low-down? Let me just get that email sent out, and I'll see you in the Seven Stars in ten minutes.'

The Seven Stars was a small pub behind the Royal Courts of Justice, and at five-thirty on a Friday it was getting busy.

Anthony managed to find a table, while David went to buy a round of drinks. Ten minutes later Leo arrived.

'So,' said David, 'tell us more.'

'I'm not sure there's much more to tell,' said Leo. 'He asked to meet me for a drink last weekend, and when I arrived, there he was, in a dress and make-up. It's something he's been doing for years, privately, and now he wants it to be a permanent thing.'

'Is he intending to – to change sex properly? I mean, have surgery?' asked Anthony.

'I've no idea.'

David frowned. 'So it's basically just cross-dressing?'

'You could put it like that. But it's not a Grayson Perry thing. It's not as though he wants to be a woman part of the time and a man at other times. He intends to be Stephanie full-time.'

'Bloody hell.' David took a thoughtful pull of his pint. 'To change your gender identity after thirty years at the Bar. That takes balls.'

'You might want to rephrase that,' murmured Anthony.

'You know what I mean. I just can't envisage Stephen as a woman. I mean, it's not as though there's anything especially feminine about him.'

'He looks quite good, actually,' said Leo. 'Homely. It's not like he's in drag. I think you'll get used to it fairly quickly.'

For a while the three of them discussed Stephen's decision, and the implications it would have in terms of work and clients.

'I suppose we'll have to have the noticeboard repainted,' observed David, thinking of the hand-painted list of tenants' names at the entrance to 5 Caper Court.

'Yes,' said Leo. 'I imagine so.' Would the Bar Standards

Board have to be told? he wondered. There might be any number of technicalities that Stephen probably hadn't thought of yet.

David finished his drink. 'Well, frankly, it's beyond me. Stephen, of all people.'

'I think,' said Leo, 'it might be a good thing if we were to start using the name Stephanie. And saying "her" as opposed to "him".'

David sighed. 'This is all going to take a bit of getting used to. Anyway, I need to make tracks.' He stood up and put on his coat. 'Have a good weekend, all.'

'You, too.'

When David had gone, Leo lifted his nearly empty glass. 'Another?'

Anthony shook his head. 'I have to be heading back. I'm meeting someone later.'

Leo nodded, and swallowed the remains of his beer, trying to ignore the little pang he always felt when confronted with the thought of Anthony with someone else. 'A new girlfriend?'

Anthony hesitated. 'Not exactly. I'm seeing Gabrielle.'

Leo said nothing for a moment, turning the empty beer glass in his hands, conscious of the pang deepening into something much more painful. 'I thought you two broke up a while ago.'

'We did. That was because she thought I was having an affair out in Singapore.' He regarded Leo. 'Where do you suppose she got that piece of fake news?'

'I believe it was a general rumour.'

'Which you did your best to endorse when Gabrielle asked you about it.'

Leo said nothing. The knowledge of what he had done lay unspoken between them. Anthony dropped his gaze, allowing Leo to contemplate him, to trace with his eyes the lean curve of Anthony's jaw, the contours of his mouth, his dark, serious eyes. He experienced a rush of longing, and at the same time an intense sense of desperation. It had been some years since he and Anthony had last been lovers, and that all too briefly, one night in the whole panorama of days and months spent working alongside one another. Expressing love for another man physically had been a capitulation for Anthony, and one he had done his best to reject ever since. The emotional difficulty of admitting that his sexuality might have more than one facet had been too much for him. Leo knew that. He was prepared to wait. He continued to hope, to work carefully towards a time when Anthony would belong to him entirely. But he knew too that the chances of that happening would fall away, the more Anthony saw of Gabrielle. For Anthony to develop a serious relationship with any girl was an inevitable obstacle. But an involvement with Leo's own daughter, however brief, would probably render any future emotional and sexual relationship with Leo too strange for Anthony to handle. Perhaps it already had.

'I gave her the best advice I could. In the circumstances.'

Anthony lifted his eyes. 'You mean you didn't have some other agenda?'

Leo rubbed his hand wearily across his face. 'No,' he lied. He stood up and put on his coat. 'No, I didn't.'

He left the pub without another word, and walked back into the Temple to where his car was parked. Enough of this, he told himself savagely. He had to let it go. He had always conducted his private life with discipline, allowing people to get emotionally close to him only as a means to an end, usually a sexually pleasurable one. Even his marriage to Rachel had been a matter of expediency. He had lost control of a love affair only once – to this day he couldn't think of Joshua without pain – and it had nearly wrecked his life. He wouldn't allow the thing with Anthony to go the same way. It could end in disaster. He should abandon ideas of being with him, bow to the inevitable. But even as he told himself this, he thought of the way Anthony looked at him sometimes; everything he felt was reciprocated. So how could he let it go? How could he possibly?

He switched his mind to other things. He was picking up Oliver in the morning and spending the weekend with him – that at least was pleasure in its simplest form. He must focus on that. He would go home and get an early night. He would not think about Anthony and Gabrielle. He pictured the empty Chelsea house, and for an instant wished Sarah was still there.

The next morning Leo picked up Oliver from his mother and they drove to Leo's second home in Oxfordshire. It was an old, weathered stone house set in an acre of garden, surrounded by countryside, with low-beamed rooms and mullioned windows. Unlike his place in Chelsea, with its cool, modern interior and minimalist furniture, the house at Stanton had a cosy atmosphere. The living room was haphazardly furnished, with deep, comfortable sofas and beautiful worn rugs scattered on the dark polished boards, and on either side of the low, stone fireplace stood two big bookcases containing an assortment of books collected over the decades.

In this restful place, and with Oliver for company, Leo felt his troubled soul grow calmer. The dynamic between father and son had changed since the days when Oliver was a little boy, but they were still easy and happy in one another's company. On Saturday morning they drove into the nearby market town to have breakfast and shop for food, and after lunch Leo left Oliver to his own devices, to text his friends and play online video games with them. He understood Oliver's deep involvement with his school friends, on the cusp of his teenage years, and their importance in his life. Later they played chess, then ate supper and watched a movie together, and the next day, after a long hike through the woods, they drove back to London. As they neared Chiswick, Leo felt the usual impending sense of loss. He parked the car outside Rachel's house and accompanied Oliver up the path to the front door.

Rachel opened it. She was a slender woman in her late thirties, with a pale, pretty oval face and long hair, silky and dark like Oliver's, and a grave, cautious manner. 'Would you like to come in for a drink?' she asked, as Oliver dumped his rucksack in the hall and headed upstairs to his room.

'Sure.'

'Simon's in Amsterdam,' she said, as he followed her through to the kitchen.

She poured them both a glass of wine. Leo pulled out a stool by the breakfast bar and sat down.

'How was the weekend?' Rachel sat opposite him and took a sip of wine.

'Very good.' Leo recounted all that he and Oliver had done.

'Sounds like you and he had a lovely time.'

'We did. How was your weekend?'

'Tiring. I have a Court of Appeal case starting on Monday, so I've been working.'

'Tell me about it.'

Rachel worked as a solicitor in the same field of commercial law as Leo – it was what had first brought them together – and he always found this point of connection made for their most amicable conversations. They talked for a while about the case, then Rachel let a pause fall. 'I've got something to tell you.'

'Oh?'

She tucked a strand of hair behind one ear. 'I'm having a baby.'

'Congratulations. That's wonderful news. When's it due?'

'The end of August.'

She was gazing at him. There it was – that expression, the one he had first seen years ago, when he had first realised she was in love with him. It was a look that was almost fearful, as though she was unwilling to accept what she felt, and at the same time beseeching. She had never stopped loving him, despite his infidelity, because she couldn't help herself. Even now that she was married to Simon and having his child, he knew what she still felt. If he didn't detest that look so much, it might have awed him, that he could provoke such depth of feeling. He glanced down at his wine, simply to escape it.

'It won't make any difference to the arrangements with Oliver,' she added. 'You seeing him every other weekend—'

'I should bloody hope not.' He could feel the amicable mood slipping.

'—but there are going to be some changes. Simon and

I are in the process of buying a house. We're moving to Tunbridge Wells.'

Leo's jaw tightened. On days when he worked from home he often picked Oliver up from school and gave him tea and helped him with his homework, returning him to Rachel at bedtime. It was an arrangement that suited everyone, and he treasured those hours. Now they were to be taken away. 'I see.' He drained his glass.

'I'm sorry you won't see so much of Oliver. But it can't be helped.'

'Christ, it really gives you pleasure, telling me this, doesn't it?' He set the glass down on the breakfast bar. 'Any little way in the world you can get back at me, you relish.'

She closed her eyes briefly. 'You're such an egotist.'

At that moment there was the thump of feet on the stairs, and Oliver appeared, brushing his dark, silky hair from his eyes. He yawned, and gave his father a hug. 'That was a great weekend, Dad.'

'It was. Don't forget I'll be picking you up on Wednesday after football.'

'Oh yeah.' Oliver flashed him a smile. 'I love coming to your house.'

Leo gave Rachel a glance, then dropped a kiss on Oliver's head. 'Night,' he murmured, and left the house without another word.

When Henry arrived at chambers on Monday morning, he found the clerks' room agog.

'Have you seen Mr D's email?' Felicity said. 'The one about Stephen Bishop?'

Liam, the junior clerk, gave a grin. 'Stephanie, you mean.'

'That's right, Liam,' said Henry calmly, as he hung his coat in the closet. 'And from now on, when you're talking to solicitors and the like, it's *Ms* Bishop. We all have to start remembering that. Respect and kindness will be the watchwords, won't they? As Mr Davies says in his email, diversity is something to be embraced. These are the times we live in.'

'Yeah, but Mr Bishop – he's the last person you'd expect to be doing something like this,' said Liam.

Carla, the office manager, frowned. She was a middle-aged woman with a conservative disposition, and she had her own private reservations about the whole business. 'Is he going to be going the whole hog, d'you suppose?' she asked. 'I mean, hormones and surgery, and all of that? You know, proper transitioning?'

At that moment Leo put his head round the door of the clerks' room. 'Felicity, I just spoke to Fred Fenton – the other side want to have the date for the Transpac mediation brought forward. Can you check my diary, and see what works?'

Felicity tapped her keyboard and nodded. 'By the way, Mr D—' She glanced up at him.

'Yes?'

'We were just having a bit of a discussion. About Mr – I mean, Ms Bishop.' She gave Carla a glance. Leo came properly into the room. He had been expecting this.

'We were wondering,' said Carla, 'whether this is a first step. Whether, you know, he'll be having surgery, and all the rest of it.'

'Does that matter?'

Carla glanced uncomfortably at the others. 'I suppose not.'

'As I said in the email, Stephanie is perfectly happy to answer any questions people might have, on a personal level, if it helps them understand things better.'

'Well, we're hardly likely to ask that one, are we?' said Felicity.

'There you are, then,' said Leo. 'It's not really important. What *is* important is that we treat Stephanie in exactly the same way we treated Stephen. Everything just carries on as before.'

'It'll take a bit of getting used to,' said Felicity.

'Maybe. But changes happen all the time at 5 Caper Court,' said Leo. 'This is just another one.'

Felicity sighed. She really liked Stephen. He was one of the nicest, most approachable members of chambers. What would it be like talking to him when he was dressed up like a woman? What he was doing was really brave, and she couldn't imagine what he'd gone through to come to this decision. She just didn't like the thought of being embarrassed around him, or behaving awkwardly. He would hate that as much as her. She hoped she could rely on herself to behave normally. She glanced at the clock. 'Don't forget you've got a con with Andrew Howard and the people from Seascope in half an hour,' she told Leo.

'I won't forget.' He left the clerks' room. How could he forget? He had only just learnt the other day that the previous case handler dealing with the litigation involving the grounding of the iron ore bulk carrier had left Seascope, and had been replaced by none other than Sarah. He hadn't seen or spoken to her since the day she had left. He hoped it wasn't going to be an awkward encounter.

CHAPTER SIX

Since moving out of Leo's house, Sarah's sense of humiliation had gradually subsided, and she'd found herself hoping he would call. From that hope, expectation grew. What might come of any call, she had no idea. But two weeks had slipped past without a word; it seemed her departure hardly mattered to him. Perhaps he even welcomed it. She didn't quite believe that. Whatever delusions she'd had about making things more permanent, they were good together. And she knew he knew it, too. In the early days of their on–off relationship, it hadn't bothered her that he had affairs with other people, because back then she didn't want or expect anything from him. Now things were different. But recent events had reminded her that although she might have changed, Leo hadn't. His time and attention were only available on his terms, and she wasn't sure she could live with them. That, it seemed, was academic. The phone call hadn't come.

'You say he's good, this fellow Davies?' Danylo Ivanov, the shipping operations manager of Montial, was seated anxiously on the edge of one of the sofas in 5 Caper Court's reception area. He was in his mid-thirties, fair and slim, with a thin, handsome face and blue eyes, and in his expensively cut, tight-fitting suit he looked every inch the successful young East European businessman. His English was fluent, his accent light. He regarded Sarah and Andrew Howard, the instructing solicitor, intently.

Andrew looked up from his mobile phone and nodded. 'About the best there is.'

Danylo knotted his hands together and frowned down at the carpet. 'It seems hopeless to me.'

Sarah liked Danylo. She had worked with him on cases before, and most of the time he was placid and easy to deal with, but in times of crisis he became infected in top-down fashion by the character of his boss, the head of Montial's global operations, an irascible bully who shouted down the phone at Sarah on a regular basis. The grounding of the *Alpha Six*, laden with a cargo of 80,000 tons of iron ore, was one such crisis, and since flying in to London yesterday Danylo had been in a constant state of agitation. Instructing Leo Davies, albeit on the recommendation of Montial's solicitors, was his ultimate decision, and if the case was lost, the blame, whether fairly or not, would fall on him.

'We have the shipper's declaration saying that the moisture content was below the TML, remember.' Sarah felt she was running out of encouraging things to say.

Danylo gave an angry sigh. 'You know they will say we mis-declared the cargo, that it was too wet, that we didn't do enough to protect the stockpiles from the rain. I don't see how this can be anything but a disaster for our new Liberian operation.'

Sarah usually found the cardocentric passion of the Ukrainian temperament attractive, but when it manifested itself in fervid despondency, it could become a bit wearing.

'Well, let's see what Mr Davies has to say in the light of the lab reports.' She felt a tightening in her throat at the imminent prospect of seeing Leo.

'Mr Davies is ready to see you,' called out Lauren, the receptionist. 'Just take the lift up to the third floor.'

Leo's door was open, and he was seated at the round conference table, his laptop open, a bundle of papers next to it. He rose and shook hands first with Andrew, then Sarah.

'Nice to see you again, Sarah.' He said it with the detached cordiality of a business acquaintance. Which, in this context, was all he was. The fleeting, warm touch of his hand made her feel, for some unaccountable reason, a little lost, as though it marked the end of something.

'This is Mr Ivanov,' said Sarah. 'Mr Ivanov, Mr Davies.'

Danylo reached forward and shook Leo's hand. 'Mr Davies, I'm glad to meet you. I believe you are going to be the saviour in our hour of need, yes?'

Watching the two men shake hands, Sarah felt her heart turn over. Leo's swift glance of sexual appraisal, the quickening of his interest, would have been missed by anyone but her.

'I'm afraid I can't make any promises,' replied Leo, returning Danylo's smile, 'but the owner's case isn't necessarily as cut-and-dried as might first appear. Please have a seat. Can I get anyone a coffee?'

Coffee was poured. As he stirred his, Danylo asked Leo, with a bright flicker of hope, 'So you think we can be optimistic?'

'That's perhaps too strong a word, Mr Ivanov. We lawyers prefer to be cautious. But the lab reports look promising, and beyond that, there are aspects of the surveyor's report on the condition of the hull that raise questions about the master's loading plan.' Leo tapped the keyboard of his laptop, bringing up some detailed diagrams, and turned it so everyone could see. 'There's evidence that torsional stresses caused a certain amount of fretting of the attachment welding in three of the holds. If you look here, and here . . .'

For the next hour they pored over every aspect of Montial's case. Sarah found the technical detail wearisome, but at least Danylo seemed to be picking up crumbs of comfort from it all.

'So you think maybe it was the master's fault?'

'Let's just say it's a possibility,' replied Leo. 'Perhaps the Chief Officer didn't carry out the critical inspections properly. We have to commission a more detailed survey, and we'll need to get expert engineering advice on the stress calculations. There's a very long way still to go. But we have grounds for cautious optimism.'

'Ah! You used my word – that's good.' Danylo grinned, buoyed up by what he'd heard, ignoring Leo's cautious note. From past experience Sarah knew that he would now be unduly confident about the prospects of success in the case, and would oversell it to his boss. She just hoped that

Leo was right in his thinking. She'd been surprised he could see even a glimmer of hope for Montial.

In the closing minutes of the meeting she let her mind drift, conjuring a departure scenario in which Leo detained her for a moment while the others went downstairs, suggesting a drink, saying something about how they needed to talk.

Leo closed his laptop and everyone rose. He shook hands with each one of them and opened the door. Sarah turned to look at him, waiting for the possibility of a moment alone, but he looked straight past her at Danylo. 'Might I have a quick private word with you, Mr Ivanov?'

'Of course.'

'Sarah and I will wait for you downstairs,' said Andrew.

Sarah could do nothing but follow Andrew to the lift.

As they waited in the reception area, Sarah responded mindlessly to Andrew's observations about the meeting. After a few minutes the lift door opened, and Danylo emerged, shrugging on his coat, a smile on his lips.

The three of them walked up to Fleet Street and caught a cab back to the City. The taxi dropped Andrew at his office and carried on with just Sarah and Danylo.

'When are you flying back?' Sarah asked.

'Tomorrow morning.' He leant forward to speak to the driver. 'You can drop me on the next corner.' He sat back with a sigh. 'I have meetings all the rest of today.' Then he smiled. 'I like your Mr Davies. I have a feeling that with him, we might win this case.'

'Well, there's still a long way to go. A lot of technical hurdles to overcome.'

Danylo nodded. 'Some of the technical things are

very complex. I told Mr Davies I didn't quite understand them all. I want to be able to explain it properly to my boss when I get back. So he offered to come to my hotel this evening to go through a few things.' He turned to Sarah. 'That's very nice of him, don't you think? To give up his free time?'

Sarah glanced out at the traffic. 'Very.'

At the end of the day Anthony, on his way back from court, put his head round Leo's door. 'How did the con with Montial go this morning?'

'Not bad. Nothing like cheering up a doom-laden Ukrainian. You know what they're like. Either utter despair or wild optimism.' Leo leant back in his chair with a lazy smile. 'Their head of shipping is a charming man. A lot younger than I expected. I'm meeting him at his hotel later to go over some of the finer technical details.' He said this purely out of mischief, to see what response it would provoke.

But Anthony merely said, 'So you actually think the charterers are in with a chance?'

'They could be.' Leo swivelled in his chair. 'If they're going to win this case, it's because I will make it happen.' He paused. 'That's me channelling my best Harvey Specter, in case you hadn't noticed.'

'I really didn't have you down as a *Suits* fan.'

'I used to watch it with Sarah. I found it rather moronic, but I definitely identify with Harvey.'

'I never know when you're being facetious.' There was a pause, then Anthony said, 'Anyway, I have to get going.'

Leo gave a barely perceptible nod. 'Don't let me keep you.'

When Anthony had left, Leo sat staring unseeingly at the screen of his laptop. No doubt he was off to see Gabrielle. Christ, to feel such bitter jealousy of one's own daughter – it was unhealthy. But he couldn't help it; the thought of her being with Anthony tore at him. He tried to remind himself of his earlier resolution. No good would come of feeling this way. He would focus instead on seeing young Mr Ivanov in an hour's time. It was just the kind of welcome distraction he needed these days.

Anthony returned to his room. He went to the window. It was already dark outside, and the lamps in the courtyard below cast their glow on the flagstones, and on the occasional figure hurrying through on their way home. He gazed down, brooding on his brief exchange with Leo. That comment about Montial's head of shipping hadn't escaped him; he hated it when Leo made these sly sexual references, as if to test him. Just when he thought the battle over his feelings about Leo had been won, and the memories of those times they had slept together laid to rest, something would happen to resurrect it all, to throw him back into confusion. He remembered the other night, when he and Gabrielle had been talking. He had been lying on the sofa, she'd been sitting cross-legged on the rug with a glass of wine, her hair tumbled about her shoulders. He had asked her a question – about what, he couldn't now remember – and the way she had looked up at him, frowning slightly, bright blue eyes beneath dark brows, running her fingers through her hair before answering, was so like Leo that his heart had turned over. He had wanted Leo there so badly that it felt like a betrayal, a secret betrayal. It had eaten at him in the days since.

He turned away from the window and sat down at his desk. It wasn't just a sexual thing, either. It operated on any number of levels. He leant back in his chair and shut his eyes. What a mess he was. And Leo wasn't the answer. Leo would always need other people, other lovers, tantalising distractions that would be the death of happiness. Better just stick to the conventions, find someone to love enough to marry, and have a family with. Throughout his fractured childhood, having divorced parents, a lack of money, and a father who was unconventional to the point of embarrassment, all he had ever wanted was normality, stability. It was why he had become a barrister, to have a respectable, well-remunerated career, and be accepted as an intellectual and social equal in an elite world. To be safe.

He opened his eyes and sat forward, tapping his keyboard, bringing up on the screen his latest brief. He would do what he always did, work diligently through it, identifying the issues, separating out the arguments on both sides, marshalling his case. There was no reason why life couldn't be dealt with in the same well-ordered fashion. All he had to do was to stick to the rules, and things would be fine.

Chay's mobile phone vibrated on the sofa in the upstairs living room. Jocasta picked it up and waited till it fell silent, then went to the recent calls list and deleted Anthony's name. She lifted her head, listened, and sure enough, her own phone trilled from the coffee table. She crossed the room and picked it up.

'Anthony, hello.' A pause, then she said in a soft, regretful voice, 'No, he's not well enough to take calls at the moment. To be honest, his last treatment has drained him so much that he says he'd rather not have any visitors for the coming fortnight. His next treatment is in three weeks' time, and he always feels better just before each one. Maybe you could visit then?' Another pause. 'Of course. I'm sure he'll ring you when he's feeling up to it. I'll tell him. Bye for now.'

She went to the kitchen, made a herbal infusion, and took it down to the basement, where a bed had now been installed, and a living area arranged so that Chay wouldn't have to make trips up and down stairs. He was lying in a reclining chair, grey-faced, shrunken, his eyes closed. The television was playing unheeded. Jocasta switched it off and sat down next to him.

'Chay, darling, I made you some tea.'

He roused himself, glanced unenthusiastically at the tea, then to the far end of the room, where his work had lain untouched for several days. He sighed. 'I want so badly to work.'

'You know you're not well enough. Maybe in a few days, when you're feeling stronger. Each bout of chemo is bound to leave you feeling washed out. Forget about work for now.' She pulled up a chair and gazed at him lovingly. 'I'm fixing us a nice supper. Then afterwards we can have a game of backgammon. Or we can just watch a film, if you like.'

He smiled. 'You look after me so well. Unlike my sons. They haven't been near me for the past fortnight.' He frowned. 'I wish I could find my phone.' He cast his

74

eyes around the workroom. 'I know it's not down here. I've hunted everywhere. And you've had a look upstairs, haven't you?'

'Yes, of course.' She stroked his hand with gentle fingers. 'It'll turn up, don't worry.'

'They haven't rung you, have they?'

'I'd tell you if they had.'

'Not even a phone call.' He shrugged. 'They're probably just waiting for me to die.'

'Everyone has busy lives.'

'So busy they can't even look in on their own father?' His head gave an angry twitch. 'If they're calculating on getting anything from me when I'm gone, you'd think they'd work out that a few visits wouldn't go amiss.'

'I'm sure they'll come when they can.' She paused. 'Would you like me to ring them, suggest they come over?'

'No! Why should I beg them? If they can't be bothered, they can't be bothered.'

'Children can be thoughtless.'

'Thoughtlessness is one thing. Ignoring your dying father is another.'

'Don't talk like that. You have to stay positive. The treatment might well work.'

'That's not the point. I probably am going to die, and they know that. So where are they?'

She continued to stroke his hand. 'I really think I should ring them, if you're going to get in a state about it.'

'No! I told you, I shouldn't have to ask!' He leant his head back. 'Callous little sods.' He clasped her hand. 'At least I have you. Thank you for everything you do.'

She kissed his bald head. 'I've always been there for you.'

'I'm sorry I behaved so badly back in California.'

'Don't. We've been over all that. I forgave you a long time ago. The present is what matters.'

Anthony worked late. It was after eight when he closed his laptop and sat back in his chair. Everyone else had long gone home, and the building was silent. He found himself remembering a similar evening, in those early, ambitious days when he'd just gained his tenancy, and had been working late. He'd just left his room, thinking himself alone in chambers, when he'd heard Leo's light, energetic tread on the stairs. A second later, there he was on the landing, whistling under his breath, a sheaf of documents in his hand. He couldn't now remember what had been said at the time, but they'd finished up going for a drink, and then dinner. In those days he had been dizzyingly happy, always, to be in Leo's company. He imagined stepping out of his room now, meeting Leo on the stairs, and felt a small ache in his heart. He dismissed the fantasy. Right at this minute Leo was with some other young man, doing what he had always done, pursuing his own desires. That was all that life was about for Leo. His thoughts shifted to Gabrielle, and it was like a gear change in his feelings, a sense of relief, of something simple and free of pain. He should call her, go round and see her. But he had a difficult hearing tomorrow morning, and he needed to sleep.

Something was at the back of his mind, irritating him. He searched for its source, and realised that it was the conversation earlier with Jocasta. She was fencing off his father, keeping visitors away. Maybe it was done from the best of intentions, but it irked him to think he was being kept at a distance. He glanced at his watch, and picked up his mobile phone. He rang Chay's number, but, as expected, it simply went to voicemail. He rang Jocasta's number, and she answered.

'Anthony.' Her voice was wary.

'Hi. Listen, I know you said earlier that Dad wasn't feeling at his best, but I'd like to see him, anyway. I'm going to come over now.'

'It's really rather late—'

'No, it isn't. I'll see you in twenty minutes.' He clicked his phone off, and went to put on his cycling gear.

Jocasta, who was upstairs in the kitchen, stood for a thoughtful moment, mobile in hand, then went downstairs to where Chay was dozing in his recliner. She sat down next to him and laid a hand on his arm, and he turned and opened his eyes.

'I was thinking about what you said earlier. I hate seeing you unhappy. I rang Anthony a moment ago, and he's coming over.'

'Why did you do that? I told you not to.'

'Because I don't see why you should suffer just because he and Barry are being thoughtless.'

'Either they want to come or they don't. I wish you hadn't done that.'

'Well, it's done now. Try to be nice.'

Anthony cycled slowly up Brushfield Street, past Spitalfields Market. He remembered the time he had spent working there years ago as a market porter, lugging crates of produce in the early hours of the morning. The fruit and vegetable market had long been relocated to impersonal warehouses in Nine Elms, and the great Victorian market space was now home to fashion shops, restaurants and street food outlets, and stalls selling vintage clothes, jewellery and bric-a-brac. He felt a certain wistfulness as he reflected on how radically the area had been transformed, just as he had, in the space of fifteen years.

He turned into Fournier Street and slowed his bike outside his father's house. As he was locking it to the railings, Jocasta came to the door. She was dressed in a crimson silk tunic and boots, her cropped hair bound in a long scarf.

'Don't expect too much of him. He's really terribly tired.' Anthony followed her into the house. 'By the way, I told him that I asked you to come over.'

'Why?'

'Because, as I said, he's not welcoming visits from anyone at the moment. I thought it would be better if he blamed me, not you.' She smiled her gentle, ethereal smile. 'Can I get you a drink? A glass of wine, maybe?'

'Thanks, that would be nice.'

He went downstairs and found Chay in his chair, a cashmere rug over his thin knees, watching television.

'How have you been, Dad?' he asked, pulling up a chair next to Chay's recliner.

Chay picked up the remote and turned off the television. 'Hellish. Tired. Sick. Without Jocasta, I don't know how I'd get through this.'

She appeared at that moment with a glass of red wine. Chay eyed it as she set it down, and she caught his expression. 'Would you like one?'

'What's the point? The medication makes everything taste like shit.'

She drew something from the pocket of her tunic. 'Look what I found.' She handed Chay his mobile phone.

'Where was it?'

'Behind the espresso machine.' She turned to Anthony. 'Can I get you a snack, or something?'

'No, thanks. I won't stay long.'

This was said in concession to his father's tiredness, but to Chay it betokened impatience to get away.

'You didn't have to come if you didn't want to.'

'Of course I wanted to.'

'If you can't be bothered to visit, the odd phone call would be nice.'

'I have called you. But it's not much use if you lose your phone, is it? Anyway, I'm here now.' Anthony dipped into the conversational topics that he'd been mulling on the way over, stuff from the news, politics, the latest Trump drama, doing his best to brighten his father's mood, but Chay remained morose and monosyllabic. After twenty minutes Anthony gave up. Evidently the chemo treatment was taking an enormous toll. Perhaps he'd been wrong to insist on visiting.

'Look, I can tell you're tired. Perhaps it's best if I head off.'

'As you like.'

Anthony drained his wine and got up.

'Thank you for taking the trouble to come,' said Chay.

The sarcasm was lost on Anthony. 'I'll visit again soon. Hope you feel better in a few days.' He leant down, hugged his father, and headed upstairs, followed by Jocasta.

'I'm not sure I did him much good,' said Anthony, zipping up his jacket.

She made a rueful face. 'I did say. Maybe it's best if I let you know when is a good time to visit. That way he'll enjoy it more. Tonight wasn't a good time. It's a struggle for you both when he's sick and exhausted.'

'Sure.'

She watched him cycle off into the night, then closed the door and went back downstairs. Chay was scrolling through recent calls on his mobile.

'He said he'd tried ringing me. Not one missed call. Nor any from Barry.' He dropped the phone into his lap and sighed. 'I can't blame them, I suppose. I'm not exactly worthwhile company.'

'Don't be silly.' She sat on the arm of his recliner and stroked his brow. 'Remember years ago, when we were living in that squat in Islington? They didn't come around much then, either.'

'No. No, that's right, they didn't. They never thought much of me. Not until I became worth something.' He reflected for a moment. 'Maybe they still don't think much of me. Maybe the only reason they've ever bothered with me is because of the money.' He looked up at her. 'I've given them a fair bit, here and there.' He looked away again. 'They probably take it for granted that they'll get everything when I'm gone. Why bother visiting the old fool when he'll be dead in a few months, and we can cop the lot?'

'I suppose all children are the same. Taking things for granted.'

He picked up her hand and kissed it. 'You, on the other

hand, you take nothing for granted. You're here for me. You look after me, and you don't ask for a thing.'

She kissed the hand that held hers. 'Chay, looking after you is reward in itself. I never stopped loving you. And now I'm here for you.'

CHAPTER SEVEN

Hilary term gave way to Easter term, and spring unfolded in gentle splendour in the Temple gardens. Leaf buds swelled on the roses, and spring flowers bloomed in the herbaceous borders. The cherry and almond trees that edged the lawns came into blossom, and in Fountain Court the young leaves unfurled on the mulberry trees. Office workers, clerks and barristers made the most of the mild weather, coming out in their lunch hour to sit on the benches with their sandwiches and wraps, and to stroll the gravel paths.

The peace and serenity that reigned in the gardens was not, however, reflected within the walls of 5 Caper Court.

'It's a fucking travesty.' Leo, sitting in his shirtsleeves at his desk, swivelled his chair in irritation. 'She talks about transparency, and then sits in on the interview to make sure her favoured candidate gets pupillage. When I recused myself from Alistair Egan's interview, it didn't occur to me that she wouldn't do the same.'

His audience consisted of Anthony and Arun Sikand. They were reporting back from the meeting of the pupillage committee that had just taken place, and at which a majority had voted for the one remaining pupillage to be awarded to Sian Attwood, Natalie King's protégée.

'Sian did exceptionally well in the advance written exercise. She's generally pretty impressive,' said Anthony. 'I'm not sure whether Natalie being at the interview made any difference.'

'Of course it must have swung things,' retorted Leo. 'How could it not?'

'I suppose she has an argument about gender balance,' observed Arun. 'You know, having more women in chambers.'

'She's been pushing that agenda for all it's worth, hasn't she? She'll be demanding quotas next.' Leo got up and put on his jacket. 'I have to get to court. You can let it be known that I think she had no business sitting in on the interview.' He picked up his robing bag and laptop, and left the room.

'No love lost between him and Natalie, then,' said Arun with a sigh.

'Not since they had that row last month.'

'Well, Sian Attwood is to be our new pupil and he's just going to have to suck it up.' Arun, who had himself voted for Sian, eased himself away from the windowsill where he'd been leaning. 'See you.'

A couple of hours later, over coffee, Arun told Lisa Blackmore how Leo had reacted. 'He was absolutely furious that Natalie was there at Sian Attwood's interview. He sees it as a complete stitch-up.'

Lisa, who had recently been instructed as Natalie's junior on a multi-jurisdictional hedge fund fraud and was assiduously nurturing a relationship with the older woman, conveyed this information to Natalie later that day over a drink after work.

'Of course he's angry,' said Natalie. 'Leo Davies is someone who's used to getting his own way. He'd much rather chambers remained a male bastion. You know, despite his reputation with women, I suspect he really doesn't much like them. I can always tell. There are far too many misogynists like him at the Bar. I'd personally like to obliterate every pale, stale male from 5 Caper Court. The more women we can bring into chambers, the better. Don't you agree?'

Lisa, who was a leading member of a recently established forum, *No Barriers*, set up to promote female equality at the Bar, agreed with the last sentiment, but not necessarily with the one preceding it. She hesitated. 'Yes, we need more women. But trying to get rid of men might be seen as a form of discrimination.'

'Masculine dominance is one of the most widespread causes of inequality. We can't make progress without a few male casualties.' She slipped from her bar stool and gathered up her Max Mara coat. 'Now, I have to get home. We have our case management conference first thing in the morning, don't forget.' She drained her martini glass. 'See you tomorrow.'

Natalie lived in an apartment on the fifth floor of a glossy new waterside development in St Katharine Docks, overlooking the marina. She parked her car in the private car park and took the lift up. As she opened the door, she could hear music coming from the living room. She chucked down her keys and hung up her coat, and went in. A young woman in sweatpants and a vest top was sitting cross-legged on a wide sofa, working on a laptop. The lights of the dock twinkled through the long, curved window beyond her. She was in her early thirties, slight, boyish, with black hair that grazed her cheeks and hung in a silky fringe over dark, luminous eyes. She had a rosy dusting of freckles on her nose, and on the silken skin of her shoulders and upper arms.

'So,' Natalie said to her, 'congratulations. I take it you got my text. You didn't answer.'

Sian Attwood barely glanced up. 'I'm sorry. I've been so busy on this article.'

'You know I hate it when you don't answer my texts.' Natalie went across to the stainless steel and glass drinks trolley, turning down the volume of the music on the way, and uncapped a bottle of Grey Goose. 'A drink to celebrate?'

'I'm not drinking this month, remember?'

'So boring.' Natalie poured herself a drink, then glanced at Sian and said irritably, 'Do we have to have the heating up so high? Maybe it would be an idea if you were to put more clothes on.' Sian picked up a sloppy sweater lying nearby, and pulled it on. Then she got up and went across to the thermostat on the wall and reset it. She sat down again without a word and returned to her laptop screen. Natalie watched her as she did these things. 'Anyone would think you weren't that bothered about getting the pupillage. I mean, I can't believe you've never even bothered to check out the chambers' website.'

Sian closed her laptop and put it to one side. She could read Natalie's mood and she didn't want an evening of bickering. When Natalie behaved like a mildly petulant child it was because she wasn't happy with the balance of the relationship; she hated being the needy one. Sian, for her own part, enjoyed her power over the older woman, but was clever enough not to abuse it.

'I'll get round to it. My joining 5 Caper Court was your idea, remember?' She stretched her arms above her head and yawned, then got up from the sofa and padded over to Natalie and put her arms around her and kissed her. 'I'm thrilled about the pupillage. You know I am.' She picked up the vodka and poured some into a glass, then added tonic to both their glasses. 'Maybe I'll have a night off.' She chinked her glass against Natalie's. 'To 5 Caper Court.' She lifted Natalie's hand and led her back to the sofa, and they both sat down.

'You very nearly didn't get it, you know,' said Natalie. 'The vote was close.' She drank some of her vodka. 'I can't tell you how satisfying it was to stick it to our head of chambers. He was absolutely furious at not getting his way. An entitled male QC in his comfortable world, chauvinistic and arrogant, who thinks because he's the highest fee earner in chambers that he's intellectually superior in some way. Everyone seems to find him formidably charming, but I can't see it, frankly.'

'Sounds quite a dinosaur. How old is he?'

'Mid-fifties? Though he looks younger.' She paused. 'He has quite a reputation, sexually. With men as well as women.'

'Really? How interesting.' Sian sipped her vodka

and regarded Natalie over the rim of her glass. 'Do you fancy him?'

Natalie gave her a scornful look. 'Are you joking? I told you, I can't bear the man.'

'Hmm. The one doesn't necessarily preclude the other.' She stroked Natalie's cheek. 'I can't bear you, for instance.' She kissed her mouth. 'Simply can't stand you.'

'Don't say that. Even if it's not true. You know how it makes me feel.' Natalie returned the kiss. 'It's not true, is it?'

'You know it's not,' replied Sian softly. Though she had to admit, she did sometimes wonder.

Natalie never stopped to ask herself what it was about Leo that roused in her such strongly antagonistic feelings, but ever since that first run-in with him at the pupillage committee meeting, she had marked him down as an enemy. It was her way of dealing with the world – anyone who was not with her must be against her, a threat that needed to be neutralised. She had identified Leo's scepticism of those tenants whom he referred to as 'the young turks', the ones who wanted to see 5 Caper Court develop itself from a loose association of self-employed barristers into something altogether slicker and more corporate, as a weapon to use against him. Through Lisa Blackmore, who was now her ardent acolyte, she began to build up a connection with the younger tenants, listening sympathetically to their ideas, promoting herself as someone who would champion them amongst the more senior members of chambers. She liked to think it reflected well on herself to be on their side, but in fact her manoeuvrings began to sow discord in chambers.

Henry was quick to pick up on this. As senior clerk, he prided himself on running a tight ship. His job, apart from managing the professional lives and egos of each and every one of the barristers in chambers, from the loftiest QC to the lowliest junior, was to ensure that the machinery of 5 Caper Court operated at all times smoothly and harmoniously.

'I suspected she might be trouble,' he observed to Felicity. 'The clerk at her old chambers did say she had a talent for putting the cat amongst the pigeons. He was upset to lose her on one level, because she brings in the fees, but I could tell he was relieved on another.' He scratched his head. 'Still, I didn't expect her to be rocking the boat this early on.'

'What will you do about it?'

'Watch and wait,' said Henry. 'Watch and wait.'

The incarnation of Stephanie had so far caused next to no fuss in chambers. Like many tenants, she worked a good deal from home, and her fleeting appearances, dressed in Caroline Charles suits and Ferragamo heels, were met with calm, friendly smiles. Ann Halliday, the only other female QC at 5 Caper Court apart from Natalie, found herself admiring one of Stephanie's dresses and asking her where she'd got it. Only later, when she was googling the retailer, did she worry whether the enquiry had sounded patronising. She would have been reassured to know that Stephanie was in fact quietly delighted that she'd asked. And it turned out the dress had been so popular at John Lewis that it was currently out of stock.

Henry had been concerned as to how Stephen's new

persona would be received in the wider world, and although it seemed to be accepted without a murmur in the courtroom, he did notice at first a certain falling-off in the quantity of work coming Stephanie's way from solicitors. He concluded that, despite professing to be all for inclusivity and diversity, individuals at certain firms harboured nervous reservations about how clients might react to Stephanie. He could only hope that things would pick up in time.

Then came the fateful Tuesday in mid-May, when young Dee, the admin assistant whose main job, amongst other menial tasks, was to print out the huge volumes of documents generated by the work of the barristers, breezed into the ladies' loo to find Stephanie emerging from one of the cubicles 'adjusting his tackle', as she put it to those in the clerks' room five minutes later.

'I mean, I didn't know where to look! I just came straight out.' She appealed to Henry. 'It's not right, him using the ladies'. Her. It's really not.'

Henry wasn't entirely sure how to deal with this unexpected crisis. He was surprised that it hadn't cropped up before now. He glanced to Felicity for support; her instincts were with Dee, but she hesitated to say so. Henry decided to stick to the approved line. 'If we're accepting Stephanie for who she is,' he ventured, 'then I can't see we can deny her access to the ladies'.'

Dee folded her arms. 'You can say what you like, but Stephanie is definitely not a lady. Not so long as she still pees standing up.'

Natalie came into the clerks' room at that moment, and picked up on the argument. 'What's the problem?' she asked.

Felicity wasn't a fan of Natalie, but as she was a senior woman in chambers it was worth appealing to her. 'Dee went into the ladies', and there was Stephanie – well . . .' She paused and glanced at Dee.

'He had his skirt up and he was sorting himself out. I mean *she* was sorting *herself* out.'

Carla, the office manager, observed grimly, 'It's one thing to accept Stephanie for who she wants to be, but this clearly presents a problem. Frankly, I think it's an insult to every woman in chambers.'

'I'm sure Stephanie never intended to insult anyone—' began Felicity.

Dee interrupted her with customary directness. 'I went into the ladies' loo, and there was a bloke in there. No other way of putting it.'

'Dee, that kind of talk is completely inappropriate,' said Henry, though he knew he was in difficult territory. 'What happened was just unfortunate.'

'No,' said Dee stoutly, dredging up from somewhere an expression that stymied everyone, 'it's a safeguarding issue, isn't it?'

Henry had no answer to this. Natalie, who had been listening to the to-and-fro, said, 'Dee may have a point. Chambers has an obligation to ensure the well-being of its employees. Female staff should have a right not to feel threatened in any aspect of our environment.'

Felicity tried to imagine what Stephanie was feeling right now. All she could summon up was a picture of Stephen in his pinstripes and black-rimmed glasses, looking mortified. 'Look, of course Stephanie didn't mean to threaten Dee—'

'That's not the point. The question is whether Dee felt threatened.' To this Dee gave a vigorous nod. Natalie turned to Henry. 'I really think this is a matter for the head of chambers.' Henry agreed, relieved not to have to resolve the problem himself.

Natalie smiled to herself as she left the clerks' room. She looked forward to watching Leo try to sort this one out.

Half an hour later, Henry, Felicity, Natalie, and Carla were seated around the conference table in Leo's room. Dee had agreed to let more mature voices speak for her. Leo listened as the matter was fully explained to him.

'That's tricky,' he murmured. 'Obviously Stephanie meant no harm—'

'We can't ignore the fact that a junior member of staff was very upset, Mr Davies,' said Felicity.

'It's more than just a question of people being upset,' said Carla. 'It's entirely inappropriate that a male member of chambers should be allowed to use the women's facilities, just because he puts on a dress and a bit of lipstick.'

Leo, startled, said, 'I like to think we all see what Stephanie is doing in a more sympathetic light than that.'

Natalie saw her opportunity and smoothly picked up the baton. 'That's really a question of perspective, isn't it? Yours is that of the male majority in chambers. As one of the only two female QCs at 5 Caper Court—'

'Three. Don't forget Stephanie.'

Natalie gave him an angry stare. 'As one of the female QCs at 5 Caper Court, I see this as yet another example of women's interests in these chambers being obscured by those of men.'

'I thought Stephanie's identity as a woman was accepted by all of us. But perhaps not by you?' Leo knew he was being deliberately provocative, but the sense of Natalie's personal hostility had provoked him to an unusual degree.

'I sympathise with Stephanie's predicament as much as anyone.' Natalie seemed to be simmering with suppressed anger. 'But this attempt at inclusivity, permitting a man to trespass on female territory simply by virtue of putting on a dress, diminishes the rights of all women in chambers. I think that's what Carla is saying, and I support her. I'm afraid every male instinct seems to be to erode women's power, and of course, that's intensified in a set of chambers where women are in the minority.'

Leo, momentarily at a loss, was reminded of the talents that made Natalie such a formidable courtroom opponent. 'Are you seriously suggesting that Stephanie is somehow' – he let out a laugh – 'I don't know, trying to use her position to exert control on behalf of men in these chambers?'

'There's nothing remotely amusing about any of this—'

'I think we may be making something of a mountain out of a molehill,' interrupted Henry, in his best conciliatory manner. 'There's a problem here that needs to be sorted, but—'

'Forgive me,' said Natalie, turning to him, 'but what may seem to you as a man to be a trivial matter can have far-reaching implications for women on a political level. Allowing male-bodied persons to use women's facilities is an erosion of hard-won female rights.'

Felicity and Carla were startled to find their concerns characterised in quite this way, but they could hardly take issue.

'Right,' sighed Leo. 'The point is taken. We'll have to try to find a solution acceptable to everyone. And that includes Stephanie.'

When everyone had gone, Leo sat pondering the problem. At length he got up, took a deep breath, and went to Stephanie's room.

Forty-five minutes later he emerged, and went downstairs. It was lunchtime, and only Henry and Felicity were in the clerks' room. 'I've just spent the better part of the past hour with Stephanie,' said Leo.

Felicity folded her arms. 'And?'

'And the situation is going to be harder to resolve than I imagined.'

'I don't see why she can't use the gents',' said Henry. 'No bloke in chambers would mind.'

'Well, quite. I'd thought that it might simply be a question of asking her not to use the ladies' loo until – well, until her transitioning moves on a bit. Perhaps that was naive of me. She doesn't want to use the men's room while she's, as she put it, still learning to be female. She sees it as important that she has access to female facilities.'

'The women won't stand for that,' said Felicity. 'You saw that from the meeting. And they've got Natalie on their side. It's a slam dunk for the girls, Mr D.'

Leo was pretty sure that Natalie was merely using the situation as another stick to beat him with, but he felt he could hardly say this.

'What about the disabled toilet?' asked Henry. 'Wouldn't that be a compromise?'

'Well – one, it's on the ground floor, and Stephanie's on the fourth,' said Leo, 'and two, offering that as a compromise rather suggests that she's suffering from some kind of disability.'

'True,' said Felicity.

'Back to the drawing board,' sighed Henry.

They continued to mull it over, and eventually concluded that, of the two men's toilets on the first and third floors, one should be designated as gender-neutral, and that Stephanie should be encouraged to use that. Leo, who in his conversation with Stephanie had detected a little more militancy than he had expected, only hoped he would be able to sell the idea to her.

While this was going on, Natalie was canvassing the views of other women in chambers. She suspected there might be some inclined to support Stephanie in principle, but succeeded, by virtue of her seniority and power of personality, in getting them to agree, one by one, that the need to safeguard the sensibilities of a junior female member of staff trumped Stephanie's right to use the ladies' loo.

The last person she went to see was Ann Halliday.

'What was Leo's take on all this?' asked Ann. She was an attractive woman in her late forties, outwardly gentle in her disposition, but a tough character who regularly fought the corner of more junior women in chambers.

'Sympathetic to Stephanie, of course. But only in terms of protecting the male patriarchy in chambers.'

'Sorry?'

'Well, she's part of it, if you think about it. Let's not pretend that in her previous incarnation, she had anything like as hard a time gaining acceptance and respect at the Commercial Bar as we women have.'

'I hadn't thought of it in that way.'

'She has my sympathy in what she's doing, but accepting her for who she wants to be doesn't exactly advance the cause of greater female representation in our profession.'

'Well, no one is suggesting it does.'

'Leo's trying to. He took some satisfaction in observing that we have three women QCs in chambers now. A nice attempt to obscure the fact that this is a male-dominated set. But of course, he wants to keep it that way. You know he tried to prevent chambers from selecting a woman for pupillage this coming autumn?'

'What?' Ann was startled. 'I can't believe that Leo would do that.'

'Oh yes. He tried to persuade the pupillage committee to reject her and instead take some young man in whom he's taken a special interest – for reasons we can all imagine.'

Ann made no reply to this. She had confused feelings about Leo. She had known him for a long time, she liked and respected him as a lawyer of exceptional talents, but she knew his sexual reputation with both men and women. She remembered that time when he had made a pass at her – an instinct for self-preservation had made her reject it, though not without reluctance. She supposed that what Natalie was telling her shouldn't surprise her.

'Fortunately,' Natalie went on, 'the pupillage committee decided to go with the female candidate. Apparently Leo was furious. I don't know about you, but I feel we need a big push to get more women into chambers. The balance as it stands is entirely wrong. And I think it's absurd of Leo to portray the Stephanie business as a step to redressing that balance.'

'No, I agree.'

'It hardly reflects well on our diversity profile to have so few female tenants. I'm trying to come up with an initiative to change things. Can I count on your support?'

'Of course,' said Ann.

'Thank you.' She left Ann's room, pleased to have manoeuvred into position another strong ally in what she now saw as her battle with Leo.

CHAPTER EIGHT

May was a busy month for Anthony. He had been working flat out on a multi-million-dollar shipbuilding dispute which, although it had earned him a considerable amount in fees, had eaten into most of his free time. On the last Friday of the month, when the case was finally over, he rang Barry.

'I haven't been to see the old man in a while. I thought we might go round this evening.'

'I can't,' said Barry. 'I'm doing a gig in Bethnal Green.'

'What about one night next week?'

'I'm in Cardiff all next week. I did try calling round the other day to see him, just on the off-chance, but I couldn't get past Jocasta. She said he was sleeping and she didn't like to disturb him. The time before that she said he was out, had some appointment at Guy's. I've texted him, but he never gets back.'

'OK. Well, I'll see what I can do. Enjoy Cardiff.'

What Barry had said reinforced Anthony's belief that Jocasta was fencing Chay off from the rest of the world. From a charitable view, perhaps she was just being protective, but the sense of being marginalised made him uneasy. He might not like his father much, and he was grateful to Jocasta for sparing him and Barry the burden of looking after him while he was ill, but they shouldn't have to fight to see him. He decided he would go round that evening, and he wouldn't ring Jocasta first to clear it with her. If she didn't appreciate an unannounced visit, that was tough.

But Jocasta welcomed him with a hug and a wide-eyed smile. She was barefoot, and wearing a long, white linen dress. 'What a nice surprise. Chay will be so pleased to see you.' She led the way down to the basement.

Now that his six months of chemotherapy were over, Chay seemed stronger and less lethargic.

'You're looking good, Dad,' Anthony told him.

'I wouldn't go that far,' said Chay, 'but I'm definitely better than I was. It'll be a while till the poison's out of my system. But who knows? Maybe it's done its work.'

Anthony noticed that as he spoke, Chay's gaze never left Jocasta as she floated around the studio, replacing old flowers with fresh ones, straightening the blinds, and generally tending things. Good for him to have someone to love, he supposed, at such a tough time. When she had finished her tasks, Jocasta slid open the glass doors at the far end and sat on the terrace in the evening sunshine with her book. Although she left them alone, it was as though she was constantly present.

At the end of the visit, as Anthony rose to go, she came

back into the studio. 'I was just about to suggest to Chay that he should have a nap.'

'No,' said Chay, 'I'm going to work. I've done enough napping over the past few months. I want to get on with things while I can.' He rose from his chair with something of his old briskness.

'Well, not for too long,' said Jocasta. She slipped her arm into his, as if to guide him.

'I can walk perfectly well,' said Chay, disengaging himself.

'Good to see you've got so much of your energy back,' said Anthony. He gave his father a farewell hug and went upstairs, followed by Jocasta.

'Thank you for looking after him the way you have,' said Anthony. 'You've been amazing.'

She gave one of her soft smiles. 'He's always been very dear to me.'

'Still, it must have been pretty relentless, the last few months.'

'I haven't minded.'

There seemed something implacable about her goodness. But maybe, thought Anthony, she really was this incredibly kind person.

'Well, I'm going to talk to Barry, suggest that we take Chay away for a holiday in a couple of weeks. You know, while we can. We all hope the treatment has done some good, but – well, he may not have that long. Who knows? And it would give you a break. You must need it.'

'You mean you want to take over?'

'What?' He gave an uncertain laugh, not sure what she meant. 'Look, Barry and I haven't exactly been hands-on. He's our father. We need to look after him better.'

99

'That's a kind thought, if rather late in the day.'

Just for an instant, he glimpsed something behind her unfaltering smile, though he couldn't say what it was. 'I know we should have done more, sooner. But it's been difficult. We'll make up for it.' She nodded. There was a silence. He opened the front door. 'OK, as I say, I'll talk to Barry and we'll arrange something. I'll be in touch.'

Jocasta closed the door and went back downstairs. Chay was seated at the end of the studio working on her portrait. She stood behind him, resting her hands lightly on his shoulders, rubbing the thin bones of his shoulder blades with her thumb.

'That was nice of Anthony to drop round,' murmured Chay. 'More than his brother does. Just sends me texts now and again to salve his conscience.'

'I told him your treatment was finished, and that it would be a good time to visit.'

'You asked him to come?'

'You're always saying they wouldn't bother otherwise.' She felt his shoulders droop slightly. She stood gazing at her portrait for a moment, then dropped a kiss on his head. 'As long as it cheered you up. That's the important thing. I'll make us some supper.'

When she had gone, Chay put his brush and paints down and went out to the terrace overlooking the sunken garden. It was a stark, sculptured area with rectangular wooden planters ranged on marble slabs, filled with astelia and peregrinans. The evening air was still warm. He sat down in a wicker chair and closed his eyes.

Twenty minutes later Jocasta emerged bearing a tray laden with bread, cheese and fruit, and a carafe of rosé wine. She set it down on the wooden table. Chay opened his eyes and sat up. She draped a cardigan around his shoulders. 'In case it gets chilly.'

'What a thoughtful girl you are.' He held her hand for a second. She sat down and poured a glass of wine and handed it to him.

He took a sip. 'Thank God I'm beginning to taste things again.'

'That's wonderful.' She watched as he helped himself to bread and cheese. 'You know, now that your treatment's over, maybe you should take a break, go on holiday somewhere.'

'That's not a bad idea,' mused Chay. 'I could go to my house in Madrid. I haven't been there for over a year.' He sat back in his chair, and contemplated her. 'Would you come with me?'

Her expression grew wistful. 'Chay, you know I adore you, and I've been so happy to help you during your treatment—'

'I know, I know, you've put your life and your work on hold to look after me, and I haven't done enough for you in return.'

'I never expected anything.'

'It's just I – I find I don't want to be without you. I need you. After all, I can't depend on my useless sons.' When she said nothing, his tone grew anxious. 'I would pay for everything. It could be a sort of business arrangement, if you like.'

She hesitated, then said, 'These last few months have been special. We were always good together.' She gave him one of her tender smiles. 'But a business arrangement?

That sounds so ugly. It's not really who we are, is it?'

'If you come with me, if you go on caring for me, I wouldn't expect you to do it for nothing.'

She reached out a hand to his. 'Well, let's see. But I think Madrid sounds a wonderful idea.'

A week later, Anthony, Gabrielle and Edward Choke were sitting at the bar of a City pub having post-work drinks. The conversation had come round to Edward's forthcoming wedding, which was to be held later that month in Italy.

'Annabel's family keep faffing around with the arrangements, but I stay well out of it,' said Ed. 'I seem to be largely an irrelevance, anyway. We're having the civil thingy here in London, but the villa has its own chapel, so now her parents have decided we should have some sort of a ceremony there, too – local priest, and all that.'

'Who's going to be best man?' asked Gabrielle.

'I can't exactly choose one of my brothers over the other, so I've asked Piers.'

'Hunt-Thompson?' Anthony made a face.

Ed gave a grin. 'You've never been his biggest fan, have you?'

'I think he's a supercilious twat.'

'I suppose he can be a touch arrogant,' said Ed. 'But I like him. Besides, we've known one another since prep school.'

'I think he's fun,' said Gabrielle, with a pointed look at Anthony.

'Really? After everything that happened at that party in Mount Street, with those appalling Saudis?'

'That wasn't Piers' fault,' replied Gabrielle. 'He didn't organise it.'

'No, but they were his friends.'

Gabrielle shrugged and finished her Diet Coke. Edward waggled his own empty glass. 'Who's ready for another?'

'Sorry, I have to go,' said Gabrielle. 'I've got a yoga class.' She slipped from her chair and kissed Anthony. 'See you later. Bye, Ed.'

When she had left, Ed scooped some peanuts from a dish and observed, 'I wasn't going to say it in front of Gabby, but let's face it, Tony, the real reason you hate Piers is because he nicked your girlfriend.'

Anthony swallowed the remains of his drink. He was long over Julia, whom he'd once thought the love of his life, but he hadn't forgotten the pain and humiliation of it all. He'd been hard up, struggling to find his place amongst the well-heeled young people that seemed to populate the Bar, and Julia's love had shored him up. At the time he'd assumed Piers had set about seducing her merely as a way of humiliating him, something that he seemed to delight in doing, but in fact he'd gone on to marry her.

As though reading his mind, Ed added, 'You know they're getting divorced?' He munched his handful of peanuts. 'Bit awkward on the wedding front, having them both there, but I couldn't *not* invite Julia.' He mused. 'I just hope they keep it civilised. You know how full on they can both be.' Anthony said nothing, and Ed went on, 'Anyway, I always thought Julia was a bit of a bitch. You're way better off with Gabs. Fantastic girl. Glad you're back together.' He signalled to the waiter for two more drinks. 'So, why did the two of you bust up?'

'Something of a misunderstanding.'

Ed nodded. 'By the way, have you booked a hotel room for the wedding yet? It's just that there's a spare room at the villa. Hugo's broken up with his girlfriend, so he's coming on his own and he won't need the double room. You can have it, if you want.'

'Yeah, that would be good, thanks.' Anthony picked up his fresh drink. 'Cheers.'

'Must be funny, going out with Leo's daughter.'

'In what way?'

'I dunno.' Edward ate a few more peanuts reflectively.

Anthony cast his mind back to the time when he and Edward had been at 5 Caper Court together as pupils, those heady days when he had fallen completely under Leo's spell. As far as he was concerned, no one, except Gabrielle, knew the full extent of their relationship. Was Ed implying that he knew more than he'd ever let on? Anthony studied his friend's bland, affable features. No, if he did, and if he wanted to signify that fact, it would be more his style to make some excruciatingly clumsy joke.

Edward went on, 'I mean, she's so like him. Must be a bit weird, no?' He chuckled. 'Always thought he was a top bloke, if a bit scary. But then, I didn't exactly measure up to his intellectual standards. How is he these days?'

Anthony thought for a moment. Just last week he'd been instructed as junior counsel on one of Leo's cases, involving a collision between an oil tanker and a cargo ship. It had been over a year since the two of them had worked together, and he'd been looking forward to sharing the electric rush of enthusiasm and adrenalin-filled urgency that Leo always brought to everything he did. But when they'd had their meeting to go through the papers, Leo had seemed harassed, distracted, and far from his usual energetic self.

'I'm not sure, to be honest. Sometimes I think he's a bit tired of it all. Clients come to him with big cases that look hopeless, and expect him to work miracles and turn things around. Once you get his kind of reputation, you have to sustain it. It must be quite relentless, staying at the top of one's game.'

'Don't know why he doesn't pack it in, in that case. I mean, he must be absolutely loaded,' said Ed. 'That's what I'd do. Buy a nice yacht, pootle around the Med, enjoy myself. What else has he worked so hard for, if not to have a good time?'

Anthony smiled. He couldn't begin to explain to someone like Edward the thing that drove Leo on – that drove him on, too – the hunger for the next challenge, taking facts and evidence, shaping them, winning cases, especially against the odds. The pleasures of life, the things that Edward cared about, were secondary to that sense of fulfilment. Work. It was all about the work.

'I don't think having a good time is what motivates him,' said Anthony. 'In fact, I'm not entirely sure what his idea of a good time is.'

Leo, a few hours later, found himself wondering the very same thing. He had left a private members' club in Mayfair in the company of Jessica, a thirty-seven-year-old investment broker whom he had known for some time. She was a slender brunette with a waspish sense of humour, and together with her friend Phil, a young music producer, they had taken a taxi back to Leo's house in Chelsea. When

Leo came back from the kitchen with ice for their drinks, he found Phil neatly racking up lines of cocaine on the glass coffee table. Jessica had kicked off her shoes and was curled up on the sofa, watching.

'Sorry,' said Leo, setting down the dish of ice, 'that's not something you can do here.'

Phil looked at him with a puzzled smile.

'I'm a barrister,' replied Leo. 'I can't afford to break the law, or let others do it in my house.' He loosened his tie. 'Tedious, I know, but there it is.'

By way of response, Phil ducked his head and snorted up one of the lines. In a gesture of irritation, Leo swept the rest of the coke off the table.

'I said, not in this house.' He dusted his hands.

'What the fuck, mate?' Phil seemed appalled at the waste.

'Leo,' said Jessica, 'the police aren't going to come breaking down the door. What's your problem?'

Leo sighed inwardly. He had been quite taken with Phil when he'd met him at Loulou's earlier in the evening, spare and darkly handsome, giving off a promising sexual vibe. Leo had imagined that after a few drinks the three of them could go to bed and enjoy themselves in any number of ways. It was the kind of default hedonism in which he generally indulged to obliterate life's complications and anxieties – which right now consisted mainly of his increasing sense of alienation in chambers, and the prospect of seeing so much less of Oliver. But suddenly bedding Phil didn't seem such an attractive prospect. Leo was irked by his belligerence, and even by his very youthfulness. He felt tired. 'Maybe you should go,' he said. 'But please, finish your drink first.'

Phil knocked back his whisky and picked up his jacket. He glanced at Jessica, but she merely gave him a little wave, murmuring, 'Nighty-night.'

When Phil had left, Leo sank down next to Jessica, leant back and closed his eyes. She reached forward and dropped cubes of ice into both their drinks, then took a sip of hers. She settled back, slipping one hand into Leo's unbuttoned shirt, and kissed him on the mouth. He returned the kiss, running his fingers lightly over her body. She gave a little shiver and kneaded his hand against her breast.

'It's a shame you asked Phil to leave. It could have been a lot of fun. It's not like you to get so heavy over one line of coke.'

'My house, my rules. What he did was rude.'

'He's a sweet guy, really.'

A Harvey Specter line that Sarah had particularly liked came back to him. 'I could agree with you,' he murmured, 'but then we'd both be wrong.' He kissed her again, more hungrily this time, willing himself into the mood. But a bit of him wished that he was lying on this sofa with Sarah, watching *Suits*. In hindsight, that had been a good time.

CHAPTER NINE

The following Monday morning, Felicity came into the clerks' room and saw Henry gazing at his computer screen, his customary expression of mild harassment transformed into one of unusual cheerfulness. She felt a little pang as she realised that the last time she'd seen that look on his face was during their brief, and to her mind ill-advised, affair. He was such a lovely man, but it had all been a bit close to home, and she hadn't been ready for another relationship so soon after the spectacular fallout from living with Vince, her previous long-term boyfriend. Now she sometimes wondered wistfully if it might have worked out if the timing had been better.

Pushing this thought from her mind, she went over to his workstation. 'What's got you looking so pleased?' she asked.

'The London Legal Awards have just come out. They've named Mr Davies shipping silk of the year, and guess who the commercial litigation set of the year is?' He looked up at Felicity with a grin. He looked so sweet and boyish she had a sudden urge to kiss him, but let it pass. Then what he'd said sank in, and her eyes widened.

'Not us?'

Henry turned back to the screen. '*Amongst the elite commercial sets in England, 5 Caper Court is rated as one of the most high-performing and dynamic. The intellectual and academic calibre of its members is second to none, combining a robust, punchy approach with supreme practical rigour.*' Henry scrolled down, searching. '*The clerks' room, led by senior clerk Henry Dawes, sets the bar for responsible, intelligent clerking and is in a different league to most commercial chambers. Henry takes the time to cultivate excellent relationships with solicitors and develop innovative fee structures. On-the-ball deputy senior clerk Felicity Waller never fails to find a solution and always impresses with her helpfulness in overcoming challenges with court listings.*'

'There's impressive stuff about Mr Davies in the nominations,' added Henry, doing some more scrolling. '*Unquestionably the best at the Commercial Bar, a charismatic advocate of consummate ability . . . the difference between winning and losing*'; '*urbane, funny and devastating in the courtroom*'; '*a fantastic lawyer*'; '*an enormously impressive guy with a really supreme mind*'; '*a tenacious, disciplined and rigorous advocate, with phenomenal intelligence, amazing forensic skills and a good sense of humour.*'

'That's lovely for Mr D,' said Felicity. 'He needs something to cheer him up. He's been going around looking like a wet weekend lately.'

Henry got up. 'I think I'll pop upstairs now and tell him.'

Henry found Leo at his desk, surrounded by documents from the ship grounding case.

'Some nice news, sir,' said Henry. 'You've been named shipping silk of the year.'

The news wasn't received with quite the enthusiastic delight that Henry had hoped for.

'Have I now?' Leo took off his glasses with a sigh. 'They seem to hand out awards like sweets these days. Still, it's good publicity for chambers. Which outfit is it?'

'Legal London. Go on – have a look. Should do your ego good.'

Leo logged in to the Legal London site and clicked through the various categories. He glanced up at Henry. 'You didn't say we'd been named best commercial litigation set as well.'

'I was coming to that. I thought you'd like to read about yourself first.'

'The less of that the better. I might start to believe my own publicity, and that would never do.' He smiled as he read the screen. 'They say some nice things about you and Felicity. And well deserved, too.'

'Nothing in comparison to you.'

Leo sat back. 'I suppose I should be pleased, but frankly, Henry, I'm beginning to wonder whether all this is worth it.'

Henry leant against a bookcase and folded his arms, studying Leo's face, noting how tired and dispirited he looked.

'Come on, I've heard that from you before. A case starts to wear you down, but then when it's all over and you've won, you're back to your old self. I knew when you took on this grounding case it would be a tough one.'

'Oh, it's not the case.' Leo glanced at the documents piled up on his desk. 'I actually think we're in with a chance, which certainly wasn't the way it looked at the outset. No, it's something else entirely.' He paused. 'Natalie has got it into her head that 5 Caper Court projects too masculine an image. She thinks it would be a good idea if we had joint male and female heads of chambers.'

'I suppose there's something in that.'

'I have no particular objection. If someone wants to share this godawful burden, they're welcome to. Thank Christ it can't be Natalie – she hasn't been here long enough. The only other woman with enough seniority is Ann Halliday.'

'She'll be fine.'

'Of course she will. Natalie says she intends to update our equality and diversity policy, too. Again, she's entirely welcome. But she seems to regard it all as some kind of palace revolution, with Ann helping to spearhead the radical feminist cohort. Not quite Ann's style, but there we are. Natalie can be very persuasive. She's certainly rallied the troops amongst the younger members of chambers, and seems to have persuaded them that there are other changes that need to happen. Apparently, she thinks we focus too much on contract law. She wants us to try and bring in more human rights work.'

Henry rubbed his chin. 'I suppose it's the up-and-coming thing. Mr Vane's been taking on a few cases of that kind.'

'But Henry, contract law is what we do. We're a commercial set.' Leo gestured to his laptop screen. 'The best in London, some people seem to think. We should leave civil liberties and human rights stuff to the likes of Matrix and Blackstone. Why should 5 Caper Court have to change its entire ethos and image? She's also proposing something she calls a "diversity lateral hire sub-committee", to increase the number of women in chambers. Says we're in danger of looking misogynistic. This from the woman who thinks Stephanie is operating from a base of male privilege.' Leo turned to Henry. 'Do you think we're misogynistic, Henry? I mean, really? I sometimes think I don't have a proper perspective on this.'

'I suppose we're a very traditional set, sir,' mused Henry. 'But no one could accuse us of that.' He shook his head. 'Definitely not.'

'I don't get it. And as I told them, the last thing we need is another sub-committee, on top of the marketing sub-committee, the data practice sub-committee, the IT sub-committee, the practice development sub-committee – there's no end to the sodding things. Maybe it was my mistake to tell them so. It wasn't a happy meeting, I can tell you. I'm definitely getting the feeling that there's an element in chambers that would like to see the back of me. Natalie King, in particular.'

'I'm sure that's very wide of the mark, sir. You know how well regarded you are. Just look at that award.'

'I don't know, Henry.' Leo shook his head. 'I really don't know. I'm beginning to think it might be as well to just pack it in, leave at the top of my game. I'm pretty sick of the way things are going round here. Anyway, enough of my moaning. Thanks for letting me know about the award.'

Henry left the room and went back downstairs. Over the years he'd grown used to Leo's black moods, but that was the first time he'd heard such a tone of resignation in his voice. Ever since her arrival, Natalie King had been quietly stirring things up, and the eddies of discontent were brewing into an ugly tide – one that seemed to be turning against Mr Davies. The time for watching and waiting was over.

Towards the end of the afternoon, Henry went to see Natalie, ostensibly regarding a hearing date that had been brought forward, causing a mix-up in Natalie's diary. When that had been disposed of, as he was rising to leave, he took the opportunity to add, 'I understand from Mr Davies there's an idea of setting up a new committee to get more women into chambers.' He said this in his most affable tone, and with a smile that suggested he found the idea an interesting and welcome one.

'Yes, it's been mooted. The junior tenants seem to be in favour. What do you think?'

Natalie regarded Henry as she waited for his answer. Her view of him was that he belonged too much to the old school of clerking. She had been weighing him up ever since her arrival a few months ago, and had decided that certain attributes were lacking. True, he was excellent at his job, but in her view he was too circumspect and unadventurous in his management of the clerks' room. When she had suggested the introduction of appraisals and personal development targets he had been polite but dismissive. Natalie had not forgotten that.

'I suppose that depends on how it's done,' replied

113

Henry, resuming his seat. 'I mean, we have a fair number of excellent female tenants already, two of last year's pupils were women and we take all our pupils on merit, so—'

'You don't detect some unconscious bias amongst the more senior members of chambers?' Without waiting for an answer, Natalie went on, 'We're never going to achieve gender equality unless there's equality of power. That's as true of 5 Caper Court as it is of society in general. Which is why I proposed we have joint male and female heads of chambers.'

'So I heard. I'm all in favour of that. As is Mr Davies.'

'If he's so keen on the idea, I wonder why it hasn't happened before now. In any event, I think we need to go further, which is why I proposed the diversity lateral hire sub-committee to bring in more women.'

'You mean quotas?'

He meant it as a challenge. Natalie met his level gaze. 'That's such a loaded word. But yes, I suppose I'm saying we need to take positive steps to redress the gender balance in chambers. There's a change in culture, Henry, in case you hadn't noticed. Certainly, our head of chambers doesn't seem to have. He doesn't seem particularly au fait with the "me-too" mindset. With his reputation one might even say he's something of a liability.' She paused, weighing her words. 'A kind of Kevin Spacey figure, one might almost say.'

This was her response to his challenge, and it altered the atmosphere in an instant. Henry suddenly understood that Natalie's ambitions extended far beyond the rebalancing of perceived inequalities. Mr Davies was right. She wanted him gone, so that she could shape chambers in her own preferred image. He felt mildly shocked at the realisation, aware that the threat extended to him, and to everyone who did not share her vision.

'That is, if I may so, a rather disagreeable remark,' replied Henry. If this was to be a power struggle, he would have to assert himself, and confrontation was not in his nature.

'Well, of course I would expect you to support him,' replied Natalie.

Henry regarded her, sitting behind her desk in her elegant suit, smiling and fingering her silver necklace, and felt a smoulder of rage, an unaccustomed sentiment for him. That this woman should insidiously and single-mindedly go about the business of undermining and changing what had, until a few months ago, been a happy and well-balanced set of chambers, angered him deeply.

'It's not a question of supporting anyone. That suggests some kind of division. It's my job to see that this set of chambers runs harmoniously. We've always rubbed along very well here, until recently.'

'I hope you're not characterising my attempts to rebalance dangerous inequalities and promote the image of chambers as being in some way divisive.'

'Let's just put it this way, madam. 5 Caper Court has always thrived on a spirit of co-operation. It's the way with all successful chambers. We clerks bring in the work, you carry it out, and we all support each other. When there's friction or division, it destabilises things. If some member of chambers rocks the boat, they may find themselves not getting the support they need.'

Natalie's chilly smile faded. 'Is that some kind of a threat?'

Henry assumed an expression of pained surprise. 'Not at all. I'm just saying we need to keep one another's best interests at heart. Saying that kind of thing about Mr Davies doesn't help. So probably best not to repeat it.' He got to his feet. 'As for the business of quotas, that's up to you and the other tenants.' When he reached the door he added, 'Of course, since it's image improvement you're after, I'll make sure to put your name forward for some pro bono work. It makes a good impression for senior tenants to be seen doing work for free.'

Henry left and went back downstairs, satisfied that he had delivered Natalie a timely reminder that it was the clerks, and her senior clerk in particular, on whom she relied for work, and that if she pushed things too far, life might become a little difficult. But he was alarmed by the current of feeling that seemed to be running against Leo. It might be an idea to find out just what was going on with the junior tenants. At the end of the day he sought out Anthony and suggested going for a drink, and they repaired to a Fleet Street pub where, over beers, Henry recounted to Anthony all that had happened with Leo and Natalie.

'She may have a point about getting a better balance of women in chambers, but the way she talks about Mr Davies – it's like she's got some kind of a vendetta against him. I wondered what you thought.'

'I have to say there seems to be a fair bit of discontent amongst the junior tenants,' said Anthony. 'For one thing, they don't like Leo's history. You know the kind of thing I mean.'

Although Henry had had in the past to deal with

problems caused by Leo's sexual proclivities, he replied stoutly, 'What Mr Davies gets up to in his private life is his business.'

'Yes, but they're remarkably prudish, the younger lot. They think Leo's reputation reflects badly on chambers. And on top of that, they've been grumbling about money, the percentage they have to pay in rent and overheads, when Leo gets the lion's share of the work.'

'Which is why his contribution is so much bigger than theirs. Fifteen per cent of what they earn might seem a lot to them, but they'd be paying a damn sight more without Mr D's share. They should be careful what they wish for.' Henry supped his beer, then asked with real worry in his voice, 'Do you think there's genuine feeling against Mr Davies?'

'I hate to say so, but yes. For whatever reason – and I personally think it's just that they don't like his style, they think his approach to chambers is too laissez-faire – they'd be quite happy to see him ousted.'

'I had no idea it was that bad,' muttered Henry.

But things were to get worse. A few days later Henry came into the deserted clerks' room at lunchtime, and found Felicity crying at her desk. When she saw Henry she hastily wiped away her tears and forced a smile. He came over to her with a look of concern.

'What's the matter?'

She shook her head, as though unable to speak.

'Come on. You've always been able to talk to me.'

Tears welled up again in Felicity's eyes. 'Don't be nice to me, Henry. It just sets me off.'

At that moment Ayisha and Carla came in with their sandwiches and coffee, chatting and paying no attention to Henry and Felicity.

'Let's you and me go round the corner for a coffee and you can tell me what's up,' said Henry in a low voice. 'Carla can man the phones.'

They went to the nearest Pret A Manger and sat at stools at a corner counter. Henry bought coffees.

'Right. Tell Uncle Henry what's made you so miserable.'

Felicity almost laughed. 'That's a really weird way to refer to yourself, you know.'

Henry looked embarrassed. 'Hmm. I suppose so. I'm not sure how you think of me these days.'

She shook her head and smiled sadly. Then after a pause she said, 'Natalie King's been saying stuff about me to Carla. I suppose Carla thought she was doing me a favour, telling me, but I honestly wish she hadn't.' She dabbed her eyes with a tissue.

'What kind of stuff?'

'She says she's not being clerked properly, that I'm not getting her good enough work. She even said I wasn't the right image for chambers, going on about how the other big sets are getting in people with university degrees, and that. All I've got is six GCSEs. And two of those are PE and RE,' she added miserably. 'Apparently at her last chambers the deputy senior clerk was some QC's daughter with an MBA, or whatever, and she thinks that's the kind of person we need, not me.' She gave a sniff and dabbed her eyes again. 'Maybe she's right.'

'She's a stuck-up bitch. And she's far from right.' Henry placed a hand on Felicity's shoulder. 'Look at what they said about you in the London Legal Awards. It's what clients and solicitors think that matters, not the self-important bollocks she comes out with.' He paused. 'The fact is, she's got some campaign going. I don't exactly know what's behind it, but she's gunning for Mr Davies. From what Mr Cross says, she's got the younger lot behind her.'

Felicity nodded. 'Yeah, Liam said something about that.' She sighed heavily. 'It was all fine before she came. You know, if she forces Mr D out, I'm not sure I'd want to stay at Caper Court. It wouldn't be the same.'

'Hey, come on. You're blowing it out of all proportion. Mr Davies isn't going anywhere. And neither are we.' He lifted his hand from her shoulder and pushed a stray curl of hair from her face. 'We've been in this together for too long to let that happen.'

A deep, welling sense of affection opened up inside Felicity as she gazed at Henry, surprising her with its intensity.

'You know, Fliss—' Henry went on. Then he paused, frowning uncertainly at his coffee. His tone had altered, and she realised whatever he was about to say had nothing to do with chambers, or Natalie, or any of that stuff.

'What?'

'When things ended between us – well, I suppose they'd hardly begun, really – at the time I told myself it just wasn't meant to happen. But I always wondered – you know, because we never, like, talked about it, or anything – I always wondered, if things had been different, if you hadn't just been through all that awful stuff with Vince, whether we might not have stood a better chance.' He lifted his eyes to hers, his expression hopeful and hopeless all at once.

'I've wondered that, too.'

'Really?' Henry leant towards her, gazing at her intently. 'I mean, really?'

Felicity smiled at him. This was possibly the nicest man she had ever known. 'Really.' She leant forward and kissed him.

CHAPTER TEN

'I'm going to Italy this weekend for a wedding. Why don't we take Dad on holiday somewhere when I get back?'

'Fine by me,' said Barry. He and Anthony were having a drink at a riverside pub in Hammersmith. 'Where were you thinking?'

'I don't know. He always liked Greece. It'll have to be somewhere he can get about easily. Last time I saw him he looked pretty frail.'

'Greece sounds good. We can sort out something suitable.' Barry pulled out his phone. 'I'll give him a call now and see if he's up for it.' He keyed in his father's number. 'Dad, hi – it's me. Yeah. How are you? Good, good. Listen, I'm with Anthony, and we were just talking – now your chemo's finished, how about the three of us go away somewhere for a week or two? Bit of a holiday, you know.' There was a long pause. 'Oh, right.' Another pause. 'OK, no worries – it was just a thought. You enjoy yourself. Let's speak when you get back.' He clicked his phone off and looked over at Anthony. 'He's at his house in Spain with Jocasta. He's going to be there for the rest of summer.'

'Oh, really?' Anthony cast his mind back to the last conversation he'd had with Jocasta. He'd definitely told her that he and Barry intended to take their father on holiday. He remembered she'd reacted strangely.

'She's quite a permanent fixture, isn't she? I suppose it's a good thing he's back with her,' said Barry. 'Someone to look after him. I feel I've been next to useless.'

'Me too. But there's a limit to what we can do. No, you're right, she's a good thing.' Anthony drained his beer. 'Anyway, I better head home and pack. Got an early start tomorrow.'

When Anthony and Gabrielle headed to Gatwick for the early morning flight to Verona, they were part of a crowd of young people marked out from the other passengers by their assuredness, their youth and attractiveness, and their clear, confident voices. Anthony sat in the departure lounge, reading *The Times* on his iPad, while Gabrielle chatted and laughed with girlfriends. He glanced up at them occasionally. They weren't loud or boisterous, but they drew glances from other people. They gave off, he realised, a kind of glow, the one that comes from having a comfortable background and a certain kind of education. It occurred to him that none of them, including Gabrielle, had ever been troubled by not having enough money, or by the peculiar, dragging notion that they might not be good enough. They had been taught all their lives that they were better than good enough, which was why they behaved as they did, in that faintly entitled manner, with that arrogant ease in which he himself could not share.

They were joined at the last minute by Piers Hunt-Thompson, who, to hoots and cheers, came pushing to the front of the Speedy Boarding queue trailing his expensive leather cabin bag. He was tall, with floppy brown hair, and his big, ugly face with its long, broken nose managed somehow to be attractive. He greeted everyone extravagantly, air-kissing girls and bear-hugging the men, demonstrating a playful superiority of manner that seemed to endear him to his friends but drew irascible glances from other passengers. It irritated Anthony to see Gabrielle greet him with so much enthusiasm.

Everybody was in high spirits on the flight, Piers just a little rowdier than everyone else, treating the cabin crew with charm and condescension. He was, thought Anthony as he watched him, one of those men who made his way through life in the full belief of his own worth. It was a kind of talent in itself. The man was unsinkable.

Anthony had hired a car at the other end, a two-door four-seater Peugeot, and after he had finally got the keys and located the car, and as he and Gabrielle were putting their cases in the boot, Piers sauntered over with his case.

'Any chance of a lift?' he asked.

Anthony closed the boot and gave Piers an unfriendly look. 'Didn't you think to hire a car yourself?'

'Anthony, don't be a dick,' said Gabrielle. She gave Piers a sunny smile. 'Of course you can have a lift.'

There then followed a brief discussion about seating arrangements and leg room, and Piers and Gabrielle ended up together in the back seat, the front passenger seat rammed well forward to accommodate Piers' long legs. Anthony drove, while Piers and Gabrielle gossiped and giggled in the back. He glanced at them from time to time in the rear-view mirror with a sinking sense of déjà vu. There had to be a reason why Piers hadn't cadged a lift from any one of the others who had hired cars. History wasn't going to repeat itself, surely? Of all the things he most detested about Piers, it was the effect the man had on his own behaviour. His dislike of Piers seemed to stifle him, rendering him savagely mute and reducing him, as Gabrielle had pointed out, to behaving like a dick. He would just have to do his best to avoid him over the weekend.

After a few issues with the satnav, they eventually reached the villa.

'Oh my God!' exclaimed Gabrielle, craning forward from the back seat as they drove between massive stone pillars with wrought-iron gates into a long straight driveway. 'Look at this place!'

The seventeenth-century Villa Lanciatto, set in a mixture of woodlands and formal gardens, was an elegant three-storey building in pale stone, with two curved wings extending at either side, fronted by flagged terraces with stone balustrades. Pale green wooden shutters were open at all the windows, and on the lawn in front of the house the waters of a fountain danced in the sunshine. To the right, set back from the main house, was the chapel, and to the left, beyond low box hedges, lay prettily whitewashed outbuildings with green shutters that matched those of the villa. The grounds of the house sloped away to a small lake, some three hundred metres from the villa.

As they got out of the car, they could hear the sounds of laughter and splashing from a swimming pool somewhere beyond the hedge. Edward came out to greet them, dressed in chinos and a white T-shirt, a glass of beer in hand.

'Wise move, hiring a car,' he said, slapping Anthony's shoulder. 'Hugo and Patrick were mad enough to take a taxi, and it cost them a hundred and forty euros. Come on, I'll show you where your rooms are.'

Piers was directed to a room in one of the converted farm buildings adjacent to the villa, where Ed's single male friends were being housed, and Edward led Gabrielle and Anthony upstairs to one of the top-floor bedrooms overlooking the parkland at the rear of the house.

'Come down when you're ready,' said Ed, 'and you can grab some lunch and have a swim.'

When Ed had wandered off, Gabrielle flopped back on the four-poster bed.

'This place is amazing. Must be costing Annabel's parents a fortune.' She wound a thick lock of dark blonde hair round one finger and smiled at Anthony. 'Come over here.'

He lay down on the bed next to her, kissing her as she unbuttoned his linen shirt and slipped it back from his shoulders. They made love effortlessly, almost drowsily, tired by the day's travelling, their minds elsewhere. Afterwards, Anthony rolled onto his back and Gabrielle straddled him, kissing his chest and pushing his dark hair from his forehead. She contemplated his well-muscled body, his dark eyes and sensuous mouth.

'I can see why my father's so fond of you,' she said.

He sat up, gently pushing her off him so that he could get off the bed and go to the bathroom. Through the half-open door he could hear her voice saying, 'I'm sorry, I'm sorry. I don't know why I said that. It was stupid.'

He flushed the loo and came back. She was sitting naked on the edge of the bed, her hair tumbled around her shoulders, looking like a penitent nymph. He placed his hands on her shoulders. Did she have any idea how much she reminded him of Leo? Maybe that was why she said these things, testing him, testing herself.

'Can we keep Leo out of this? Please? Apart from anything else, I don't want to think about chambers, or anyone in it, right now. Things are not good there. OK?'

She reached up her face and kissed him. 'OK.' She smiled. 'Come on, let's unpack and go and get something to eat.'

Downstairs, they found people coming and going in the big kitchen, helping themselves to food from the platters of cheese, cold meat, salmon and salad laid out on the scrubbed wooden table, pouring drinks from an array of bottles of wine and beer chilling in ice buckets. They had taken possession of the place much as if it had belonged to them, unfazed by the grandeur of their surroundings, the panelled rooms, the enormous fireplaces and sweeping stone staircases. They were entirely at home.

Anthony and Gabrielle helped themselves to food and drink, and went out into the sunshine. Anthony spotted Edward's parents at a table on the terrace with some other people, and suggested joining them.

'You can introduce me later,' said Gabrielle. 'Julia's down at the pool, and I haven't seen her in ages. I'll see you in a bit.'

126

The swimming pool lay beyond the terrace, and Anthony could see Julia, with her short blonde hair, lying in a red bikini on a sun lounger amongst a group of friends. At the opposite corner of the pool, next to a covered bar area, Piers was horsing noisily around with some other young men, while Julia studiously ignored him.

In the evening there was an informal supper on the terrace. Anthony, by dint of staying well away from Piers, found himself better able to relax. Edward's friends were his friends now, too; he no longer felt out of his depth in the way he would have ten years ago. A handful of couples at their table had become recently engaged, and much of the talk revolved around weddings and house prices. As he sat with his fourth glass of wine, Anthony found himself considering what it would be like to be one of them, embarking on the exciting joint venture of marriage, with houses and babies and all the rest of it. He realised, as he looked around the table, that for these young people the prospect of treading the same path as their parents, with the same middle-class expectations, was a comforting one. The reassurance of perpetuating the things they had always known, within the circles in which they moved, was strong. He glanced at Gabrielle. Her hair was loosely swept up, silky tendrils glinting in the candlelight against the softness of her cheek, and she was laughing at something someone had said, her hands clasped before her on the table. She looked very pretty, very happy, and so much a part of it all that he was suddenly filled with a rush of longing, a need to belong, to share in the safety and happiness of these people and their world. He could marry Gabrielle, have a wedding just like this, buy a family house in Wandsworth, have children, send them to good schools, buy a second home in Dorset, go skiing in Val d'Isère every winter, rent a place in The Hamptons, or a villa on a Greek island in summer. He already earned, and would with luck and diligence go on earning, the kind of money to live just such a life. The thought was beguiling, and at the same time suffocating, frightening.

'We went there a couple of weeks ago,' Gabrielle was saying. She turned to Anthony. 'Didn't we?'

'Where?'

'That new place in Mayfair, the one that's just got a Michelin star.'

'Oh yes. Forgotten its name. It was amazing.'

'Isn't it fabulously expensive?' asked someone.

'Fabulously,' laughed Anthony. 'But who cares?'

He heard himself, hated himself, and then forgave himself. The chatter about London restaurants continued. He put out a finger and traced a gentle line across the skin of Gabrielle's shoulder. She turned again to smile at him. It was a soft, radiant smile.

'What?' she murmured.

'Nothing. Just thinking about you. About us. About all this.' Maybe it was the answer. Right now, at this point in his life, he couldn't think of another.

After supper Edward had, perhaps ill-advisedly, but with the idea of bringing together the generations, organised a quiz. The thirty or so guests sat in groups at the long dining table indoors, while Edward tried gamely to marshal proceedings. A lot of people were quite drunk by this stage, Piers in particular. He was in a team that included Annabel's aunt Lauren, an attractive woman in her late forties, who looked ten years younger, and who was flirting with the young men on her team with the provocative good humour of an older woman who knows she is still desirable. Piers took to referring to her as 'Mrs Robinson', but failed to pick up on the chilly warning smile she gave in response to this. Some people said later that it was Lauren's fault for flirting so shamelessly, others blamed Piers for overstepping the mark, as usual, but all agreed that it was hugely embarrassing and unfortunate when Piers tried to make a drunken pass at Lauren, which ended with him spilling an entire glass of red wine into the lap of her ivory silk dress, then tumbling off his chair and pulling her down with him.

The quiz descended into a shambles, Lauren exited in wine-soaked fury, and Annabel's father took Piers aside to give him a good talking-to, which Piers accepted with appropriate, albeit drunken, humility. However, he then compounded his error by going to Lauren's room to try to apologise, which did not go down well.

Everyone at last went to bed, and peace reigned over Villa Lanciatto.

Around 2 a.m. the peace was broken by high-pitched buzzing from the direction of the lake. Lights went on all over the villa, and Annabel's father and uncle went out in dressing gowns with torches to discover Piers and four others, armed with bottles of beer and wine and a couple of flashlights, racing remote-controlled toy boats on the lake. There were angry remonstrations, the miscreants were ordered back to their beds, and everyone went back to sleep.

Breakfast the next morning was a makeshift meal of coffee and rolls. After last night the atmosphere was subdued but cheerful. Piers appeared, badly hungover, unshaven and unapologetic, sporting a pair of Cartier Santos sunglasses and complaining loudly about the quality of the coffee.

As they breakfasted outside on the terrace, Anthony and Gabrielle watched as Piers tried gamely to make amends with Annabel's parents for his behaviour the previous night; they seemed grudgingly forbearing.

'God, the man's a nightmare,' said Anthony.

'It's only because the divorce is making him so utterly bloody miserable,' said Gabrielle, licking her finger to pick up the remaining crumbs of bread from her plate.

Anthony hadn't given any thought to the effect on Piers of his divorce. The man seemed so unassailable that the idea of him being rendered vulnerable and unhappy seemed a strange one.

'He didn't seem particularly miserable when he was flirting with you in the car yesterday.'

'That's just his way. Piers being Piers.'

Anthony gave her a glance. 'Do you find him attractive?'

'Sort of. I mean, he's fun to be with – up to a point. But he always pushes things too far. He's cruel to people. He was cruel to Julia, and now he's paying for it.' She pushed her plate away and gave him a smile. 'That's enough about him. Let's have a swim.'

Some people spent the morning by the pool, some in the games room, and others in the peace and quiet of the villa's library and drawing room. Then in the early afternoon the caterers descended to take over the kitchen, and a small army of staff bustled about on the terrace, spreading snowy cloths on a sea of tables, laying out cutlery and wine glasses and floral centrepieces. Guests took themselves off to their rooms to get ready for the ceremony.

Annabel and Edward's wedding took place late that afternoon in the chapel adjoining the villa, with a local priest officiating. The sun shone, the bride looked delightful, Ed was pink-faced and proud, and everyone felt happy and jovial in their finery. The wedding was followed by champagne on the lawn, and by dinner a couple of hours later. Piers' speech as best man was amusing, and surprisingly short on ribaldry. Anthony suspected Annabel's father might have taken Piers aside to remind him that he'd already pushed tolerance to the limits. As night fell, and after the tables had been cleared away, there was dancing on the terrace that carried on into the small hours.

It was around two o'clock that Anthony wandered away from the noise of the party to find some solitude, leaving Gabrielle, who loved to dance, amongst the crowd on the terrace. He strolled down the grassy slope to the lake, the thump of the music fading behind him. The trees at the water's edge were hung with lanterns, making the warm night air soft and ghostly. He sat down on the grass, his back against a tree, and let his thoughts drift tipsily. Moments later he became aware of indistinct voices nearby, the sound of a man and a woman arguing. After an angry, quick-fire exchange the voices fell silent, and a few seconds later Julia walked quickly past him to the edge of the lake. She stood by the water, unaware of his presence, her shoes in her hand, evidently recovering herself. He contemplated her. He'd been struck earlier by how lovely she looked, in a strapless dress of pale blue silk that clung to her slender figure, setting off the milky skin of her neck and shoulders and cropped blonde hair. As though somehow alert to his unspoken thoughts, she lifted her hand to the back of her neck, and as she did so she staggered slightly. He realised she was pretty drunk. Just like the rest of us, he thought.

'Hi,' he said, and she turned, startled, then saw who it was.

'Oh, hi,' she replied, something like relief in her voice. She padded across the grass and sat down next to him. She gazed at the shoes in her hand. They were pink, high-heeled. 'God, I hate these. Don't know why I bought them. They're so bloody uncomfortable.' Suddenly she lifted them above her head and flung them into the lake. Anthony watched them bobbing in the light from the lanterns, and let out a laugh.

'What did you do that for?'

'I don't know.' She giggled, then leant back against the tree next to him and closed her eyes. 'I'm so drunk.' After a moment she opened her eyes. 'I've just had a frightful row with Piers. Did you hear us?'

'If you mean, did I hear what you were saying – no.'

'Good.' She plucked some blades of grass. 'Honestly, I wish he'd leave me alone. He's either following me around wanting to talk, or trying to get my attention by arsing around with his friends. It's pathetic. I don't know why he can't just accept the fact we're divorcing and deal with it like a grown-up.'

Anthony could not imagine two less grown-up people than Julia and Piers. He remembered the circumstances in which she had betrayed him; the recollection had long ceased to be painful.

'I'm sorry your marriage didn't work out.'

'No, well – it's a miracle it lasted as long as it did. I don't even know why we got married in the first place.' She sighed. 'I suppose it was because so many of our friends were doing it, and it seemed like a laugh at the time. You know, having a wedding' – she gestured in the direction of the villa, where music was still pumping out – 'inviting all our friends, having a huge party, Daddy paying for it all. I mean' – she slurred her words a little, speaking with drunken emphasis – 'it's what we sodding well do, isn't it? People like us, when we get to a certain age. We get married, and we buy nice houses, and we have nice kids, and we send them to nice schools . . .' She drew a deep breath. 'And then they grow up and they do the same thing all over again.' Anthony was startled by how clearly her words reflected everything that he'd been thinking the night before. 'Mind you, I did love him once. Before I realised what a sod he really is. I suppose we're just lucky we didn't do the kids part. That would have been a mess.'

Anthony couldn't think of anything to say. She turned to look at him. 'I sometimes think I was stupid to give you up for Piers.' Her blue eyes swam with incipient tears.

'Oh, well . . . You and I had just about reached the end of the road, don't you think?' Anthony hoped this wasn't going to turn into one of 'those' conversations. 'I actually thought you and Piers were well suited.'

She shook her head. 'You're a far more decent person than Piers. Gabrielle's lucky.' She was very close to him, her shoulder against his, and Anthony knew that she was waiting for him to turn and kiss her. She'd always followed the desires of her empty heart. It had led her to where she was right at this moment. He gazed straight ahead, saying nothing, and after a moment she realised he had no intention of doing what she wanted.

'I'm going to bed,' she said.

'I think that's a good idea.'

She gazed at the lake and gave a little giggle, her faint humiliation already forgotten. 'Oh, look at my stupid shoes! Why did I do that?'

Anthony glanced to where the shoes still floated. They seemed as silly and aimless as Julia herself. And yet he had once loved her, truly and desperately. He felt a pang of sorrow for those days, and for the person he had been then.

'I can fish them out, if you like.'

'No point. They'll be ruined.' She gave him an untroubled smile and got to her feet, stumbling a little. 'Night-night.'

When she had gone, Anthony sat reflecting, remembering the evening years ago that had ended everything, when he had come across Piers and Julia having sex in the shadows beneath a tree, after some chambers' cricket match. It seemed absurd now, a crude, ridiculous betrayal, but at the time it had been raw and devastating. Leo had been with him. He had witnessed and understood it all, rescued him from his misery, taken him back to his house in Stanton. They had sat up, drinking brandy, talking. About what, he could no longer recall. Then Leo had kissed him. He could remember still the power of that moment, the gentleness of it. It should have been shocking, but it wasn't. And nothing had happened, anyway. Not that night. But that was the moment he understood that Leo loved him. Looking back, he realised that if he had wanted, Leo could have taken and discarded him as carelessly as all his other lovers. Instead he had loved him with restraint and care, never wanting to damage him, or limit his career.

Thoughts and memories drifted together into a painful, inconclusive muddle. He opened his eyes with a sigh and stood up. He didn't much want to go back to the wedding revelry. He decided to walk the long way round to avoid the terrace. The underwater lights of the swimming pool were still on, and as he passed by it he noticed, by the ghostly blue light from the water, someone sitting in the half-darkness on the edge of one of the sun loungers.

'Hello, Anthony.' It was Piers' voice, with its usual light edge of mockery. 'Come and have a drink.'

Anthony paused. 'I'm just on my way to bed. I won't stop.'

Piers' reply stabbed each word with emphasis. 'Come and have a bloody drink.' Suddenly Piers' weight caused the sunbed to tilt, and as he half fell he let out a laugh. He righted himself, then held out a partly drunk bottle of champagne. Oh God, thought Anthony, first her, now him. Reluctantly he sat down on the lounger and took a swig from the proffered bottle.

'You really don't like me, do you?' said Piers. The tone of his voice was challenging, but curious and sad at the same time.

'Not much.'

Piers nodded. 'I suppose I can't blame you. All the stuff with Julia.'

'Oh, there's a lot more to it than that.'

There was a pause, and to Anthony's surprise they both laughed. Then Piers said, 'I don't like myself much, to be honest.' He took a drink from the bottle and passed it back to Anthony, who drank some more.

'You're not that bad.' Anthony cast a sideways glance at Piers. With sudden insight he realised that what he felt about Piers was simple envy. He envied him his ease of manner, the arrogance and insouciance with which he dealt with the world, knowing exactly what he wanted and how to get it. A part of him wished he could be so assured. But with a similar flash of clarity he could see how Piers had become who he was, starting no doubt as a pushy toddler, then a swaggering little boy masking his fears by bullying others, then an ugly, insecure teenager anxious to make his mark, hiding behind a veneer of arrogance, learning to use the weapons of class and money to dominate boys and girls alike. It all made sense. There was really nothing to envy at all.

'Try telling Julia that. She hates me. I love her, and she hates me. I mean, I left it too late, didn't I? Finding out.'

'Finding out what?'

'That I bloody love her. Far more than I realised. Far more than I understood. God, I must be pissed to be telling you this. You of all people.'

'I'm sorry.' Anthony passed the champagne back.

'I know what you dislike about me,' Piers went on. 'It's what a lot of people don't like about me. They think I'm an arrogant, loud-mouthed toff. Well, fair enough. It's what I am. And I can't stop being the person I am. I don't know how. I don't know how else to be.'

'Don't worry about it too much.'

Piers turned and looked quizzically at him. 'You're not like us, Anthony. You don't really belong, do you? I mean, I've watched you trying to fit in. You've worked hard at it. You make enough money, you've learnt to do and say all the right things, you're good-looking, and people like you. But you're not one of us.' Anthony started to get up. He wasn't in the mood for a bullying tirade. But Piers laid a hand on his arm. 'No, I don't mean it in the way you think. I'm not having a go. I'm telling you something truly and honestly. You're lucky. You don't have to follow the fucking rules, not if you don't really want to. Us, we' – he flung an arm out towards the villa – 'people like us don't have a choice.' He upended the champagne bottle and drained it. 'I envy you. I truly do.'

Anthony didn't know what to say. Piers set the empty bottle carefully on the ground. They both sat there for a while, saying nothing.

'Come on,' said Anthony at last. He helped Piers to his feet, and they walked back together to the villa in companionable silence.

CHAPTER ELEVEN

Once upon a summertime, when life was lived at a more sedate pace, and the practice of law was still a stately business, lawyers and judges luxuriated in a thing known as the Long Vacation. For a two-month period from the end of Trinity term on July 31st, to the beginning of Michaelmas term in October, the law courts would close, the City would fall into a drowse, and the denizens of Middle and Inner Temple, and Gray's and Lincoln's Inn, would down tools to relax their bodies and refresh their intellects at home or abroad. Such indulgence is now a thing of the past. The demands of litigation require courts to sit and barristers to work throughout the summer months, with only two or three weeks' respite to sip rosé in Provence or to lounge in rented villas in Vale do Lobo.

Thus life at 5 Caper Court continued at an only marginally slower pace throughout June and July. Leo, despite his workload, was determined to spend a fortnight of the summer with Oliver. He expected resistance from Rachel, since generally he had him for no longer than a week at a time. When he mooted the idea one Sunday as he was dropping Oliver off, she merely said, 'That should work. We're completing on the Tunbridge Wells house soon, so maybe we can do the move while Ollie's on holiday with you. It'll be much easier.'

Leo glanced down the hallway to make sure Oliver was out of earshot. 'You know he bitched all weekend about moving schools. It's not a great time, at his age, to be leaving his friends.'

Rachel sighed. 'It can't be helped. He's got a place at an excellent school there. He'll soon make new friends.'

Leo shrugged. There was no point in saying more. He detected a subtle shift in the balance between them, adding to his already unsettled nervous state. He was used to being the one who was disengaged, wary of any emotional contact, but her pregnancy seemed to have reversed things. It was she who had the air of remoteness. Suddenly feeling the need to make more of a connection, he said, quite unnecessarily, 'You're looking very well. Remind me again when the baby's due?'

'August the twenty-eighth. Though it's hardly an exact science, as you know.'

Her words evoked for both of them the memory of Oliver's birth twelve years ago. Leo felt a wrench of terror at the memory of how he'd tried to persuade her to end that pregnancy. If he'd succeeded, there would be no Oliver. The idea seemed unthinkable. Guilt flooded him, numbing him.

In the same instant Rachel was recalling how entirely and trustingly in love she'd been then, so happy to be having Leo's baby. She had only found out later that he'd been having an affair with some young man throughout her pregnancy. He'd ended the affair, and she had forgiven him, had tried hard to make the marriage work, desperately keeping Oliver at the heart of it, knowing how much Leo loved him. For that brief time she had, in her way, been happy, constantly hoping against hope. But things had inevitably fallen apart, the culmination being Leo's bedding of the nanny, before Oliver was even a year old. It seemed farcical in retrospect, but it had destroyed her at the time.

She gazed at Leo, amazed at how, despite everything, she had never quite fallen out of love with him. He looked rough, unshaven, tired, dispirited, far from his usual assured self.

'Are you OK?'

'Yes, fine.' He paused. 'Actually – no. Not so great.'

'Work?'

Leo rubbed his chin. 'Partly. There's a lot going on in chambers.'

'Do you want to come in and talk about it?'

Again Leo hesitated. She had that intense look on her face. It was a long time since he had talked to her about anything, apart from Oliver. He was usually careful to avoid any closeness. But she was married to Simon now, she seemed very content, there could be no harm.

He nodded, and followed her into the house.

Simon was sitting at the kitchen table, his long legs propped on a chair, reading the sports section of the *Sunday Times*. He was in his early forties, tall, with thinning brown hair, an easy manner and a quick sense of humour. Leo liked him. He was perfect for Rachel, and an excellent stepfather to Oliver. When the new baby came, they would be a cosy family unit. Leo could foresee how it would swallow Oliver up, how he himself, despite being his father, would become a kind of adjunct. The thought had a sad inevitability about it.

Simon and Leo shook hands.

'I'm just making Leo a cup of coffee,' Rachel told Simon. 'Do you want one?'

Simon folded up the paper. 'No, thanks. I've got some work to do upstairs. I'll leave you two to it.'

Leo sat down at the table. 'He has good instincts.'

'He could tell we wanted to talk.' Rachel made coffee and brought it over. 'So,' she said, 'tell me what's happening.'

It was a strange relief to be able to talk about the situation with Natalie, and the growing tensions between him and the younger tenants. As head of chambers, he hadn't felt he could really discuss it with anyone, apart from Henry, without potentially inflaming matters.

'I've instructed Natalie King a few times,' mused Rachel. 'She's good, but I can't say I like her much. Do you think she's deliberately stirring things up?'

'I suspect there's an element of that. She's on a crusade of some kind, and she perceives me as getting in the way of it.' Leo took his coffee. 'Thanks. Maybe she's right to want to take 5 Caper Court in a different direction, to turn it into some sort of sleek, corporate outfit. But I'm too old for change.'

Rachel smiled. 'You're not old.'

'I'm heading that way.' He rubbed his eyes and sighed.

'What about the Bench? They're crying out for commercial judges. Sorry, I didn't mean that the way it sounded—'

'Come on, Rachel, you know I've been turned down once, and I don't intend to be humiliated twice. Julian Hooper told me that Sir Vivian Coleman pretty much stitched me up with the Judicial Appointments Committee, for whatever reason. He never liked me much when he was Master of the Rolls.'

'Maybe so, but . . . why don't you try again?'

'Are you joking? I made that application because I saw becoming a judge as a way of giving something back to the profession, despite the inflexible hours and the rubbish money, and the Ministry of Justice buggering about with judges' pensions. Having been told I'm surplus to requirements – well, frankly, they can stuff it. Anyway, the whole thing has become utterly devalued. Society used to take judges seriously. But then they turned the office of Lord Chancellor into just another stepping stone for career politicians, and now the judiciary doesn't even have a voice in government. No wonder they're struggling to recruit people.' He sighed. 'I'm seriously wondering if I shouldn't just pack it all in, leave Natalie and the Hitler Youth faction to it.'

'You can't give up your practice. You're too good.'

'Kind of you to say so. But the work doesn't excite me the way it used to. For instance, I have a hearing in September that would have had me all fired up a few years ago, but now all I can think of is what a nightmare it threatens to be.'

'What's it about?'

'You remember the oil tanker that collided with a cargo ship off Shanghai eighteen months ago?'

'The *Pasanto*? The one that caused the massive oil spill?'

142

Leo nodded. 'We're on for the owners of the cargo ship. It looks like there was blame on both sides, but of course the other side have the error in navigation defence. We're going to have a hard time arguing that the tanker should have taken evasive action, given the size of the thing—' He stopped and gave her a glance. 'Sorry, you don't really want to hear all this on a Sunday night.'

'No, go on.' She smiled. 'I do this job, too, remember.'

As Leo began to recount the details of the case she was only half listening, her mind still on what he had said a moment ago. He might talk about giving up his practice, but without it, what would he be? Who would he be? He deliberately made his sexual life complex and promiscuous as a means of avoiding emotional attachment to anyone, but if he went on that way he would end up a lonely man. An old one, too, in a mere matter of years. His relationship with Oliver was, so far as she could tell, the only intimate relationship he had with anyone. She could see why the problems in chambers were affecting him so badly. 5 Caper Court was his home, his world. To feel himself being eased out by hostile forces must be painful. She traced his features with her gaze, thinking with a pang that if he had been a less selfish, less driven man – driven by every heedless appetite you cared to name – they might still be together. Their marriage, when he wasn't destroying it, had been good enough. For just an instant she allowed herself to remember what sex with Leo had been like, and felt a shiver of longing. She switched her mind guiltily away. Why couldn't he just have accepted life on the terms that most people did? Because then he wouldn't have been the man he was, insatiable and compulsive, the man she had fallen in love with.

She fastened her attention on what he was telling her about the case, rapidly absorbing the details, throwing out a couple of suggestions on tactics.

'If you can establish the tanker master was negligent in some way, you get round the error in navigation defence. That's the way to go.'

'Easy enough to say, but the difficulty is in finding any proof. And ours is the vessel that veered to the right fifteen minutes before the collision happened. It's going to be an uphill struggle. Anyway,' he sighed, giving her a quick smile, 'enough of me and my problems.'

She returned the smile. 'So, where are you thinking of taking Oliver on holiday?'

'We'll probably head down to the house in Antibes for a week or so. I've got the boat there. Alasdair and Jenny have rented a villa in Juan-les-Pins,' he added, referring to an older couple whom they both knew. 'They're having their grandchildren to stay, and they're about Oliver's age, so he'll have company. Then we might come back and just muck about at Stanton for a few days. I haven't booked any flights, so let me know what fits in with your move. I'm easy.'

She nodded, then lifted her eyes to his. 'Can I ask you . . . ?' She hesitated.

'What?'

'Please don't take him out on the boat.'

'Oh, for God's sake – I've got life jackets. I wouldn't take any risks. We'll only go out to the islands. He needs a bit of adventure.'

The pleading look in her eyes became steely. 'Leo, I absolutely insist that you don't.'

'Rachel, you're overprotective. Or maybe it's that you don't trust me, not even where our son is concerned.' He could feel the amicable atmosphere evaporating, as it always did.

'Trust you? That's a pretty bad joke.'

'OK, enough.' He drained his coffee and stood up. 'Let me know what dates suit you, and I'll try to arrange the holiday around them. But don't tell me what I can't do with my son in the time he's with me.'

She was helpless to prevent her own temper rising. 'You know, if I'd taken it upon myself to tell a court exactly what you got up to during our marriage, you probably wouldn't even be allowed to spend time with him.'

'Our marriage?' His blue eyes flashed with anger, and his tone was mocking.

'Yes, the one you wrecked with your cheating and lies. Remember?'

'Our marriage, as you call it, was a fabrication from the start. If it hadn't been for your pregnancy, and the fact I was applying for silk and needed to appear squeaky-clean to the Lord Chancellor's office, it would never have happened. So don't talk about it like it's some holy fucking relic you need to keep in a cupboard to grieve over.'

He left the house. Outside, he sat for a few moments in the car. He couldn't believe he'd told Rachel that. How hurtful. How cruel. But then, the truth so often was. He switched on the engine, then hesitated. He had no wish to return to the empty house in Chelsea. He felt, as he always did after returning Oliver on a Sunday evening, completely bereft. There was only one person he wanted to see, to talk to. Well, why not? Why not go round to

Anthony's on the off-chance? He felt beyond pride, beyond caring. He just needed his company.

Twenty minutes later, just as Leo swung the Aston Martin off Old Brompton Road and cruised into Onslow Square, Anthony was emerging from the Anglesea Arms with Gabrielle and some other friends.

Leo drew the car to a halt in the street opposite Anthony's flat. He sat for a moment, unsure of what he was doing there. What was he going to say when he rang the bell? What absurd excuse was he going to come out with? As he hesitated, he saw half a dozen young people coming round the corner, chatting and laughing. He recognised Anthony's tall, dark-haired figure, and saw he had his arm round Gabrielle. The group paused outside Anthony's place, and after a few minutes of banter and farewells, four of them carried on up the road, and Anthony and Gabrielle went up the steps to the flat.

Leo put the car in gear and moved away, but not before Anthony, as he put the key in the door, turned and saw the silver Aston Martin disappearing up the street. He paused, sure that it had been Leo's car, and sensing immediately that he had been in need of something.

Gabrielle went inside, then turned and saw Anthony standing on the doorstep, his eyes on the street. 'You OK?'

'I'm fine.' He turned and closed the door, then went down the hall to the kitchen. 'You want a coffee, or a glass of wine, or something?'

'No, thanks. I've had enough to drink for one day, and coffee will just keep me awake.' She moved close to him, putting her arms around him as he stood motionless, the house keys in his hand. He didn't respond. 'Are you sure you're all right?'

Anthony made an impatient gesture. 'Yeah, no. Sorry. Just

146

tired, I suppose.' It was as though Leo's sudden appearance and disappearance had created some invisible link, an attachment that seemed almost telepathic. It was unsettling.

'Well, look.' Gabrielle stepped away from him, feeling a quickening of resentment. It was as though Anthony was suddenly at a distance, not wanting to be with her at all. 'If you're that tired, perhaps I should go.' She took out her phone, adding briskly, 'I'll take an Uber.'

'What? No, look, I didn't mean—'

'Done now.' She switched her phone off with a tight little smile. 'You know, you've been in a funny mood ever since we got back from Italy. It's like sometimes you want to be with me, and other times you don't. Was it something I said or did while we were out there?'

'Oh God, don't be ridiculous. I'm sorry if I've given you that impression. Come on, why don't you stay?' He tried to put his arms round her, but she shook her head.

'I've got a busy day tomorrow, anyway. Let's just say goodnight.' Her phone buzzed in her bag and she took it out. 'My car's going to be here in a second.'

He walked outside with her, and watched as she got into the cab and left, feeling oddly relieved. He returned to the kitchen and stood gazing out over the communal garden, where the people from the flat above were having a barbecue with friends. He tried to connect his mind to Leo's. For a moment he wondered whether he should call him, then decided against it. Every time he saw Leo these days, he seemed like a man adrift, and it frightened Anthony. He wanted to know what to say or do to set things right, but he was utterly at a loss.

* * *

147

Natalie and Sian were sitting on the balcony of the flat in St Katharine Docks, cradling glasses of wine. The evening sky was faintly streaked with traces of sunset coral, and out in the marina a sheaf of small yachts bobbed sleepily. Smoky music drifted from Sian's Bluetooth speakers. But the mood was far from being as relaxed and tranquil as the picture suggested.

'It was entirely inappropriate for you to behave that way around him,' Natalie said angrily. The low-level argument had developed in the wake of the recent departure of a handful of people whom Natalie had invited over for lunch.

'Since when do you tell me how to behave? Anyway' – Sian drank some more red wine – 'I think it's nice that you get jealous.'

'Oh, so you admit you were doing it just to provoke me?'

Sian gave a sigh. As usual, her attempts to defuse yet another disagreement prompted by Natalie's insecurity were going to be turned against her. She couldn't win. 'Whatever you choose to think.'

'Well, it's either that, or you fancied him and you didn't mind letting him and everyone else know all about it.'

Sian turned to look at Natalie. 'You really hate it that I can actually find a man attractive, don't you? You simply hate it that I might want to sleep with one now and then.'

'Don't you think that just wanting to is a betrayal of me? Of us?'

'What, so if I came on to one of your female friends, that would be all right?'

'You're deliberately twisting what I'm saying.'

Sian set her empty glass down on the deck. She let a few

minutes' silence elapse, then said, 'I think maybe we need a break from one another.'

Natalie turned to her in alarm. 'What does that mean?'

Sian clasped her hands and stretched them above her head. 'I need a holiday. Writing this paper has exhausted me. My aunt and uncle have taken a villa in the South of France for a couple of months, and they've invited me to spend a couple of weeks down there. I half suspect they want me to help out with their grandchildren, but I'm cool with that.' She relaxed her clasped hands into her lap. 'I love the Med. And it will give you a nice break from me.'

'What if I don't want a break from you?' Natalie's voice sounded bleak.

Sian turned her eyes to Natalie's and gave her a reassuring smile. 'As I said, I think we both need one.' She laid her hand on Natalie's. 'And it'll make it all the nicer when I come back.'

Natalie tugged her fingers from beneath Sian's. 'Don't assume I'll be here.'

'Oh, and where might you be?'

'I might take a holiday myself.'

'Well, then – that will be perfect for both of us, won't it?' She picked up her empty glass from the deck and got up. 'I'm off to bed. You want me to take your glass?'

'No. I might have another drink,' said Natalie sulkily.

'OK. Night.' Sian went to the kitchen, cleared up the last of the lunch debris, and set off the dishwasher. As she went from the kitchen to the bedroom she glanced out to the balcony where Natalie still sat, silhouetted against the now-rosy sky, glass in hand, bottle at her side. *She's thinking about me*, thought Sian. The knowledge filled her with fatigue. An escape from the neediness, the watchful anxiety, was what she craved. Maybe what she really wanted was a permanent escape. But then, she thought, as she closed the bedroom door and slipped out of her clothes and into the baggy T-shirt she wore at nights, going back to living on her meagre earnings as an academic wouldn't be much fun. It was lovely living here during the vacation, enjoying the waterside flat while Natalie worked, being taken to expensive restaurants and gigs, having things bought for her, a car always at her disposal. No, a break was all she needed, and a break was what she would have. Tomorrow she would check flights and car rentals, email her aunt, and by the end of the week she would be in Juan-les-Pins, a free woman. For a while at least.

CHAPTER TWELVE

Two weeks later Sian was lounging on a sunbed with her Kindle, watching ten-year-old twins Noah and Emily fighting over an inflatable turtle in the swimming pool, and reflecting how lucky she was not to have children. Her aunt appeared with plastic tumblers of squash and a dish of crackers and set them down on the table next to Sian, calling to her grandchildren. Noah and Emily scampered out of the pool and over to the table.

'Must you splash water everywhere?' exclaimed Sian. The children began to squabble over the crackers and Sian lifted the plate aloft, stuffing some into her mouth. 'No more till you stop fighting.'

'Come on, you two, pack it in.' Jenny sat down and Sian lowered the plate to the table. 'I meant to tell you, we have a neighbour coming to lunch today. I think you'll like him. He's a lawyer, like you.'

Sian lifted her sunglasses to her forehead and helped herself to some more crackers. 'French?'

'English. He's a barrister. He has a house in Antibes, a lovely place, right next to the market. He's down here on holiday with his little boy.'

'What's his name?'

'Leo Davies. Al used to be one of his clients. We've known him for years.'

The name meant nothing to Sian.

Jenny's husband, Alasdair, emerged from the house at that moment, sporting baggy shorts, a blue shirt with a silk cravat, and a battered panama. He settled himself in the shade of the parasol with a copy of the *Daily Telegraph*.

'I was just telling Sian that Leo's coming to lunch,' remarked Jenny.

'Oh, he's a great chap. First-class lawyer, too. Much-sought-after – in more ways than one.'

'Oh, Alasdair, really.' Jenny watched as her grandchildren drained their tumblers of squash and raced back to the pool.

'Jenny, don't pretend you don't know his reputation. Anyway, he's very likeable, extremely witty, seems to know something about everything. We're very fond of him.'

'Sounds a paragon,' murmured Sian, envisaging some loud-mouthed bore. 'Let me know what help you need with lunch.'

Leo decided he and Oliver should walk from Antibes to the Suttons' place on the Cap, and by the time they got there around noon, Oliver was hot and grouchy. He immediately cheered up when he saw Noah and Emily playing in the pool. He tugged off his T-shirt and threw it to Leo, then dive-bombed into the water. As Leo tucked the T-shirt into the rucksack he had brought, he glimpsed a girl through the kitchen window. He could see immediately that she was tall and attractive. She had her head bent over a chopping board, and he took a moment to observe her, the dark, silky hair cropped to her jaw, the suntanned slim shoulders, the skimpy pink vest top and denim shorts. Very pretty. This must be Jenny's niece, Sian, whom she'd mentioned on the phone.

He crossed from the pool to the open patio door, and she looked up at him with a cool, unsurprised smile that told him she had seen them arrive, and had been quite aware of his appraisal of her.

'Hi,' he said. 'I'm Leo.'

'Hi.' She put out a hand. 'I'm Sian Attwood, Jenny's niece. I'll let her know you're here. She can't have heard the car.'

'Oh, we walked.'

'Really? Then you must be thirsty. Would you like a beer?'

'Thanks.' He watched as she took a beer from the fridge, noticing the dusting of freckles on her nose and on the curve of her shoulders. Why was the name familiar? He'd certainly remember if he'd met her before. He tried to guess her age, and put her somewhere in her early thirties.

Jenny came in at that moment, in a sky-blue caftan. 'Leo! I didn't hear you arrive.'

'I came by stealth.' He kissed her. 'Darling Jenny, lovely to see you looking so well.' He gestured towards the pool. 'As you can see, my son's made himself right at home.'

'Well, that's perfect. Maybe he can stop Emily and Noah fighting. I tell you, it's constant, and it's getting on my nerves. To think we volunteered to have them for a whole fortnight.'

Sian uncapped a beer and handed it to Leo.

'Now, I can see you two have introduced yourselves,' went on Jenny. 'Has Sian told you she's a lawyer, too? More on the academic side. Where is it you lecture again?'

'Cambridge,' replied Sian. 'Trinity. But I'm going into private practice in the autumn.'

In that moment the penny dropped, and he realised that by some strange coincidence this was the girl whom Natalie had recommended for pupillage. But she didn't seem to have made the same connection, or recognised his name as that of her future head of chambers. He was bemused. One would expect a future pupil to have researched that much. But she merely smiled and asked, 'And you? What's your field of practice?'

'Commercial. A fair spread of everything.' He decided against giving anything more away. The situation had the potential to be amusing.

Sian nodded, and let her smiling glance brush his eyes in a vaguely flirtatious manner before returning her attention to the melon she was slicing. He wasn't at all what she'd been expecting. She'd imagined the usual boring, slightly pompous middle-aged type that seemed to populate the Bar, but instead here was this strikingly lovely man with intense blue eyes, silver hair, and a very nicely honed body for someone of his age. A most interesting proposition.

'I'll just take the ham and melon out,' she told her aunt. 'Everything else is ready.'

Lunch was long and lazy, the ham and melon followed by a large platter of tagliata, then cheese, strawberries, and a plate of macaroons from the local patisserie, Jenny remonstrating each time Alasdair pottered off to open yet another bottle of rosé, Alasdair pointing out by way of excuse that Leo wasn't driving. By four o'clock the children were fractious and lethargic, bored with the pool, and Jenny herded them inside to cool down and watch a DVD.

Jenny returned to the lunch table and poured coffee. 'Peace. But probably only for an hour or so.'

'Why don't you let me take them down to the beach for a bit?' said Leo. 'Let them muck about and buy them ice creams.'

'Oh, Leo, that's a marvellous offer. Maybe you could go, too, Sian.' She glanced at her niece. 'Three's rather a lot for one person to manage.'

Sian, who was at that moment preoccupied with the particular point on Leo's body where the muscles of his chest met the coarse weave of his white linen shirt, glanced at her aunt. 'Yeah, great. The sea will be a nice change from the pool.'

When the children emerged, Jenny packed a beach bag with towels and sun lotion, and the five of them set off. Leo headed for a beach bar with a deck where he and Sian could sit while the children played in the sand.

'Drink?' he asked.

Sian shook her head. 'I've had more than enough wine. Just a coffee for me.'

He ordered two coffees and sat back, contemplating her. She was quite the loveliest girl he'd seen in a long time. He would have to steer the talk away from work, and 5 Caper Court at all costs, in case she worked out who he was; he strongly suspected she was the type of girl who would put her professional interests well ahead of the uncertain

155

prospect of a fling with someone who ultimately had the power to affect her career.

He indicated her Kindle, lying under her phone. 'What book are you reading?'

'*Bonjour Tristesse*. Françoise Sagan. Do you know it?'

'A teenage girl trying to depose her father's mistress, as I recall.'

She smiled. 'It seemed appropriate, since it's set down here.'

'Do you like it?'

She shrugged. 'It has momentum. I definitely want to find out what happens. But I'm not entirely sure I buy her version of young love – her own romance, I mean. She's so detached and clinical. The voice is too mature. I certainly wasn't like that at seventeen.'

'What were you like at seventeen?'

It was a sudden switch to intimacy. The expression in the glance he gave her was unmistakeable, and she felt a pure thrill of excitement. She had to turn away, as though afraid it might show on her face. Rarely had she come across someone so instantaneously attractive, so capable of projecting a subtle sexual vibe undetectable by anyone but its object. She was utterly intrigued, beguiled by his looks and his personality.

'Oh – I suppose I was intensely passionate, and much more unsure of myself than the girl in the book.'

'And are you less passionate now?'

She turned to look at him. 'I'm less unsure of myself. But just as passionate.' She paused. 'It's all a question of control, don't you think?'

'I couldn't agree more.' They smiled at one another.

Leo talked about books, films, plays – anything to steer her away from the possibility of her finding out who he was. She asked no direct questions about his work – but then people rarely did. The world of commercial litigation wasn't the most exciting or personal of topics, and he was conscious that she wanted to keep things on a personal level. That, he thought, boded well.

When she had finished her coffee she went for a swim. She slipped off her top and shorts, and made her loose-limbed, casual way to the water's edge, where the children were playing. She stopped to say something to them, and Leo watched as she waded into the water, admiring her tall, lightly tanned figure, her white bikini making her hips fuller and breasts larger, for some reason he couldn't fathom. He knew she knew he was watching her, and he liked that. He liked everything that lay unspoken between them. It was tantalising, delicious, a feeling he had been badly in need of these past few months. What happened in September when she began her pupillage wasn't something he concerned himself with. It would only be a problem if she chose to make it one. And she seemed clever enough to ensure none of what he hoped was about to happen need ever matter to either of them, not in the real world.

As they walked back to the villa Leo said, 'Why don't you come over to dinner one evening?'

'I'd like that.'

'How about tomorrow, around nine? Not too late?'

'No, that's perfect.'

He gave her his number and the address of the house. It was the most prosaic of exchanges, but it cast a delicious spell of anticipation over them both, and they scarcely spoke for the rest of the walk. Leo delivered Noah and Emily back to Jenny, and after thank yous and farewells, he and Oliver walked back to Antibes. Leo found himself dwelling on the possibilities of tomorrow evening with the same excitement he had felt as a teenager, the evening he had taken his first girlfriend to the pictures. He could recall still the candy scent and taste of her cheap lipstick. That was the beauty of being single and uncommitted; every new sexual encounter was exciting and fresh. Nothing staled, the way it did in a marriage, or a long-term relationship. He thought fleetingly of Sarah. That was the closest he had come to keeping the excitement alive, but even that hadn't worked out. Better the shock of the new, than the tedium of the familiar. Besides, he always liked it best when it wasn't just about the sex, but about the person, too. He'd enjoyed talking to Sian as much as looking at her. She had a good mind and a quirky sense of humour, which he liked. Tomorrow would be fun, in every conceivable sense of the word. Or so he hoped.

The next day he took Oliver out in the boat. He knew it was more likely to tire Oliver out than any other kind of expedition, and ensure that he would be in bed by the time Sian arrived. He made up a picnic, and they went to Île Sainte-Marguerite and spent the afternoon trekking around, swimming and exploring. By the time they got back and moored in the harbour it was six o'clock, and Oliver was too exhausted after supper to do anything but go to bed and sleep.

Leo's house was set in a quiet backstreet behind old wooden gates guarding a cobbled courtyard planted with jasmine and oleander. The house had three storeys, the bedrooms and bathrooms on the upper floors, with a large living area and kitchen on the ground floor adjoining the courtyard. Leo set some candles on the big oak table outside, and arranged a few fat, coral-coloured cushions that Gabrielle had bought the previous summer on the chairs. It looked comfortable, low-key, but not too overtly seductive.

Sian texted him just as he was preparing supper to say she had arrived. He opened the gates as she was paying off her taxi, they exchanged a light kiss, and she followed him across the courtyard to the kitchen. She was wearing a simple, lemon-coloured shift dress that set off her lightly tanned skin and dark hair, with sculpted silver earrings and a matching necklace.

'What an amazing place,' she said admiringly, glancing around. Her gaze fell on his half-finished food preparation. 'I see you roasted a chicken.'

'It's only rotisserie, picked up in town. Oliver and I went out for the day, so I haven't had time to cook properly. So it's just the chicken, with some mesclun, and bread and cheese. Oh, and these tomatoes. I always think weird-shaped tomatoes taste better, don't you?'

She gave a smile. Food was the last thing on her mind. She was so pent-up she only hoped she would manage to eat something. She'd been quite relaxed in the taxi here, but the sight of him, hair slightly damp from the shower, dressed in chinos and a blue linen shirt, was heart-stoppingly intoxicating. It seemed absurd to feel this way.

Leo took some wine from the fridge and opened it, and poured two glasses. 'Have a seat outside,' he said. 'I'll bring the food out in a minute. I work best without people watching me. Would you like some music?'

159

'Mm. That would be nice.'

She settled herself against the cushions in the courtyard. Some anonymous jazz floated softly through the open windows. The evening air was warm, perfumed with the vanilla scent of jasmine, and after a couple of mouthfuls of wine she felt the tension in her body ease.

She relaxed even more over supper. He was so easy to talk to, endlessly interested and interesting, funny and thoughtful by turns, not once doing or saying the kind of suggestive things that some men might have, under the circumstances. The conversation never strayed near the law, or his work. She began to wonder whether she hadn't perhaps misunderstood. Maybe he'd simply planned nothing more than a pleasant, platonic dinner. She felt a little squeeze of panic at the thought.

But that fear was laid to rest. At the end of the meal she went inside to the loo, and when she came out to the courtyard again, he had drawn his chair nearer to hers, and as she sat down he reached out and lifted one of her hands to his lips.

'Thank you for being my guest,' he said. 'Possibly the most beautiful one ever to grace this somewhat shambolic household.'

'It's not shambolic. It's quaint. I love it.' She glanced up at the walls of the house, then back to him, fingering one of her earrings. He held her hand still. Then he leant forward and kissed her. It was light and soft, but charged with everything she had hoped for.

He drew away and gazed at her for a moment, so intently that she felt her face flush slightly. 'Would you like to see the rest of it?'

'Please.' She could feel a pulse beating in her throat.

He rose, and picked up their glasses and the bottle. 'Let's take the wine.'

She followed him up inside, and up the wooden staircase to the first floor.

'There are two bedrooms and a bathroom above this. But we won't go up there, because Oliver's asleep. This' – he opened the door to a large, airy room – 'is where I sleep and work.' A desk sat in one corner of the room, a couple of plain wooden chests of drawers against two other walls, and in the centre of the room stood an enormous four poster bed with a canopy of draped white muslin, and white bedding and pillows. 'My daughter, Gabrielle, decided on the decor. She likes to keep everything clean and simple.'

'I didn't know you had a daughter.'

'Twenty-seven. She comes down here regularly. Any good taste in the house is entirely down to her.'

'I find that hard to believe,' murmured Sian. 'You seem to have perfectly wonderful taste.'

He set the glasses and the wine bottle on a small table by the bed, and drew her towards him and kissed her for a long, thorough moment. She gave herself up to it entirely. He lifted her dress over her head in one swift, smooth movement, and she tried with trembling hands to unbutton his shirt. He moved her hands gently away and tore the thing off, then his trousers. His mobile fell from his pocket, and as he put it on the bedside table she kicked off her knickers. Within seconds they were on the bed. As they kissed she felt a sense of accomplishment and power. He was hers, and she would make him feel it. She would relish possessing him, enjoy having both their passions under her control.

161

She sat lightly astride him, looking down at him with a smile that he knew she intended to be endearingly wicked. He indulged her, tracing a light line between her nipples, thinking how incredibly sexy she looked, naked except for the silver that gleamed at her throat and ears.

'You are sensational,' he whispered.

'I could be,' she replied. '*We* could be.' She was about to move on top of him when he stopped her. He sat up and pushed her down onto the bed beneath him, then knelt to kiss first her breasts, then her stomach. She lay back, closing her eyes, surrendering herself to his mouth and fingers. She had only to utter the lightest of sighs, and he seemed to know exactly what to do next, and where. One fractional lifting of her hips, one exhaled breath, and he understood her every need. Pleasure mounted with each second, until she was letting out little moans and cries of ecstasy, at which point he suddenly relinquished, letting things slow unbearably. She gave an agonised shudder, and with a faint laugh murmured, 'Oh, Natalie, what a lot you have to learn.'

Leo, distracted from the task at hand, paused and lifted his head to ask, 'Who's Natalie?'

Sian propped herself up on her elbows, and said with her knowing, tantalising smile, 'I'm not sure you really want to know.'

He tried to arrange his expression appropriately. Could it really be possible that Fortune had dealt him such a lucky, unlikely card? 'Why ever not?' he asked, and waited.

'Natalie's my partner. I'm her live-in lover.'

Oh, thank you, God, thought Leo. *Thank you.* Lying there between her slim thighs, he couldn't help smiling at the mysterious, worldly expression on her face. 'Wow.'

'You're shocked, aren't you?'

'You could say that.' He inched his body upwards. 'Tell me about her.'

She arched her back lightly, longing to have him inside her, and breathed, 'What do you want to know?'

'Everything.' He stroked her lightly, liquidly with his fingers, readying her, so that she let out a gasp and closed her eyes. The idea that she thought it excited him to know she slept with another woman, and that he wanted to hear the details as an additional turn-on, amused him. He reached out a hand to the bedside table and, conscious of the movement, she opened her eyes. 'Just getting a condom,' he murmured.

'I'm prepared to trust your clean bill of health, if you'll trust mine.' She wanted only him, as close and as naked as possible, inside her. 'I'm not going to get pregnant, if that's what's worrying you.'

He gave a little shrug, and after a second took his hand from the bedside table. 'Fine. Now, where were we?' His fingers did their work again, and she gave an ecstatic shudder. 'Oh yes, Natalie. You were going to tell me about her.'

'Only if you—'

He moved a little way inside her, and her hips sank. 'Oh God, yes . . .' She began to talk about Natalie, what she looked like, who she was, anything she could think of. She had never felt so deliriously on the brink in her life. She wanted to prolong every second.

'Tell me what she does,' urged Leo, sinking further inside her, beginning to move rhythmically. She talked on, and he listened, trying with detachment to work out exactly what he could most usefully do with this interesting

163

and fortuitous information. Then he reminded himself that it was perhaps rather poor etiquette not to devote himself more single-mindedly to the business at hand. She was, after all, a very lovely and desirable creature, and it would be a somewhat incomplete pleasure if he didn't pay closer attention to her needs and his own. Thinking could come later.

'A QC, you say?'

She gave a gasp as he drove deeper inside her, then laughed. 'You like that idea, don't you? What an old pervert you are.'

'That's me,' admitted Leo. 'You've got me down to a T.' And he covered her mouth with his and gave himself up to the pleasure of the moment.

CHAPTER THIRTEEN

Leo woke next morning to find the bed empty. He picked up his phone from the bedside table and squinted at it in the shaft of sunlight filtering through the shutters. Almost nine. Tactful of her to absent herself. He rolled onto his back, rubbing his hand over his beard, yawning. What a night. They couldn't have got to sleep till the early hours, and then she had woken him again towards dawn, to make love again, twice. That was the trouble with the young – so insatiable. Still, there was nothing he needed to do today but take Oliver to the beach and have a doze on a sunbed.

But when he went downstairs he found Sian sitting with Oliver at the table in the courtyard, drinking orange juice and eating croissants. She gave him a sunny smile. 'Oliver and I went to the boulangerie to buy breakfast. There are more croissants in the oven, keeping warm. I made coffee, too.'

Leo gave a half-smile and turned and went back into the kitchen, slightly disgruntled that she was still here. But what did he expect? He had taken her to his bed, so it was only fair that she should stay to breakfast. He was slightly uneasy at what Oliver might make of the situation.

Oliver, however, was entirely unfazed and seemed to be enjoying Sian's company. They were watching a YouTube video on Oliver's phone, and Leo could hear them laughing as he poured himself a coffee. He took a croissant from the oven and went outside to join them. He sat in silence as they carried on. There was, he knew, more than one game being played, and the subtextual one was entirely familiar to him. It was one in which a woman with whom he had slept decided to make an ostentatious show of befriending Oliver – either to demonstrate how young and playful she was, or to annexe Leo and make him feel de trop, as Sian was doing now. It was tiresome, he thought, as he dipped his croissant in his coffee. Happy though he was to make love to her, he really could do without her intruding in some fake big-sister way into his space with his son.

'What are you doing with the rest of your day?' he asked, hoping it didn't sound too pointed.

She put her chin on her hand. It was a marvel how good she looked, how golden her skin without a trace of make-up, fresh as a daisy, as though she hadn't spent half the night engaged in the most energetic sex. His own brain felt fuzzy with lack of sleep. 'I don't know,' she replied. 'It depends. What are you two up to?'

'Beach, I suppose,' replied Leo, and yawned. 'Sorry. Need to catch up on sleep.'

She smiled knowingly. Oliver slipped from his chair and went to fill the watering can from the outside tap; watering the plants was one of his tasks. Sian slid a hand over Leo's.

'I have to get back to the villa. Looking after Noah and Emily for a few hours is a sort of quid pro quo for my staying there. But I could see you later.'

Leo smiled. 'Much as I hate to disappoint you,' he murmured, 'I have to be frank and say that I don't think I can do two nights like that on the trot. It would kill me.'

'We could just eat and talk. And we can sleep together without—' She smiled and shrugged. *Fucking one another's brains out*, she thought longingly.

Leo did as courtesy demanded. 'If you think I could have someone as delectable as you in my bed without making love to you, then you're insane.' He kissed her swiftly, then drained his coffee. 'The fact is, Oliver and I have been invited to friends up in the hills this evening. We might stay over. And then tomorrow evening we fly back.'

Sian felt a wrench of disappointment. This shouldn't be over before it had even begun. She eyed him, thinking that he should look somehow less desirable, with the faint haze of silver bristle on his chin, rumpled hair, dark shadow beneath his eyes. But he didn't. With those killer cheekbones and that world-weary aspect, in his unbuttoned white shirt, he looked even more attractive. She glanced to where Oliver was splashing water over the geraniums from an overfull watering can, and wondered whether she could entice Leo upstairs for one last bout of lovemaking. But the thought died as it was born. He wouldn't. Not while Oliver was awake and around. For a hopeless moment she understood what it was to be Natalie, glimpsed what it was like to feel needy and thwarted. She didn't like the feeling. It wasn't her.

'OK, that's cool,' she replied. 'You've got my number.

I'll be back in London the week after next. So maybe . . . ?'

'Yeah, maybe.' He saw the momentary lost look in her eyes and smiled quickly, reassuringly, wishing he could tell her the truth, that he would happily have her around for the next few months, and let this play out in the delightful way it should. But now that he knew what he knew, now that Natalie's part in this strange game had been revealed, he couldn't afford yet for Sian to find out who he was. His survival in chambers might depend upon it. He had to stick to his creed of ruthlessness, whatever pain it might cost and whatever loss of pleasure to them both.

Sian felt confused and uncertain, disappointed that he didn't seem to care as much as last night had led her to expect. But she returned his light, bright smile.

'OK. Well, I'd best be getting back. Jenny and Alasdair must be wondering where I am.' She got to her feet, picking up glasses and plates.

'Leave those,' said Leo. 'I'll see to them.'

It felt like a kind of dismissal. 'I'll just get my bag.'

She reappeared a moment later with her straw bag over her shoulder, sunglasses on; she didn't want him to see a single blink of her pain. He gave her a light kiss, hating himself for not being able to cut her more slack. It was brutal. 'I'll call you when we're back,' he said, not meaning it for a moment. But it gave her a little spark of hope.

'That would be nice.' She returned the kiss. 'We shouldn't let a good thing go to waste.' She turned to Oliver, who was refilling the watering can, and called out, 'Bye.'

Oliver gave her a cheerful, dismissive wave, and Leo unlocked the wooden gates. A stray cat was passing on the pavement, and Sian bent to stroke it. 'How will you get back?' asked Leo, wondering if he shouldn't offer her a lift.

'I'll walk.' She straightened up. 'Thanks for a lovely time.'

'Thank you, too.' He watched with something like genuine regret as she sauntered off down the street. But it really couldn't be helped.

August, when people drifted away from chambers on holiday, brought something of a lull, and Leo was able to get on with work with less of an unsettled feeling. Going away with Oliver had done him good, and he attacked his impending cases with renewed enthusiasm. Natalie was away for three weeks, which made for a more relaxed atmosphere in chambers. Leo couldn't help wondering if she was somewhere with Sian. Speculating on that relationship did no good, however. He was just glad to have her away from 5 Caper Court. He still hadn't entirely decided what to do with the knowledge that she had, against all protocols, used her position of influence to help her lover get a pupillage.

The parties in the *Alpha Six* grounding case had now decided to try and resolve the matter by way of a mediation, which was due to take place soon. That meant seeing Sarah for the first time since the meeting in March. He wondered how it would be. Over the years of their strange, on–off relationship, she had been a compelling presence in his life. As though there was always unfinished business between them. But when she had left last time, it had felt somehow final. In a way he regretted that, but it had been entirely his own doing.

The oil tanker collision case took up most of the rest of his time. He and Anthony spent days working on it together in the garden summer house that Leo used as an office in the balmy days of summer. It was more restful than working in chambers. The hearing date had been set for the first week in September, and there was a lot of ground to cover. The topic of Gabrielle never came up. Leo longed to ask what direction the relationship was taking, but he refrained. On the occasions when he saw Gabrielle, she always dismissed any enquiries about Anthony with the response, 'We're fine. You don't need to know. So don't ask.' It suggested to Leo that whatever shape it was taking, if it was becoming genuinely serious, they had no intention of letting him know. He wasn't sure he wanted to, either. It was in many ways too painful.

Then one morning, when Anthony was due to come round to work on the case, Leo opened the door to find him ashen-faced on the doorstep.

'You OK?' he asked in alarm. 'You look terrible.'

'Chay died.'

'Oh, Christ. I am so sorry. Come through.' He led Anthony through to the kitchen. Anthony slumped in a chair, and Leo sat down next to him and took one of his hands in his. 'When did you hear?'

'Just this morning. His – his girlfriend called from Spain.' He felt better, just for having the warmth of Leo's touch. He felt safe. 'They'd been out there on holiday. It was very sudden. The thing is, last time I saw him, just a few weeks ago, he looked so much better.'

Leo let go of his hand. 'I have some coffee on. I'll get you a cup.'

They sat drinking coffee, talking. 'I have such mixed feelings about him,' said Anthony. 'I mean, on one level

170

I thought he was a pretty appalling human being, but on another – well, he had his good aspects. I just can't believe he's gone.'

'He was your father, when all's said and done. And regardless of your relationship with him, it's going to be painful.' Leo paused. 'You must have things you need to do, so don't worry about this wretched case. It'll wait.'

Anthony rubbed a hand over his tired eyes. 'I have to go out to Madrid with my brother to bring Chay back. We can't expect Jocasta – that's his girlfriend – to worry about all that kind of thing. She'd only been in his life for the past few months. So, yes, I'm afraid the case is going to have to take a back seat for a few days.'

'I told you – don't worry about it.'

Anthony sat for a moment, coffee mug in hand, recognising how much better he felt simply for being with Leo. It suddenly occurred to him that, even if he hadn't been due to come over to Chelsea to work this morning, he would have come here anyway, turning to Leo for comfort and understanding, and not Gabrielle. Why was that? Surely the person closest to you in the world should be the one to whom you think to bring your worst news. His head felt muddled.

'Well, look,' said Leo, 'you go off and do what you have to do.'

Anthony set down his coffee cup and got to his feet. 'I don't like to abandon you in the middle of all this work. We were going to go through the master's cross-examination – it's pretty crucial.'

Leo smiled. 'You know, I've been doing this for some years. I think I can manage on my own. We'll go over it all again when you get back. You have more important things to concern yourself with.'

When they reached the front door Leo added, 'Let me know when the funeral is. I want to come.'

Anthony nodded. There was a pause, and then Leo put an arm around him and hugged him impulsively. Anthony returned the embrace, grateful for a few seconds of physical contact. He realised it was something he hungered for, constantly. He drew away.

'I'll be in touch. Bye.'

Anthony and Barry flew to Madrid later that afternoon. Jocasta was at the house, pale and stricken, looking even more waiflike than usual. Anthony noticed her bags were already packed and in the hallway.

'It was so sudden,' she said. 'I would have contacted you earlier, but there was no warning. He collapsed yesterday morning, and then a few hours after he was taken to hospital it was all over.' Her marmoset eyes brimmed with tears. Anthony gave her an awkward hug.

'Where is he?' asked Barry, dropping his rucksack on the marble floor and glancing around, almost expectantly.

Jocasta looked momentarily startled. 'At the morgue. Not here.' She went to a drawer in the hall table. 'Here's his passport. I think you'll need it for the repatriation process. I'm sorry – maybe I should have made a start on it, but it's expensive.'

'It probably needs to be done by the next of kin, anyway,' said Anthony. She said nothing. 'Don't worry.' He glanced at her cases. 'I see you're all packed.'

'I couldn't stay here on my own. Not without him.'

Anthony realised how abruptly she had been marginalised by Chay's death. Her influence in his life was over. After everything she had done for him over the past months, it seemed a little brutal. He wondered whether she didn't deserve some kind of recompense. It didn't feel like something that could be addressed right at this moment. Perhaps when they were back in London.

The doorbell chimed, and Jocasta picked up her sunglasses and bag. 'That's my taxi.' She fished in her bag for a piece of paper. 'I had to hire a funeral director to have his body moved from the hospital. That's the number. They seem to know all about the formalities.'

'Thanks,' said Anthony.

'And thanks for everything you did for Dad,' added Barry. 'We really appreciate it.'

She had put on her sunglasses, and her expression was unreadable. 'It was nothing.'

Anthony and Barry carried out her suitcases and watched as the taxi drove away.

'It was like she couldn't wait to get out of here,' said Barry.

'Awkward for her, with us on the premises.'

'I suppose so.' Barry scratched his head. 'It's gone six. Probably too late to go to the morgue, or to get in touch with the funeral guy.'

'That can wait till the morning. I'm going to see if there are beds made up, then I suggest we head out to a bar. I need a drink.'

The repatriation formalities took two days to complete, and by the time Anthony returned to London on Friday evening he realised he hadn't been in touch with Gabrielle for a week. He hadn't even told her about his father's death. He rang her to explain.

'I should have texted you, or something. I'm sorry. There's just been so much to do.'

'That's OK.' Gabrielle fought to keep the relief out of her voice. She'd spent the days agonising over his silence. It had felt like the Singapore thing all over again. She didn't understand why she couldn't bring herself to text him, to find out what was going on. Surely that was what people did in a normal relationship, without thinking twice? She couldn't help feeling that ever since the weekend in Italy something had been out of kilter between them. 'I'm really sorry about your father. Do you want me to come over?'

Anthony hesitated. He was tired and dispirited – but he told himself those were exactly the reasons why it would do him good to see her. Chay's death had left him feeling rudderless in a way he hadn't anticipated. 'Only if you want to. I mean, it's late.'

'Of course I want to. It doesn't matter that it's late. It's Saturday tomorrow. I'll see you soon.'

An hour later they were sprawled together on the sofa in Anthony's living room, the French windows open to the summer evening air, talking. Anthony was recounting everything he could remember, and all that he had ever felt, about his father. Gabrielle lay and listened, understanding that it was cathartic for him, and a way of exorcising whatever guilt he felt. When he had finished, silence fell.

'You know,' said Gabrielle after a few minutes, 'it doesn't matter that you didn't like him. You loved him, anyway. We have to love our parents. It's hard-wired into us, no matter how awful they are.'

'Do you believe that?'

'Of course. There are times when I don't rate my father at all. He can be such a dick. But I love him. I can't help it.'

'I'm confused. Do you mean Leo?'

She extricated herself from his arms and sat up cross-legged on the sofa, facing him. 'Of course not. I mean Daddy. Daniel. He brought me up. Leo is just Leo. I don't mean that in a flippant way. He's really, hugely important to me. I'm a part of him, physically. But he never had that special place in my life. The family you grew up with is everything, don't you think?'

Anthony made no reply. His childhood experiences were disjointed, not warm and secure. His mother and Barry were unquestionably his family, but they had never been a happy, cosy unit. He and Barry had never had much in common growing up. Christmases had been spent in the company of relatives he never much cared for, such holidays as they'd had had been fractious and generally joyless. Lack of money had left his mother not unaffectionate, but permanently tired and harassed. Everything he had done from the age of sixteen had been with a view to escaping. He had met Gabrielle's family, and he knew that her experience was very different from his. He put out a hand to touch her tousled hair, tumbled in that sweet way around her shoulders. She looked so earnest, so pretty as she gazed at him. The same thoughts he'd had at Ed's wedding came back to him now, reinforced by his father's death. He hungered for some kind of completeness. He knew that when people looked at him, they probably saw him as a rounded person, with a good life, a good career, and everything he wanted in his life. But when he thought of himself, all he saw was someone surrounded by blank space.

'I think your life has been very different from mine,' he replied. 'You've been lucky. You've had this big, warm, happy family, with lots of room for everyone to like one another. Mine's not been quite the same.'

'My family do mean a lot to me. But not as much as you do.' She registered his expression, and leant forward to kiss him. 'I do love you, you know.' She pushed his hair from his eyes. 'I'd quite like to create a family of my own. That's what coming from a happy family makes you feel. You want to replicate the experience.'

'You mean – you and me?'

She smiled. 'Is that such a weird idea? It's what people do when they're in love.'

He saw it all again, just as he had seen it in Italy– the way it could be, the safety of it, losing this sense of free-falling through life. The loss of Chay – whatever he had meant to him, as a father and as a person – had given him a panicked feeling of emptiness. Living with Gabrielle, making something new with her, would be a way of filling it. He saw the years stretching out ahead, conventional, busy, messy, happy. Why not follow the same patterns everyone else did?

'I like that idea.' He returned her kiss. 'Maybe it's something we should seriously think about.'

'You mean it?' A feeling of warm happiness flooded her.

He pulled her down towards him. 'Yes, I mean it.'

After all, he thought as he kissed her, what else was there left in life to do?

176

CHAPTER FOURTEEN

During the August lull Henry and Felicity went away together for a discreet week to Crete. Most people in chambers were aware of what was going on, but no one made any direct reference to it. There was no need. Everyone seemed entirely relaxed about the burgeoning romance. That was, until Natalie returned. When she discovered that Henry and Felicity were conducting 'a personal relationship', as she put it, she was dismayed, to say the least.

'It's wholly inappropriate,' she complained to Ann. She had taken to dropping in on Ann whenever she had a grievance to air. '5 Caper Court is meant to be a professional barristers' chambers, not some kind of cosy family. I think we need to introduce a fraternisation protocol, to discourage that kind of thing. Actually, I'm concerned about the ethos of the clerks' room generally. I went in there yesterday and Liam and that new junior clerk, Joe, were playing cricket with a rolled-up magazine and balls of paper. We can't have staff acting like schoolchildren.'

'Nothing wrong with letting off a bit of steam.'

Natalie sipped the coffee that Ann had poured her. 'Anyway, why are we still using the term "clerks"? It's Dickensian. They don't have clerks at 20 Essex Street. They have an administration team, with practice directors. Look at Matrix. They have a separate department for fees and finance, instead of lumping everything together under the aegis of the clerks. It's much more disciplined. And the calibre of their management teams is so much more impressive, people with actual degrees and business skills, not a deputy senior clerk who made her way up from a secretarial pool ten years ago.'

'That's rather unkind to Felicity. What does it matter what her qualifications are, as long as she's doing a good job?'

'Well, is she? I can't say I'm entirely happy with the quality of work I'm getting. And I know certain junior tenants have been grumbling about the work allocation. If she's getting sloppy, an office romance is hardly going to improve matters.'

Why, wondered Ann, did Natalie seem to have it in for Felicity all of a sudden? Aloud she said, 'Your break doesn't seem to have left you in a particularly good frame of mind. I thought holidays were meant to refresh the soul.'

Natalie made no reply. When Sian had gone to the South of France, she had decided to retaliate by taking a three-week break herself. But the Mexican resort to which she had gone alone in her fit of pique had been the wrong choice. She found herself surrounded by too many people intent on enjoying themselves, the evening entertainment was vulgar and tedious, and instead of feeling cool and independent in her solitude, she felt simply lonely. She'd had too much time to reflect on the situation with Sian. That relationship had started out with her in the position of strength, the sophisticated high-earner able to impress and indulge her new young partner, but over the months the emotional kilter had swung the other way, and now Sian was the one who seemed to be in control. There was nothing Natalie could do about it. She was too much in thrall to end the relationship, and the more casually Sian treated her, the worse it got. On her return from Mexico she had resolved to try and redress the balance, but Sian's cool behaviour, swinging between indifference one minute and displays of demonstrative affection the next, had left her more confused than ever. And in just a few weeks' time Sian would be joining 5 Caper Court, something she herself had engineered. How would that play out in their relationship? Even now she was wondering if it was something she might come to regret.

Ignoring Ann's question, she said, 'We must be the only commercial set in the Temple that still runs on old-fashioned lines. The junior tenants think our older members are positively antediluvian in their outlook.' She paused. 'I read recently that Credit Suisse have introduced a reverse mentoring scheme, and I was wondering whether that kind of thing might not work for us.'

'What on earth is a reverse mentoring scheme?'

'It's where younger employees take older people in the workplace under their wing and coach them about issues like diversity and sexual harassment.'

Ann gave her a doubtful look. 'I'm not sure our senior members of chambers would take very well to being lectured on their behaviour and attitudes by the junior tenants. Rather reminds one of the Cultural Revolution, and those "struggle sessions", when all the humbled, grey-haired professors had to sit and listen to shouty lectures from their students. Besides, we've got diversity policies, and we don't seem to have a particular problem with sexual harassment.'

'Hmm. Well, maybe 5 Caper Court isn't quite ready. But to return to the matter of the clerks' room, I really believe it needs a managerial shake-up. I intend to propose at the next chambers' meeting that we bring in a chambers' director, like a CEO, someone with a strong business background and leadership skills, to remodel the entire administration.'

'It does creak a bit sometimes,' admitted Ann. 'Henry and Felicity are solid in the traditional fundamentals, but maybe they'd welcome being relieved of some of the management burden. We've expanded the number of tenants in recent years without that being reflected on the admin side.'

'I'm glad you agree with me.' Natalie gave Ann a smile. 'Now that you're joint head of chambers, perhaps we can start getting things done around here.'

Felicity was busy preparing fee notes to submit to the solicitors in the tanker collision case that Leo and Anthony were working on. She ran through the hours that Leo had logged and found herself somewhat perplexed. She knew for a fact that he'd been working on it over the weekend – probably all weekend, knowing him – but he'd only put down four hours, when she suspected it was probably more like six, or even eight. Mr D was notoriously imprecise about time spent on a case.

Henry passed by her desk and saw her frowning at her computer screen. He paused, dropping a light, caressing touch on her neck, and she smiled up at him.

'Everything OK?'

'Yeah, fine. Only Mr Davies is doing his usual, not putting in for all the time he spends on that tanker collision case. Still, what can I do?'

'Won't hurt to bump his hours up a bit. Look at all the paper it's generated, all the days that Dee's spent photocopying documents. We must have about fifteen lever arch files, with more to come, and the solicitors don't let us charge for that. Costing's never an exact science, you know that. Half our senior lot underestimate. Natalie King's one of the worst. For such a stickler she's really slapdash in that department. Her clerk at her old chambers told me, whatever estimate she gives for producing an opinion, double it. I've had to work to keep her fees on that film finance insurance case respectable. So you have my permission to be creative.'

'If you say so.'

'I do say so.' He dropped a light kiss on her upturned cheek, just at the very moment that Natalie came into the clerks' room. Henry went to his desk and sat down. Natalie spent a few moments in conversation with Carla and as she turned to leave she said, 'Felicity, may I have a word?'

Felicity glanced up in surprise. She got up and followed Natalie out to the hallway, past the reception area.

'Felicity,' said Natalie, 'I don't think it's a good idea for you and Henry to be quite so obvious about your relationship.'

'I'm sorry?'

'The kind of thing I just saw happen between you is really quite inappropriate in an office environment.' Felicity felt her cheeks grow warm with anger. 'If I had my way,' Natalie went on, 'personal relationships between members of chambers' staff wouldn't be permitted. As it is – well, I suggest you keep displays of affection for out of office hours. We have professional standards to maintain. Oh, and while we're talking about standards, I heard you on the phone the other day referring to Mr Davies as your "guv'nor". Is it really the language to be using when referring to the head of chambers, in this day and age? It has such a touch of the barrow boy about it. Not quite the image we want to promote.'

Felicity stood speechless as Natalie disappeared through the doors to reception. Her first instinct was to flee to the ladies' and burst into tears. She felt as though she were right back in her first job, when her female manager used to bully her and criticise her for the slightest of reasons. As she stood there taking in everything Natalie had said, the insecurities of those years came flooding back, and her righteous anger dwindled into panic and self-doubt. No doubt Natalie was right. Henry shouldn't have done that. Maybe it was stupid to assume that people would be OK about their relationship. Not for the first time, she wondered whether it might not be a good idea to move to another set of chambers. She knew that it was already getting serious with Henry – when was anything not serious with him? – so maybe it would be for the best if they didn't work together. She was fed up, anyway, with the general atmosphere at 5 Caper Court. Nothing was fun any more. The junior tenants were a joyless lot, focussed on work to the exclusion of everything else. She remembered fondly how Cameron Renshaw used to crack open the sherry or a bottle of red wine at six on the dot every evening. Everyone seemed a lot jollier back then. But those days were gone. Even Mr Davies seemed to have lost his mojo. He'd once been the life and soul of the place, always ready to have a laugh, playing as hard as he worked. But Natalie seemed to have had the same crushing effect on him. She remembered with a little chill Henry confiding in her that Leo was thinking of calling it a day, and retiring from practice. If he went, she definitely didn't want to stay. Perhaps it really was time to start looking around.

Anthony knew the firm of solicitors who had prepared his father's will, so he got in touch with them, obtained a copy, and invited Barry round to go through the contents.

'How come you get named executor and I don't?' asked Barry, scanning the first page.

Anthony snapped open a can of BrewDog and set it down in front of his brother. 'I imagine because I'm a lawyer.' Chay had always been vaguely contemptuous of his eldest son's choice of profession, regarding him as an establishment sell-out, but evidently he had recognised its ultimate usefulness. More probably his own commercial success had moderated his disdain of lawyers and accountants. 'To be honest, I intend to let Dad's solicitors do all the admin. It's time-consuming and boring doing all the probate business, and I'm up to my eyes in work.'

Barry took a swallow of his beer and flipped to the second page. 'Holy fuck,' he murmured. He glanced at his brother. 'Why didn't you tell me?'

'I wanted to see your face when you read it.'

Barry grinned. 'Not such a bad old bastard after all. Three hundred K is enough for Mum to retire on. I wonder how much his estate is worth in total. He's got the house in Spain, and the place in Spitalfields. And money in the bank, presumably. There should be a fair amount over, even after Mum gets her money. And he's split it between the two of us.' He looked up from the document, his expression wondering, speculative.

'You're forgetting all the money he lost in the stocks and securities fraud.'

'Yes, but that was years ago. He's been painting and selling since then.' Barry reflected for a moment. 'Mind you, not so much.'

'Exactly. I'm just saying – I honestly don't know the full extent of what he lost to Madoff. Probably much more than he ever let on. Remember how he had to sell his New York apartment? He was so convinced he was being a smart investor, and he was really ashamed afterwards. Well, embarrassed.'

'I still reckon he was worth a few bob. Look at how much he's left Mum.'

'Yes, but the will was made three years before the fraud. Look at the date.'

Barry frowned thoughtfully at his beer, then folded up the copy of the will and handed it back to Anthony. 'So, what happens next?'

'The solicitor gets a grant of probate, we speak to a lawyer in Spain, and we find out what he was really worth. And we should arrange to go round together to Shoreditch, sort out Dad's belongings. I still have to go through all his papers. I was thinking, maybe Jocasta – I mean, she spent all those months looking after him. Maybe we should give her something. Pay her something. I don't know.'

Barry made a face. 'Sounds weird. I always thought she did what she did because she was his friend.' He drained the can of beer. 'Or whatever.'

'It was just a thought.'

'Well, I'm not doing anything on Saturday. Let's go round then.'

The following afternoon, a rumour began to swirl around 5 Caper Court to the effect that Stephanie had been seen coming into chambers that morning looking unmistakeably masculine, attired in a pinstripe suit and black brogues, and had held a conference with representatives from a Saudi petrochemical corporation and their London solicitors. Lauren on reception confirmed these details.

When the rumour reached Natalie's ears, she lost no time in insisting on a meeting with Leo and Ann to express her views.

'It's absolutely farcical. It can't be allowed to happen.'

'Yes, well, maybe you don't know what lies behind it—' began Ann.

'I don't care what lies behind it! The fact is, Stephanie is trying to have the best of both worlds. Having become professionally established as a man, with all the advantages that entails, she then decides she'll reidentify and claim female privileges. And now, when it suits her, she decides she'll switch back temporarily to avoid the impossibility of dealing with Saudi clients as a transgender woman, simply to earn some lucrative fees. Don't you detect an element of hypocrisy here?'

'Look,' said Leo, 'she's desperately trying to fund private cancer treatment in America for her son, and she couldn't afford to turn the work down. It hasn't been entirely easy for Henry to find her work over the last few months. People say they're all for inclusivity and diversity, but there's a difference between what they say and what they do. There's no question the effect on her practice hasn't been good.'

Natalie was visibly discomfited, but only momentarily. 'I'm sorry, but she can't simply switch gender at her convenience. It's insulting to every woman in chambers.'

Ann shrugged. 'I don't feel especially insulted. I think she's in a difficult position. Anyway, as I understand it, she only needs to provide a written opinion for the Saudis. It's not as though it will involve court appearances. The meeting was purely a one-off.'

'That's not the point. Women at the Bar have had to battle toxic masculine prejudice for decades. But Stephanie? All her professional power was gained as a male. She got pupillage here as a man, became a tenant as a man, and took silk as a man. And now, when it suits her to earn fees from a particular client – a client who wouldn't, by the way, instruct either you or me, Ann – she reverts to that position of male privilege. Being female is not some kind of game.'

'You talk about Stephanie gaining her professional power from a position of male privilege,' said Ann, 'but if you want to look at things in those terms, you and I gained our professional power through our white female privilege, as middle-class, educated women. There are certain struggles and disadvantages we've never experienced. Privilege doesn't just belong to men.'

'That's an utterly spurious argument, if I may say so,' retorted Natalie.

There was a silence, and then Leo asked, 'So, exactly what is it you want us to do?'

Natalie caught his half-smile, and hated him for it. 'I want you to make it clear to Stephanie that being female in these chambers isn't a mere matter of putting on a dress as and when she pleases. If she sincerely wants to identify as female, then she has to accept all the challenges and difficulties that that involves. And if that includes not being instructed on lucrative cases by unsympathetic entities, so be it. That's all I have to say on the matter.' She left the room.

Ann turned to Leo. He smiled knowingly, and raised an eyebrow. Ann had seen that look before, in courtroom encounters and chambers' meetings, charming and quizzical, intended to signify that what he'd just heard was rubbish and should be dismissed as such.

'No, Leo.' She shook her head. 'I am not your ally in this. I think Natalie is being unkind to Stephanie, but she has a valid argument. We need to speak to Stephanie and make sure it doesn't happen again.' She, too, rose and left the room.

Leo rubbed his hands wearily over his face. The truth was, he had no allies. He felt baffled by the changes happening around him. He thought about Cameron Renshaw, his old head of chambers before him. How would they have coped with this kind of thing? But it had been such a different world back then. Maybe he should just accept that time had moved on and left him behind, and go.

CHAPTER FIFTEEN

At supper that evening Natalie decided against telling Sian about Stephanie, and the stance she had taken. She was afraid that Sian might be chillingly unsympathetic, and that it would lead to an argument. In fact, in recent weeks she had stopped talking about work. Regret at ever having suggested to Sian that she should join 5 Caper Court had begun to nag at her. A few months ago, when the relationship had been fresh and loving, and she had been the one in control, it had seemed like an ideal plan. Sian would leave her not very well paid academic career, move to London, become first a pupil and then a junior tenant at 5 Caper Court, and they would build a prosperous future together, domestically and in chambers. But the dynamics had changed over the last few months, Sian's affections now blew hot and cold with savage unpredictability, and the relationship sometimes felt like a torment. Yet she was the one who had rendered it immutable. And when she looked ahead, some neuroticism convinced her that Sian might destabilise her professionally, unlikely though this possibility was. This was the place she found herself in.

After supper, they lay together on the sofa watching a travel documentary.

'We should go away together somewhere,' said Natalie, when it was finished. 'I could do with a break, even if it's just for a weekend.'

'Didn't you enjoy Mexico?' Although Natalie had said little about the trip, Sian knew it hadn't been a success.

'Not without you. I missed you.' There was a silence. Sian was fiddling with the remote, looking for the ten o'clock news. 'I bet you didn't miss me when you were in the South of France.'

Sian put down the remote. 'Sorry – what?'

'You haven't told me a thing about France. What you did, who you met.'

'Nothing to tell.' Sian smiled her mysterious smile, eyes fixed on the screen. Then she gave Natalie's hand a squeeze. The gesture was meant to be affectionate, but Natalie merely felt patronised, vulnerable. 'Anyway,' Sian went on, 'we're going to be together twenty-four seven soon.' She inched down the sofa and rested her head on Natalie's lap. 'You'll be able to boss me around, keep me in my place.'

'It doesn't quite work like that,' murmured Natalie.

'You used to be so dominating.' Sian put up a hand and stroked Natalie's face. 'I loved that. Now you let me get away with too much.'

'You always do exactly as you like, anyway.' Over the months it had been painful to discover, from dropped hints, that Sian didn't regard the relationship as necessarily exclusive. Natalie had no idea how she would react if she were to find out that Sian had slept with someone else, and so far there had been no indication that she had, but the possibility added another layer of tension and potential unhappiness. 'Are you telling me that something happened in France?'

'As if I would.' Sian smiled and reached up to kiss her.

'As if you would what – sleep with someone else, or tell me?'

'Either, or both. You work it out.'

'You're saying something happened, aren't you?' Natalie's voice was sharp with anguish.

Sian sighed. 'Oh, so what if it did? I'm here, aren't I?' She paused. 'You know, maybe you need to make me try harder. Keep me on my toes. Make me less sure of you.'

'That's ridiculous.'

'Is it? People thrive on different things. So do relationships. Just saying.' She sat up and slipped off the sofa. 'Now, I'm going to bed.' She held out a hand. 'Coming?'

Barry was the first to arrive at the house in Shoreditch on Saturday morning. The silence of the place brought home forcefully, in a way he hadn't felt in Spain, the fact of his father's death. He paced around the kitchen and living room, examining objects, glancing through the books on the shelves, filled with morbid, yet curiously pleasurable sentimentality. He went down to the studio. Everything was just as Chay had left it before going to Spain. The portrait of Jocasta still stood on the easel, virtually completed. It occurred to Barry it would sell for a fair sum, as would any other work Chay might have left. He remembered the charcoal drawings of local streets that his father had said he could have, and began a search of the shelves and cupboards. Besides the drawings, he unearthed the preparatory sketches for Jocasta's portrait, and, tucked at the back of a cupboard, a slim folder of drawings labelled 'Judith'. He leafed through the contents. They were nude sketches of their mother, made when she was very young. As he was inspecting them, he heard the sound of Anthony's key in the front door.

'Hi,' said Barry, as Anthony came down to the studio. 'Thought I might as well make a start. Just nosing around seeing if Dad left any work. I found these.'

'Wow. They're old.'

'I reckon they must be worth something.'

Even though to Anthony the drawings looked crude and unsophisticated, he knew that in the eye of the market anything of Chay's would possess significant worth. 'I'll say. We should give them to Mum.'

After a moment's hesitation, Barry nodded. 'Yeah, we probably should.' He picked up the folder of charcoal sketches. 'And there are these.'

'Dad said you could have them.' His eyes met Barry's. 'So have them.'

He glanced at the portrait of Jocasta. 'Maybe we should give that to Jocasta. Given that she looked after Dad the past few months.'

'Isn't that being a bit overgenerous? It'll probably fetch a small fortune.'

'We can decide later. I'm going to make a start on his papers.'

Despite the general mess of the studio, Chay had kept

his personal papers in a fairly orderly fashion, with bank statements, insurance policies and other documents neatly filed. Quite a change, thought Anthony, from his chaotic younger days. Maybe that was what money and success did to you. It didn't take long to go through the most recent bank statements and ascertain that, in money terms, there was a fairly healthy balance of a few hundred thousand in the bank and in various investments. But when it came to the properties, the picture was less rosy. It seemed that shortly after the Madoff crash in which he'd lost a fortune, Chay had mortgaged the Spanish property to the hilt. That left the house in Shoreditch, but as he continued to go through the papers, he discovered that Chay had taken out a hefty mortgage on that, too.

Barry appeared with cups of coffee. 'So, what's the word?'

He was about to tell Barry what he'd found so far, when they heard the sound of the front door opening and closing upstairs. They glanced at one another, and went up to find Jocasta in the hallway.

She clapped a startled hand to her breast. 'You didn't say you were coming round.'

'Why would we?' replied Barry. 'We didn't expect you'd still be here.'

She said nothing, but walked past them and down the concrete steps to the basement studio. They followed her.

She surveyed the studio and turned to them. 'Have you been going through Chay's things?'

Barry let out a laugh. 'What? You say that like we've no business doing it, when you're the one who's—'

Anthony cut him short. 'Look,' he said diplomatically to Jocasta, 'it's been a bad time for all of us, but we have to

192

start moving on. I'm sure Chay wouldn't want us to turn you out, but the fact is, you can't stay on here indefinitely. Have you got plans?'

She glanced at the folders of drawings that Barry had laid out on the work surface. Then she looked up and said, 'There's something I didn't tell you in Spain. I wasn't sure what difference it would make to my position, legally, so I waited until I could speak to a lawyer, and be sure.' She paused. 'Chay and I were married.'

Barry stared at her. 'What? When?'

'A month ago. We gave notice at the register office before we went to Spain, and came back a few weeks later for the ceremony. Then we went back to Madrid. It was Chay's idea. It was what he wanted.' She gathered the sketches together. 'So I believe these are mine. And the portrait. And this house. And everything in it.'

'Well, that's where you're wrong,' said Barry. 'Dad left a will, and we know what it says, and you're entitled to precisely nothing.'

Jocasta glanced at Anthony. 'Shall you tell him, or will I?'

Barry turned questioningly to Anthony, who was gazing blankly at Jocasta. After a few seconds Anthony said, 'Dad's will doesn't matter any more.'

'What the fuck do you mean?'

'If someone marries,' said Anthony heavily, 'the marriage revokes all prior wills.'

'So I'm afraid,' said Jocasta, 'that your father's will has no effect.'

'I don't believe this shit!' stormed Barry. 'I don't even believe you were married!'

'Oh, please.' Jocasta's expression was faintly contemptuous. 'Wait there.'

She went back upstairs.

'This is fucking surreal,' Barry said to Anthony. 'You're telling me that because she – she apparently bloody *manipulated* our father into marrying her, she can walk off with everything he owned?'

'If what she says is true, it's as though Dad's will never existed. Christ, I can't believe he did this.'

Jocasta reappeared. She handed a document to Barry. 'There.' She watched him scrutinise the marriage certificate. 'As I say, I thought it best to talk to a lawyer before I spoke to you two. I think you'll find that I inherit all of your father's property and personal belongings. There may be something leftover for you two, depending on how much money there is, but I'll let you know in due course. In the meantime' – she shrugged, the steely look in her eyes never wavering – 'I think you'll find you're the ones who have to move on.'

'You left us to do everything in Spain,' said Anthony. 'The repatriation of Chay's body, all the formalities. You effectively abandoned him.'

She lifted her chin defensively. 'I didn't have the money. I didn't know where I stood. I thought it best to leave it all to you. It was a sensitive time.'

'You couldn't attend to any of that, but you think you'll be able to sort out his estate?'

'I'm sure I'll manage. I couldn't face being here when I returned from Spain. I've been staying with friends. I only got back last night. I'll make a start tomorrow.'

Barry reached for the folder of drawings. 'You're not

bloody well having these. Dad gave them to me.'

'He never said anything to me about that. They stay here.' She put a detaining hand on the folder. 'I have the law on my side. Ask your brother.'

'Leave them,' said Anthony shortly. 'For now.'

'You're kidding. We just – what? We hand everything over to her?'

'It's not yours to hand over, Barry,' said Jocasta. She swept up the folders of drawings. 'You know your way out. Oh, in case you were thinking of dropping by again, I intend to have the locks changed.'

Out on the street, Barry raged at Anthony. 'I can't believe the way you were in there! You're just rolling over and letting this happen. You're meant to be the lawyer, and you just stood there and let her tell us the score. Why aren't you angrier about all this?'

'I am. I'm bloody furious. But taking it out on Jocasta, and antagonising her, isn't going to get us anywhere. And by the way, this isn't exactly my field of legal expertise, you know. I need to find out where we stand, but frankly, I don't think our position is great.' He let out a sigh. 'Come on – let's get a drink.'

In the pub Anthony did some googling on his phone. 'So,' he told Barry despondently, 'the position is – she gets all Dad's property and his personal belongings, the first two hundred and fifty thousand of his money, and half of what's left. The rest goes to us.'

Barry considered this bleakly. 'How much money is there?'

'About four hundred K. Roughly.'

'So' – Barry frowned into his beer as he performed some mental calculations – 'she gets two hundred and fifty thousand of that. Which leaves a hundred and fifty.'

'And she gets half of that.'

'And we get half each of what's left.' Barry's face was bleak. 'Seventy-five grand between us. Bugger all.'

Anthony contemplated his brother. He'd already had a fair amount of money from Chay over the years, but that had been spent, frittered away. Lately, ever since their father's cancer diagnosis, Barry had lived in the belief that when Chay died there would be enough coming his way to make up for his own lack of money or proper career. A rash assumption, but that was Barry for you. He thought only of himself, and for that, Anthony despised him.

Barry put his head in his hands. 'To think we were considering giving her something for looking after Dad. What a joke. I can't believe that bitch gets virtually everything – the money, the houses.'

'The houses are practically worthless. Dad mortgaged them up to the hilt. That's going to be an unpleasant surprise for her when she finds out.'

'Good.'

'It's Mum I feel sorriest for.'

'Oh yeah, Mum.' Barry shot his brother a guilty glance. 'Still, she won't miss what she doesn't know about.'

'The thing is—'

'What?'

'I told Mum. About the will. About the money she's meant to be getting.'

Anthony groaned. 'What did you do that for?'

'To make her happy.'

Anthony tried to picture his mother's reaction. He

remembered when he was younger how angry she had always been about his father's failure to provide her with any money. Even so, when Chay had become successful and had tried to make financial reparations, she had only ever accepted what she felt he owed her for the years of neglect. He wondered what she really felt about the bequest. She was a woman of some pride.

He sighed. 'OK. Well, leave it to me. I'll talk to her.'

Early on Friday evening he went to see her. Judith had lived in the same terraced house in East Dulwich for thirty-six years, working as a primary school teacher. Now in her mid-fifties, she was petite, dark-haired, and still attractive in a clean, unadorned fashion, wearing no make-up and dressing in functional, unremarkable clothes. She had a cheerful disposition, and a stoical outlook. When Anthony told her, over cups of tea at the little kitchen table, about Chay's marriage to Jocasta, and how it rendered his will ineffective, she simply shrugged.

'It would have been nice, but to be honest, it makes no odds.'

Anthony gazed at her. 'I'm sorry, Mum. It was a lot of money.'

'When has your father been anything but a disappointment?' She smiled the maddening smile of patient fortitude that he remembered so well from his childhood. Her attitude to Chay had always been that of a tolerant adult towards a difficult child, because in spite of his failings, she had loved him. It was still a matter of wonder to Anthony that his father could have inspired love in any woman. 'I've almost paid the mortgage on this place, and between us, Alan and I have enough to enjoy life.' Alan was a fellow teacher with whom Judith had been in a relationship for several years. For some reason that Anthony couldn't quite fathom, but that he suspected had something to do with Judith's determination to keep her independence, they lived separately, letting their lives coincide as and when they wanted. 'And I love my job. It's not like I want to retire.'

'You know I earn more than enough to help you out financially, if ever you need it.'

Again that smile. 'That's sweet. But you need your money to build your own life. The kind of circles you move in now, I suppose you have to keep your end up.' She had always been proud of his success, but jokes over the years about how he was betraying his humble origins had always indicated to him that she begrudged the fact his career, and the kind of people he now mixed with, put a social distance between them. She added, 'And I suppose Gabrielle has certain expectations.' On the occasions when Judith met Gabrielle, they got on pleasantly enough, but his mother's reaction to Gabrielle's breezy confidence was always guarded, reminding him of the people at the airport watching the party on its way to Edward's wedding, their expressions speaking their faint resentment.

'She earns her own money,' he replied. But even as he said this, he realised there was truth in what his mother had said. Gabrielle did have certain expectations of their relationship, and the shape that their life together should take. Just a few days ago she had suggested that they should announce to their friends that they were getting married, and have an engagement party. The suggestion had startled him. Looking back on the conversation they'd had that night when he'd come back from Spain, he supposed that she was entitled to assume from it that they would at some point get married, but he hadn't expected her to construe it as such an immediate statement of intent. They didn't even live together. So he had dodged the suggestion with some vague response. But yes, Gabrielle had expectations, and he knew what they were. So why was he reluctant to give into them? What was holding him back?

He turned the conversation away from Gabrielle, and back to Chay. They talked about him for a while, about the people who had come to the funeral, about the past. Eventually Anthony said he had to go, and kissed his mother goodbye.

Outside on the pavement he checked his phone, and saw he'd missed two calls from Gabrielle. He rang her as he walked to the station.

'Hi. Sorry I missed you. I've been round seeing my mother.'

'No problem. But you do realise we haven't seen one another for almost a week?' Her tone was light, cheerful, but the underlying reproach was there.

'Yeah, sorry. Work's been quite full on, and I've been having some problems with my father's estate.'

'Well, what about tonight?'

'Yes, fine. Where do you want to go?'

'Why don't we just stay in? I've had a busy week and I don't feel like going anywhere. I could come over to yours.'

'Fine. It'll take me an hour or so to get back. I'm all the way over in East Dulwich.'

'You know, if I had my own key, I could just let myself in and cook us a meal. It's something to think about.'

'Yes. Absolutely.' A pause. 'Anyway, I'll see you later.'

It was inevitable, he thought, as he slipped his phone into his pocket. And a natural part of her expectations.

CHAPTER SIXTEEN

The *Alpha Six* mediation was being held in a conference room on the fifteenth floor of the imposing offices of Montial's solicitors in Leadenhall Street. When Leo arrived, Sarah was already there with Danylo Ivanov and Andrew Howard. She gave Leo only the coolest of smiles, and he felt again a touch of regret. Everything about her was so familiar, so attractive and sexy, that it seemed odd for them not to be able to regard each other in the casually proprietorial way they once had.

Sarah, for her part, had come today determined to maintain a calm, professional exterior, to give nothing away. She had thought it would be painful to see Leo, but she found to her relief that the months spent getting over him had given her a new detachment. She would always feel the same hungry attraction for him, but it was good to be free of the relationship's tiring uncertainties. It seemed strange now to think of the pleasure they had once taken in tormenting one another.

There was no opportunity for anything more than small talk before the representatives for the other side arrived, and then the mediator hurried in, a small, smiling, bespectacled woman. She set briskly to work, outlining the basic points of dispute, reminding everyone of the non-binding nature of the process, and its purpose in trying to bring the parties together to find some mutually acceptable compromise. Leo began by setting out the case for his clients, keeping his statement brief and lucid, and the other side's barrister then did the same, though in a somewhat more confrontational fashion. The opposing parties then went to separate rooms, and the day unfolded. For the next few hours the mediator shuttled between the two rooms, ferrying points of view and trying to whittle down areas of contention. At one point Danylo and the shipowner's representative were closeted together, and an hour later Leo and his counterpart met separately to address legal issues. To and fro it went. Much coffee was drunk, and at lunchtime sandwiches were brought in. By mid-afternoon matters seemed to have reached a hostile stalemate, and the cool, anonymous white-walled meeting rooms were beginning to have a claustrophobic effect on everyone. Still the mediator persisted with amicable earnestness, and after another two hours, and yet another meeting between the two barristers, a thaw settled in. As the mediator continued to bustle back and forth, small accommodations were being made by both sides.

'Now the serious horse-trading begins,' observed Leo. Sarah yawned. Her head was aching from too much coffee. Danylo stared anxiously at his phone, on which he was texting news of progress to his querulous boss.

Proposed settlement figures began to be traded, at first wildly apart by millions of dollars, and then, as time ticked by, gradually moving closer. Then, at a little after six o'clock, the shipowner's side dug in their heels and refused to budge from their last offer.

'This is the best deal we're going to get,' Leo told Danylo.

'I'm not authorised to go to that figure!' protested Danylo.

'Then I advise you try and get that authorisation. Otherwise we go back to arbitration and there's no guarantee you'll ever get as good a deal.'

Danylo rang his boss, pacing up and down the room and conducting a volatile discussion in Ukrainian. Andrew Howard went off to the gents', and Leo took the opportunity to lean forward and murmur to Sarah, who was sitting across the table from him, 'I haven't had the chance to ask you how you've been.'

'I've been fine, thanks. Why wouldn't I be?' Her smile was frigid.

'Good. I just wondered.'

A few moments later Andrew Howard came back into the room, and Danylo clicked his phone off. 'It's done. I'm authorised to settle at that level.' His face looked blank with relief.

The mediator carried the news to the other side, and the parties reconvened in the conference room. After all the hours of intense discussion and negotiation, Sarah expected everyone's mood to be buoyant but, as she observed in a low voice to Leo, Danylo and his counterpart both looked grimly dissatisfied, and grudging of the outcome.

'No one's ever happy with a negotiated deal,' murmured Leo. 'Both sides always think they've come off worst. Think Brexit.'

After a few formalities, the parties shook hands and left

the boardroom. The long day was over. As he stood waiting for the lift, Leo saw Danylo and Sarah in what looked like a close, personal conversation at the end of the corridor. A moment later Danylo came towards the lift.

'Sarah not taking you for a drink to celebrate?' asked Leo.

Danylo shrugged. He looked mildly annoyed. 'She has other plans. But I have an early flight tomorrow, so maybe it's just as well.'

The lift arrived. Leo glanced at Sarah, who was still at the end of the corridor, making a call on her mobile. 'I think I've left something in the conference room,' Leo said to Danylo. 'You take the lift. Have a safe journey.'

'Thanks for your work today,' replied Danylo. He stepped into the lift, the doors closed, and Leo went back down the corridor to where Sarah was slipping her phone into her bag. Was she really busy, he wondered, or had she just made an excuse to Danylo?

'Have you time for a drink?' he asked.

She hesitated. She had spent the whole day consolidating her altered feelings, and the prospect of spending even an hour with Leo, knowing how susceptible she was, made her apprehensive.

'All right. But I can't stay long.'

'Fine. There's a place round the corner. It shouldn't be too busy on a Tuesday.'

They left the building and found a quiet booth in a nearby wine bar. Leo bought the drinks.

'Here's to a good result,' he said, chinking his glass against hers.

She nodded. 'Montial may be paying two hundred thousand more than they want to, but it's better than months of litigation and the possibility of losing altogether.'

'Which is probably what would happen. I'm not sure my arguments about torsional stresses would hold up in arbitration. Still' – he took a sip of wine – 'they did the job today.'

They continued to discuss the mediation, but it was an artificial exchange, each aware of something else waiting to be said. A pause fell, and Leo said, 'Look, I know I should apologise. About the day you left, about what happened with Sergei. I didn't mean for you to be hurt.'

'People always get hurt around you, Leo. It doesn't matter what you do to try to stop it happening, like lying and hiding things. It happens, anyway.'

'I never pretended I could be faithful to you. You knew that much years ago.'

'I know. I was stupid to hope things might change.'

'I genuinely wish it could be otherwise. You know – if you were queen of pleasure, and I were king of pain.'

'Is that a quote from something?'

'A poem by Swinburne. You should read it some time. It rather describes what you and I are like. So rightly yet so wrongly matched. We give each other pleasure, but we always hurt one another, in the end.'

'You're incapable of being hurt.'

'Ah, that's far from true.'

'Anyway, I have the feeling we're done, you and I.' She smiled at him. 'But, as they say, it was fun while it lasted.'

'In many ways, I was happier with you than anyone else. I only wish I could give you what you want.'

'Don't worry, you did. For a few years at least, on and

off. But now I need someone and something steadier in my life. I'm getting old and tired.'

'Far from it. You're young, and very lovely.' She said nothing. 'Tell me, why didn't you go for a drink with Danylo after the mediation? I thought looking after clients was part of your job. He was clearly a bit put out that you said you couldn't.' A pause. 'When evidently you could.' Sarah tucked a strand of blonde hair behind one ear and studied her wine. 'He has a bit of a thing for you, you know. I watched him all day around you.'

She glanced up at him in irritation. 'Oh, for God's sake, Leo – you can ask that question after what you've just said? Really? Yes, I like Dan. A lot. And I know he likes me. But do you really think, with all that's happened between us, that I'm going to take your leftovers?'

'My leftovers?'

'That evening you went to his hotel after the meeting in March. You couldn't wait. But then, you never can, can you? You see someone you want, and you have to have them. So that's why I turned him down. I've no wish to pick up your discarded lovers.' She stared angrily at him. 'Why are you laughing?'

'For once, you've got it all very badly wrong. Yes, I went to his hotel. Yes, we had a couple of drinks. But we spent most of the time discussing iron ore liquefaction levels. Not the sexiest of topics, you'll agree.' Leo sat back, gazing at her. 'So you've spent the last few months assuming I seduced him?'

The expression in Sarah's eyes was tempered with something like relief. 'Can you blame me? It's what you do.'

'Just because he liked me didn't mean he wanted to sleep

with me. He is very distinctly straight. I guessed that long before I got to his hotel.' Leo drained his glass. 'He's more interested in you. Very much so.' Sarah said nothing. 'Why don't you call him? He's got a flight back in the morning, but there's still this evening.'

Sarah lifted her eyes to his. 'You think?'

Leo nodded. 'It's what I would do.'

'Oh God, I'll be frank,' she sighed, 'it's what I want to do. I really, really like him. I just always thought that—'

'Well, you were wrong. So just do it.'

There was a long silence, then she asked, 'We'll still be friends, you and I?'

'When were we ever friends?' He drained his glass. 'Don't worry. I'm always here.'

She gathered her things together. 'Thanks for the drink.' She leant forward and kissed him lightly, then slid from the booth. 'See you around.'

He watched her as she walked towards the door, already on her mobile. Calling Danylo, he presumed. Well, that was good. Maybe he was someone who could give her what she wanted. But as he watched her leave, he felt a strange void in his heart, knowing that she was taking with her something that could never be replaced.

'It's not a question of backing down, Mr Kinderman. In my view, after all the time and effort spent on this case, and given the inherent dangers of going to trial, settling is Backlit Production's best option. I would say that anything in the region of thirty million would represent a good outcome.' Natalie glanced in the direction of the instructing solicitor, Abby Murphy, as she said this. Abby, a poised, smartly dressed redhead, nodded in agreement.

Mr Kinderman, a corpulent American with the build of a Chicago mobster, stirred in angry irritation, making his chair creak. 'They wrote the policies, and I want them to pay a hundred per cent. We're not budging on this one.'

Natalie sighed inwardly. This film finance insurance case had been going on for some months, and over that time it had become evident that the prospects of recovery under the policy were far from certain. She sat and listened as Mr Kinderman re-rehearsed all the reasons why the case should fight, and wondered for the hundredth time why he had ever bothered instructing lawyers, since he seemed convinced he knew best. Eventually, after some more to-ing and fro-ing, during which Mr Kinderman became more and more tetchy, the conference concluded, because he had a plane to catch.

'I don't want to hear any more about settling, Ms King,' he said, as he prised his bulk from the chair and tugged his jacket down. 'You know, if we were running this case back home, we'd be giving these insurers both barrels.' He smiled with an effort, trying to close on a pleasant note, making a fat fist with his hand and shaking it playfully under Natalie's nose. 'You London lady lawyers need more fighting spirit! Less pussy-footing around.'

Natalie smiled wanly. 'All my advice is given in good faith and in your best interests, believe me.' She and Abby rose to shake hands with him.

When he had gone, they sat down at the conference table and exchanged looks. They were contemporaries, and having worked on a number of cases together they had developed mutual respect and something approaching a friendship. As Natalie didn't make friends easily, she enjoyed the feeling of female camaraderie.

'Fat jerk,' said Abby.

'Highly unprofessional language, with which I wholeheartedly agree.' Natalie closed her laptop and sat back with a sigh.

'We're going to end up going to court and losing. And guess who'll get the blame?'

'Some clients just won't be told.'

Abby glanced at the time on her phone. Half six. The meeting, unprofitable as it had been, had lasted two hours. 'I suggest we go for a drink and try and work out a new strategy. What do you say?'

'Marvellous idea.' Sian was away in Cambridge, and Natalie had no wish to go back to the empty flat and brood over what she might be getting up to.

They left 5 Caper Court and went to the nearest pub, but on a Friday night it was packed and noisy.

'We can do better than this,' said Abby.

They walked along the Strand to the Savoy, made their way to one of the quieter cocktail bars, and ordered martinis. Over the first drink they discussed the case, but after another hour and another cocktail the conversation drifted to books and plays, and in particular a recent play that both, as it turned out, had seen and enjoyed. As they debated its themes, Natalie was conscious of a pleasure she hadn't known in a while. She felt relaxed, on equal terms with Abby, who was shrewd and quick-witted, and made her laugh. She was good to look at, too, with her sleekly short red hair and pale skin, and her pretty, sharp features with just the right amount of make-up. The fingers that curled around the stem of her martini glass were slender and white, the nails varnished with a red so dark as to be almost black, and her suit, dark blue against the creamy white of her silk blouse, was beautifully, figure-huggingly cut. Natalie, who always took strength from dressing well herself, with due care and attention to make-up and jewellery, liked the thought of the picture they must make, two attractive, sophisticated professional women, enjoying cocktails and each other's company at the end of a busy week. The restfulness of the low-lit bar, the pleasantly fuzzy feeling brought on by two martinis, and the pleasure of simply listening to and looking at Abby, who was recounting some amusing story from work, made her realise how accustomed she had grown to the tension and uncertainty that Sian generated, making Natalie work constantly for her affection, for the bestowal of kindness. That was what being in love had done to her ego. It was as though when she was with Sian, she lost any real sense of herself as the strong, serene woman she felt herself to be at this moment.

Abby leant forward and touched the geometric silver bracelet that Natalie was wearing. 'That's a beautiful bracelet,' she said. 'Very unusual.'

It had been a gift from Sian in the early days of their relationship. 'Thank you,' she said. Abby's fingers lingered, turning the bracelet gently on Natalie's wrist. She looked up and met Natalie's eyes, letting her fingers drift to the skin of Natalie's wrist.

'You know, I hadn't expected this evening to be so enjoyable. It's nice, getting to know you properly at last.' Natalie had no words. It hadn't occurred to her that Abby might be gay. She felt Abby's fingers drift from her wrist to the palm of her hand, where they rested. 'Why don't we carry on at my place?' continued Abby. 'Have another drink or two?' She stroked Natalie's palm for a second, then took her hand away, smiling.

Natalie thought of Sian, and what she had said the other night. *Make me less sure of you.* Could she do this? She loved Sian, but the passion was lopsided, unhealthy. Sian had virtually told her so. Maybe this would be a way of redressing the balance. Yet she was a woman of scruples. Betrayal did not come naturally to her. She was hesitating for words when Abby leant forward and kissed her gently on the mouth, then sat back.

'I've been dying to do that for weeks.'

Natalie looked hastily around the bar, then back at Abby. 'Really?'

'You have no idea. I knew you were gay, but I just couldn't summon up the courage to let you know how I felt. Till this evening.' She held up her empty martini glass. 'Gin helps.' There was a pause. 'So, what do you say?'

Natalie hesitated for a moment. She was sure Sian had had some kind of a fling in France, so perhaps some payback would be healthy. She drew a breath and smiled. 'Let's go.'

Two hours later, Natalie was lying in bed in Abby's Hoxton house, drowsing in a tangle of sheets while Abby, propped up on one elbow, stroked her forehead and contemplated her. She enjoyed the feeling of Abby's light fingers on her forehead.

'I love that you play as hard as you work,' said Abby. 'All the hours you've put in on this Backlit case.'

'Not so very many.'

'Hmm. I was looking at the fee notes the other day. Don't worry – I'm not complaining. You wouldn't believe the times I've had to ask counsel to bump up their fees to justify my own. It doesn't exactly look good when a barrister charges a tenth of what I'm charging.'

Natalie opened her eyes and rolled over. 'I've been charging the same hours every month.'

'I know. And very healthy sums, too.' She leant down and kissed Natalie. 'Don't frown like that. It's all fine.' She kissed her again. 'In fact, I've a good mind to bill Backlit Productions for the two hours we've spent in bed. I mean, it's all been for the good of the case, hasn't it?'

CHAPTER SEVENTEEN

On Monday morning Ann Halliday stopped by Leo's room. 'Just to warn you that Natalie intends to call a chambers' meeting later today.'

'Does she, now? I thought that was something only you and I could do.'

'We revised the constitution, remember? Any member of chambers can call one now, if it's a matter of constitutional importance.'

'Oh yes, I dimly recall that.' He sighed. 'Everything seems to be a matter of constitutional importance with that woman. This used to be a nice relaxed place. Now it's like working for a corporation.'

Ann sat down. 'This issue she wants to discuss is quite important, actually.'

'So she's already spoken to you about it? Well, that's bloody marvellous. Is there any reason why she hasn't extended me the same courtesy?'

'She says she finds you' – Ann hesitated – 'somewhat antagonistic when it comes to discussing chambers' issues on a one-to-one level. She thinks you're preconditioned to be hostile towards her. And towards women in chambers generally.'

'What, she thinks I dislike her because she's a woman? I dislike her for a whole host of reasons, but that's not one of them.' Leo sat back in his chair and regarded Ann with bemusement. 'And you? Do you share her view?'

'No, I don't. I don't think you're remotely prejudiced towards women in chambers. But whatever kind of personal animus there is between you and Natalie, that's the way she interprets it.'

'So,' sighed Leo, 'what's the burning issue?'

'Fee notes. She believes that they don't accurately reflect the hours people put in on a case. That too much is left to the discretion of the clerks. I think she's going to suggest we all start using time sheets to log our work.'

'God, this persistent meddling.'

Ann glanced at her watch. 'Anyway, I just thought you should know what's on the agenda. I'm due in court.' She rose. 'See you later.'

When Ann had gone, Leo sat mulling it over, trying to work out what it was that motivated Natalie to agitate constantly about the way in which chambers was run, particularly this latest ludicrous intervention. Maybe the clue lay in her relationship with Sian. In all probability, having a partner so much younger than herself, especially one with a penchant for casual infidelity, made for all kinds of stresses and insecurities. Perhaps it was some kind of transference, trying to exert control professionally to make up for her inability to regulate her personal life.

Anyway, the chambers' meeting wasn't something he could afford to waste time worrying about. The collision hearing was only a fortnight away, and he still hadn't made up his mind how he would run the cross-examination of the master of the oil tanker. On the face of it, there might have been negligence in the navigation of the ship, but nothing close to the level of incompetence or complete culpability required to find the master, and therefore the owners, liable. He had gone through every shred of evidence, the AIS data, video data recordings, and the statements of officers and crew members, but they yielded nothing to support his sense that this had been something more than an accident. Maybe he should simply prepare himself for the possibility that this was a case he and his clients were bound to lose.

He scrolled through the documents on his laptop screen for a few moments, but Ann's visit had disrupted his concentration. He left his desk and went to the window, and gazed out. The late summer sunshine fell with gentle melancholy on the mellow brickwork of the walls and flagstones of Caper Court. The place might be no more than a collection of old buildings, but for thirty-five years it had been his familiar home, the place where he would always soonest be. In that moment he made a decision. He would not let Natalie turn it into some ruthlessly professional organisation. He wasn't ready to give up his practice, not under pressure from this woman. He had let her relentless campaign for change wear him down, instead of galvanising him into action. She had made an enemy out of him, and it was about time she found out what a mistake she had made.

A knock at the door made him turn from the window, and Anthony came in. He caught the expression on Leo's face. 'Is this a bad time?'

'No, no. Good timing, actually.' Leo returned to his desk and sat down. 'We need to have a talk about the master's cross-examination. Despite my gut feeling, I can't find a shred of evidence to back it up.'

'Is that why you're looking so fed up?'

Leo shook his head. 'Something else entirely. Natalie King is calling a chambers' meeting this afternoon. Apparently she doesn't like the way fee notes are calculated. She wants to introduce a timekeeping system.'

Anthony groaned. 'Oh, dear God, no.'

'Quite. The woman's relentless. And I've decided I've had enough. What would you say if I told you that our new pupil, starting in a couple of weeks' time, happens to be Natalie's live-in lover?'

'Wow. I'd say that was intriguing.'

'It's more than intriguing. You may recall that she actively campaigned for her to be given the place. And she sat in on her interview. Something of a conflict there, wouldn't you say?'

'Absolutely. She's not going to look particularly good when that comes out. Her integrity will be in tatters. I assume you're going to bring it up at the meeting? I can't think of a better opportunity.' Anthony paused. 'How come you know this?'

'Oh, I just happened to find out. Yes, it's a rather useful piece of ammunition. I haven't quite worked out how I'm going to deploy it.' He sat forward in his chair. 'Anyway, enough about that woman. She occupies far too much of my time and attention. We need to talk about the cross-examination.'

At four that afternoon people began to assemble in the conference room for the chambers' meeting. Natalie was already there, seated with a look of frigid, blonde composure. Anthony arrived and slid into a seat between Leo and Stephanie. The meeting was called to order, and Natalie wasted no time in telling everyone its purpose. 'It's about fee notes. I think the practice of leaving it to the clerks to make their own rough and ready assessment of how much to charge on a case is problematic. I've been made aware, in particular relation to a case I've been working on for some months, that the fees being charged are not necessarily an accurate reflection of hours spent. I accept that this is a function of people being sloppy with recording their hours – I'm as guilty of this as anyone – but that's precisely why I feel it's something we seriously have to address.'

'Logging our time isn't an exact science, but I think we do our best,' observed David Liphook.

'And Henry and Felicity have a very fair idea of what is appropriate to charge on any given case,' added Anthony. 'I don't believe fee notes go out that are materially inaccurate.'

'I recently had a case where the solicitor actually asked me to increase my fees so they were more in line with his,' added David. 'I refused, of course.' He shrugged. 'Sometimes it's a question of managing expectations.'

'But don't you see that that kind of slapdash approach lays us open to all kinds of problems?' said Natalie. 'I firmly believe we should consider introducing a proper and accurate time-recording system.'

'What? And start doing all that billable hours nonsense that solicitors do, splitting everything into six-minute units when you may only spend a couple of minutes on something?' said Leo. 'I don't see how that's any better.'

Natalie fixed him with a stare. 'It's hardly nonsense to have a system that fairly and accurately represents the time an individual spends on a case.'

'But the amount of time spent on a piece of work doesn't always reflect its value,' countered Leo. 'You know perfectly well that you may be asked to produce a written opinion, and Henry or Felicity will negotiate a fee in advance that has nothing to do with how long you spend producing it. Every one of us works at a different pace. Some people spend a day on something that might take two hours of another person's time.'

'Exactly,' said David. 'Take Stephanie on safe ports, for example. She'll turn out in fifteen minutes something a lot more worthwhile than a junior would after four hours of research. Experience versus time saved. What's the use of a time sheet there?'

'Besides, it might not produce the intended result,' said David. 'There are some who, if I may put it this way, grind slowly yet exceeding small – they stand in theory to benefit from time sheets, but on the other hand, it would just highlight their slowness. Much better for our clerks to make a fair valuation of the work without regard to the amount of time spent on it, which in my view is often irrelevant.'

'I agree,' said Stephanie. 'Our clerks would never submit fee notes that they didn't think were entirely appropriate.'

'I'm not suggesting they do,' replied Natalie. 'But what I

am saying is that the way things are done presently, they could lay themselves – and us – open to a charge of inaccurately representing the time spent by a member of chambers on a case, and that's obviously problematic to any half-decent lawyer, I would have thought.'

'Oh, for heaven's sake,' sighed Leo. 'Your constant denigration of the clerks is becoming tiresome. They do their utmost best for us, and everyone here knows it. You seem to take every opportunity to find fault with them.'

'This isn't a question of fault. I'm simply pointing out to you that the kind of licence we allow them leaves them open to accusations of behaving – well, dishonestly.'

'That's ridiculous,' said Anthony.

'Is it? Everyone in this room seems to accept that Henry and Felicity routinely charge fees without any proper basis for their estimate. Is it such a stretch of the imagination to characterise that as a fraudulent act? Imagine if the Bar Standards Board or the Serious Fraud Office were to come sniffing around us. If we don't introduce a proper system, people in this room could, in theory, be accused of living off the proceeds of crime.'

There was a ghastly silence around the table.

'What ridiculous scaremongering,' said Leo. 'When has any instructing solicitor suggested that our fee notes are out of line?'

Arun Sikand cleared his throat. 'There shouldn't be any scope for them to do so. I take Natalie's point. I would prefer that fee notes issued on my behalf should be beyond question. I back the introduction of time sheets.'

'I'm with Arun,' said Lisa Blackmore. There was a murmur of agreement amongst the junior tenants. Some of the more senior members of chambers scoffed, and took issue, and for a few minutes there was debate to and fro across the table. At length Leo interrupted it by saying, 'I see absolutely no need to change practices that have served these chambers perfectly well for decades. I have no wish to start measuring out my hours in six-minute coffee spoons, the way solicitors do. It would be an absurd pressure. We are self-employed individuals. We're not working for some corporation. I for one am resolutely opposed to the idea.'

'I don't see what possible objection you can have,' said Natalie, in her most reasonable tone of voice. 'Having a modern, computerised system for recording our time is the simplest way of ensuring all fee notes are entirely accurate. Not leaving it up to the clerks to pluck figures from the air. Surely we have a duty to be entirely accountable and transparent in everything we do?'

Anthony glanced at Leo. This was his moment, surely? To stop her in her tracks, all he had to do was to reveal to everyone how she had concealed her relationship with Sian Attwood. It would make a mockery of her pretensions to those articles of faith, transparency and accountability that she was endlessly holding forth about. It would demolish in an instant the support she had built up for the wholesale changes she was trying to bring about. Her credibility would be shot. He waited.

But Leo simply gazed at Natalie for a long moment, then inclined his head, and said, 'If the majority here agree with you, then I won't object further. But I would like it recorded that I think you are seeking a solution to a problem that doesn't even exist.'

Ann Halliday drew a breath. 'Very well, let's have a vote on it.' A show of hands was called for, but the vote was evenly split. 'Well,' said Ann, 'in my view, as the meeting was called at such short notice, and since not every member of chambers has been able to attend or arrange a proxy, we'll have to rerun this. We'll put the issue aside for now.' She glanced at Natalie. 'Was that the only item for discussion?'

'There is another issue I would like to raise,' said Natalie. 'It's a sensitive one, but as Stephanie is here today, it seems appropriate to deal with it now.' There was a pause, in which people's gazes darted to Stephanie. 'I would like to have it formally recorded that I – and I believe I probably speak for all the women in chambers – take the strongest personal objection to her recent behaviour in deciding to abandon, for one day, her female identity and to present herself as a man to secure work that would not otherwise have come her way. That conduct not only trivialised what we had all assumed was the difficult and painful process of changing gender, it was insulting to all women in these chambers. I'd like to remind Stephanie that, for the rest of us, living the life of a woman means not having access to the privileges that come with the patriarchy. I think she should recognise that and apologise to every woman here.'

There was a shocked silence. Leo glanced at Stephanie. She was dressed in the ubiquitous female barrister garb of black suit and white blouse, but, as always, her attempts to feminise her appearance were not entirely successful, and there was a desperate pathos, given Natalie's stinging words, in the way in which the make-up did not entirely disguise the beard growth, nor lipstick the masculinity of the jowly face. It wrenched at Leo's heart to see his friend's mortification and embarrassment. It was as though Natalie had managed, despite the carefulness of her language, to ridicule her and everything about her. Stephanie got clumsily to her feet and looked around. Leo could feel the tension, everyone willing this not to be happening, for Natalie not to have said what she had just said. The sympathy was almost palpable.

'I-I am sorry. I was under certain pressures, which—' There followed a long, agonising moment in which she struggled for words. Then she simply pushed her chair back and left the room.

Everyone sat in silence.

'I think we should leave matters there,' said Ann stonily. People got to their feet and began to leave. She turned to Natalie, clearly furious. 'Was that absolutely necessary? Really?'

Natalie's composure was not in the least shaken. 'It had to be said.'

'You just wanted to take her down. It was appalling.'

Natalie gave a chilly smile, got up from the table, and left without a word.

Leo leant over to Ann. 'You know, one of the greatest strengths of the patriarchy is that you lot all seem to hate each other.'

The remark produced the wry laugh it was intended to. 'Don't.' Ann shook her head. 'Her agenda, whatever it is, is way beyond me. That was just such a bloody cruel thing to do.'

'Don't worry,' said Leo, as he got to his feet. 'She isn't going to get away with it.'

As Leo was leaving, Anthony stopped him. He waited for others to pass out of the room, then asked, 'Why didn't you say something? That was the perfect chance.'

'Something Harvey Specter said. Never destroy someone in public when you can accomplish the same in private.' He smiled. 'Be patient.'

Natalie was in her room putting her things together and preparing to leave, when there was a knock at the door. Leo came in.

Natalie gave him a defensive look. 'I assume you've come to tell me I was wrong to say what I did.' She had spent the last half-hour berating herself. Having won the sympathy of the younger tenants on the matter of time sheets, she'd then squandered it by attacking Stephanie. It didn't help that she believed herself to be entirely in the right. The fact was, she'd badly misjudged the mood of the meeting, and people's sentiments regarding Stephanie.

'Not at all. I think it's time you and I put an end to hostilities. It's creating a bad atmosphere in chambers. Toxic, I believe you'd call it. I came to invite you to dinner.'

The smile he gave her was his most charming and beguiling, and she recognised it as such. The sense of succumbing to it was hateful; she realised in that instant that one of the reasons she detested Leo was that he was so attractive. In objective terms only, she assured herself. The confusion of her emotions caused her to hesitate.

'I think it would help to have a civilised discussion,' he went on. 'And we might even find we enjoy one another's company. I believe we may have more in common than you think.'

223

Again that smile. After the miscalculation she'd made in attacking Stephanie, she had the feeling that she needed to recover ground. She and Leo might have diametrically opposed views about how 5 Caper Court should be run, but maybe there was something to be gained in sitting down with him and talking things through. He was head of chambers, after all.

She shrugged. 'I'm not sure we agree about enough to achieve anything, but there's no harm.'

'Good.' He unfolded his arms. 'I just have to finish a couple of things. I'll see you downstairs in half an hour.' As he opened the door he added, 'I think you'll like the place I've booked.'

The door closed. So he'd assumed she'd say yes. That irritated her, but only mildly. The prospect of taking on Leo on a one-to-one basis over dinner was quite exciting.

In the flat in St Katharine Docks, Sian was putting the finishing touches to the chicken dish she was cooking as a surprise for Natalie. She'd been feeling a little bad lately about not doing more to please her. When their relationship had first started, one of her chief delights had been finding ways of making Natalie happy, of gaining the attention and affection of this cool, awesome woman. Then when Natalie had fallen in love with her, she'd no longer had to try so hard. It had always been that way. She thought back to ex-lovers, ex-boyfriends, and to that moment when she had become the pursued, and not the pursuer. Taking someone's love for granted, it was easy to become thoughtless and unkind, which was what she'd been lately.

She left the kitchen, poured herself a drink, and flopped on the couch. Guilt about the one-night stand in France had been gnawing at her. It was up to her to mend the relationship, to make Natalie feel safe, to let her know that she still wanted to please her, to make her smile. Natalie had been so generous to her, even to the point of bringing her into her professional world by engineering the pupillage. Not that Sian had any doubts about her own abilities; she was more than capable of being an excellent barrister. But getting the opportunity had been the key. It wasn't that easy to make the switch from the academic world to the Bar, particularly to gain entrance to such an outstanding set of chambers, where, if she worked hard enough, she could earn serious money. Natalie had done that for her. She had to do more to show she was grateful.

She picked up her laptop. It occurred to her that since she would be starting her pupillage in just two weeks' time, she really should do a bit more research into 5 Caper Court. She'd worked hard in the run-up to her interviews to ensure her legal knowledge was flawless when it came to the written exercises, but she hadn't paid particular attention to the place itself and the people who worked there.

She brought up the website. The home page had the usual blurb about chambers, and various links. She clicked on the 'Queens' Counsel' link, and up popped a list. There at the top was the name 'Leo Davies'. She felt her heart skip. *You have to be kidding*, she thought. She clicked on his name. Since that night in France, the visual recollection of his face had inevitably begun to fade, but suddenly there it was in all its startling attractiveness – the silver hair, the high cheekbones, the intense blue eyes and the faint smile that promised and hid so much. She skimmed the description of his practice – *international trade, embracing shipping, commodities, insurance, the carriage and sale of goods, banking and related disciplines . . . appears principally in the High Court and the Court of Appeal and before various international arbitration tribunals . . . has acted in some of the largest and most high-profile trials of recent years* – and came to rest on the final words, *Leo Davies is joint head of chambers at 5 Caper Court.*

Oh God, she had slept with her future head of chambers. If either of them had had a clue, it certainly wouldn't have happened. She stared at his picture, piecing together her thoughts. She felt a prickle of excitement as she recalled the night in Antibes. Encountering one another in chambers needn't be awkward, not if they were cool enough about it. And he definitely was cool. Once he got over the surprise, he might even regard the coincidence as fortuitous. Maybe the affair they'd begun in Antibes wouldn't have to end there. It didn't necessarily matter that he was her head of chambers, barristers in chambers had affairs all the time . . . Then her excited thoughts died away. If he'd wanted to do that, he would have called her. Besides, once he found out who she was, it was the last thing he would let happen.

Her thoughts moved to Natalie. How did this complicate things with her? In a way she did still love her, but there was no question things had cooled off lately, and seeing Leo's face reminded her of how easy it had been to be unfaithful to her. It didn't say a lot about the relationship. Here she was, trying to mend it, when it was probably beyond saving. There were priorities to consider. Whatever the fallout from this bizarre situation, it mustn't affect her pupillage. She closed her laptop and rolled onto her back, staring at the ceiling. She couldn't begin to imagine how this was going to play out.

CHAPTER EIGHTEEN

The restaurant was small and French, tucked away in a Covent Garden courtyard. The cosy booth in which they were seated struck Natalie as being more appropriate for some romantic assignation than a work discussion. She sipped the wine that Leo ordered, and let him lead the conversation. Over the meal he talked about himself, about who he had been when he had first come to 5 Caper Court, and the kind of place it had been then.

'You evidently hold it in great affection,' said Natalie. 'I can't say I've ever felt that way about any of my chambers. I've been a tenant in three places in the space of twenty years, but I never regarded any of them as a spiritual home. I'm not sure it's entirely healthy to feel that way about what is, after all, just a place of work.'

'Perhaps that's why you and I take such different approaches to the way it should be run.'

'I'm not sure my approach is exceptional. I just hate

228

inefficiency when I see it, and sloppy practices.'

'But, you know' – he proffered the wine, and she nodded and let him refill her glass – '5 Caper Court isn't a company. It's a loose association of self-employed individuals.'

'Perhaps. But you can't deny that it has a collective identity, with a character and reputation to maintain. Image is everything these days. We can't afford to be seen as out of touch. We have to modernise, to streamline our services. Which is why chambers' policies need to be moulded by the younger members of chambers, not the older ones. Take the issue of bringing more women into chambers. The younger tenants fully support that. You older ones, with all respect, seem to be rather resistant.'

'Far from it. I just don't believe that quotas are the way. We should be taking the best candidates, regardless of gender.'

'That word "quotas" annoys me. I prefer to call it an affirmative gender policy, aimed at promoting confidence amongst the female members of chambers. We have to be seen to be ticking the right boxes.'

'Ah, box-ticking. You must be rejoicing in the fact that Stephanie ticks the diversity and inclusivity box very neatly.'

'I'm very proud of the fact that we have a trans person in chambers. It obviously reflects well on us.'

Leo gave her a puzzled look. 'It isn't about us, or how good it makes us look. It's about her, about being kind. Why did you behave so cruelly to her at the meeting?'

'I wasn't being deliberately cruel,' replied Natalie defensively. 'The issue was one that needed addressing. As a man you probably can't see how outrageous her behaviour was, how deeply wounding it was to the women in chambers, and how offensive to other trans people. In fact' – she lifted her chin a little, and Leo could tell that something contentious was coming – 'what Stephanie did makes me realise that she's arguably taking up a place in chambers that might more deservedly go to someone who has genuinely experienced the difficulties of being a woman at the Bar. Not someone who got to their position through the advantages of male privilege and seems prepared to resort to them as and when they like.'

Leo gave a wry smile. 'You mean, a real woman?'

'Don't try to put words in my mouth. What I'm saying is that unless she makes a proper formal apology and gives an undertaking never to revert to a male identity where work is concerned, I don't believe there's a place for her in our chambers.'

'You'd hound her out?'

'That's ridiculously pejorative.'

'How you describe it doesn't matter. It's what you'd be doing.' *But not to my friend*, thought Leo. *It isn't going to happen.*

The mildly hostile exchange triggered a pause. She gazed at him. In one of those human moments where thought processes interweave and come and go in seconds, she found herself thinking how absurdly handsome he was, how easy to look at, and the sharp involuntary tug of attraction prompted a mental picture of being in bed with him. It was the last thing she wanted to think, and she banished the image immediately, angry at her own self-exposure.

'When in fact,' Leo went on, 'I think you're the one

who should be considering her place at 5 Caper Court.'

Her eyes widened. 'I'm sorry?'

'Natalie, you've been civilised enough to come to dinner with me on the pretext of calling a truce on our hostilities. But we both know that you see this ending in only one way – with you having your way, consolidating the power base you're building, and getting rid of every element in chambers that you regard as inimical to your ambitions. Which would include me. And Stephanie, too, apparently.'

She sipped her wine and said nothing. It was close to the truth.

'I'm getting on a bit,' continued Leo. 'I have days when I'm tired of the whole game and think I should just pack it all in. You've helped to foster those feelings by creating division in chambers, by demoralising Henry and Felicity, and by making me, and other senior members of chambers, appear irrelevant and obstructive. But as I explained to you, 5 Caper Court is my life, my home. I love it in a way you can't begin to understand. So, jaded as I might be, I don't intend to let you reshape it in your desired image.'

'Leo, I think you know the strength of support I have from the younger element within chambers. Your sentimental attachment to the place does you credit. But you must see which way the wind is blowing. People back my proposals. They want to see change, even if you don't.' She picked up the wine, poured the remains into both their glasses, and raised her eyebrows in a smile. 'So I'm far from convinced that my position at 5 Caper Court is under any threat.'

Leo sat back. 'Well, let's address this. You used the words "transparency" and "accountability" at the meeting this afternoon. They're expressions you use a lot to justify the changes you want to steamroller through. But I wonder what other members of chambers would think if they knew that you used your position to help your live-in lover get a pupillage with us.' Natalie froze. 'You even sat in on the interview that helped to secure it for her. That doesn't exactly look transparent and accountable, does it?'

'She's someone I know, that's all, in the same way that you know the candidate that you were so keen on. There's no difference.'

'Ah, but I think there is. I certainly don't have the kind of relationship with Alistair Egan that you have with Sian Attwood. That is her name, isn't it?'

'I don't know what you think you know, but she's simply a friend. Someone whose talents I recognise and admire. Which, when I last looked, doesn't breach any regulations.'

'Interesting that you mention regulations. Because, as I recall, the Bar Council's Fair Recruitment Guide has something to say about avoiding bias – chapter two, I think it is. *Where issues of selection between applicants fall to be considered, the panel should not include any relative or close friend of the candidates.* I believe that's the general gist. So if it did turn out that you and Sian are closely involved, that might be a bit of a problem.' He picked up his wine. 'And I think our chambers' constitution has some provision about the need for complete transparency and lack of bias in such matters, too. I imagine Alistair Egan might feel a little aggrieved if he were to learn about what has happened. He might even take us to the Bar Standards Board. And the other tenants won't like that.'

'It's all entirely irrelevant. There is no relationship of the kind you suggest.'

'Really?' Leo reached into his pocket, drew out his mobile phone and laid it on the table. 'I don't want to cause you any embarrassment, but you're so adamant—' He scrolled to the recording and pressed the 'play' button. He kept the volume low, but Sian's voice was distinct enough. It took a few seconds for her breathy utterances to resolve themselves, then Natalie realised that Sian was talking about her, about their relationship. The background noises and Sian's intermittent gasps of pleasure made the context obvious.

Natalie slapped her hand onto the phone, as though to silence it. 'Stop it! Switch it off!'

Leo obliged. 'Sensible. I think you might find the full recording upsetting.'

She stared at him, appalled. 'When did . . . ?'

'We met in France a couple of months ago at the home of mutual friends. She had absolutely no idea who I was.' He signalled to the waiter for the bill. 'She's a very passionate girl, isn't she? Gets quite carried away. And that always leads to indiscretion.'

There was silence as Leo settled the bill. Natalie's mind was working hard. The idea that Sian had betrayed her by sleeping with a man – with Leo, of all people – was horribly painful. She thrust aside the recollection of her own infidelity with Abby. There was her professional situation to try to rescue. When the waiter had gone she said, 'If you think this is a way of ousting me from chambers, you're seriously mistaken.'

Leo shrugged. 'Work it out any way you like. I don't know how comfortable you'll find your position, with your credibility seriously undermined. Which it will be when people find out that you deliberately engineered a pupillage for someone with whom you're intimately involved. Wasn't that what you once accused me of trying to do with Alistair Egan? Ironic, really.'

He tucked his credit card away and, without another word, got up from the table and left.

When Sian heard Natalie's key in the door, she had to fight down her sense of irritation. Dinner had dried up in the oven hours ago. But it wouldn't do to have an argument. She assumed a welcoming smile. Then when she saw the look on Natalie's face, her smile died away. Natalie flung down her keys. She fixed Sian with blazing eyes.

'Why? Why did you do it? Why did you sleep with Leo Davies? Leaving aside the fact that you cheated on me, why him, of all people? What on earth possessed you to sleep with your future head of chambers?' Sian was too bewildered to say anything. 'Do you realise I have been utterly humiliated tonight? Finding out from him what happened between you in France, being told he knows I helped you get your pupillage – you've almost wrecked my position in chambers. After all I've done for you. I have loved you, looked after you, done everything I could to help your career – and you repay me like this.' Natalie's angry eyes filled with tears. 'How could you? How *could* you?'

'It was a one-night thing. It didn't matter. I'm sorry.' Sian stood up and tried to put her arms around Natalie, but Natalie pushed her away. She went to the drinks trolley and poured herself a drink with trembling hands.

Sian followed her across the room, trying to assemble her thoughts. None of this made sense. 'Look, I didn't know he was anything to do with 5 Caper Court till tonight, when I went on the chambers' website. And he didn't know who I was, either, when we met in France.'

'He most certainly did. He even recorded you on his mobile, talking about me, just so he could blackmail me.'

'He – what?' Sian stared at her, appalled at the thought of how she had been played.

'Evidently you were too carried away to realise what was going on.' Natalie's voice dripped with angry sarcasm. She flung a handful of ice cubes into her vodka. 'Well, it's not going to happen. I can retrieve the situation. I'll tell Leo you won't be taking up the pupillage. With any luck he won't take it any further. Another humiliation for me, but if it's what it takes—'

'I'm not giving up the pupillage.'

Natalie set her drink down. 'Sian, look' – she pressed her hands together tightly, as if trying to quell her emotions – 'we can get past this. I hate what you did, but I'm willing to forgive you, because I love you. But if we're going to save our relationship, it means you have to make this sacrifice. There's no alternative. I can make this go away, but only if you contact chambers and let them know you won't be taking up the pupillage after all.' It was Natalie's turn to put her arms around Sian. 'You're marvellously bright and well qualified. You'll get a pupillage somewhere else.'

'Not in time for this year. I resigned my teaching post on the strength of this pupillage. What am I supposed to live on?'

'You know I'll look after you till you find something.'

Sian shrugged away from Natalie's embrace. 'Don't you see that Leo Davies is just using this as a means to get

235

rid of you? You've told me enough about the way you're trying to change things there, and the hostility you're encountering.' She gave a despairing laugh. 'If only you'd mentioned his name, just once. But that doesn't matter now. Whether or not I take up the pupillage makes no difference. He wants you out. You're the one who's going to be sacrificed, Natalie.'

'You mean you won't even try, for my sake? I know I can turn it around—'

'You threw yourself under this bus. I don't see why I should lose my opportunity because of it. I mean, I'm sorry it's worked out this way, but I have to protect my interests.'

Natalie stared at her. It was true. Blinded by love, she'd done a foolish thing, and now Leo was able to use it against her, because the other stupid thing she'd done was to set herself up against him.

'What makes you think he'll let you take up the pupillage?'

'Well, we'll just have to find out, won't we? It seems he's known about you and me for a while, but I've heard nothing to make me think the offer has been rescinded. No, as I say, I think you're the victim here.'

'I can't believe, after everything I've done for you, all the love I've given you, that you can be so utterly selfish—' She broke off tearfully.

Sian put her arms around Natalie, as if to soothe her. 'I am truly sorry, but you're asking me to do something quite pointless. You do whatever you have to do, make whatever decision you have to make. But' – she kissed Natalie lightly, almost regretfully – 'I don't see how we can stay together.'

'Why not?' asked Natalie in a tone of panic, searching Sian's face with fearful eyes. 'I don't care that you slept with Leo. I told you, it doesn't matter—'

'Ah, but it should. You shouldn't be so ready to forgive me. It's not healthy. I love you, Natalie, but not enough. I can't guarantee I won't hurt you in the same way again. It's not fair to you to keep this going.'

She moved away, picked up Natalie's drink, took a swallow, and set it down. The casual gesture spoke volumes. 'I'll sleep in the spare room tonight, and pack my stuff up tomorrow. I can stay with friends for a while.' She glanced at Natalie. 'That's a thing, you know. I've missed my friends. I've missed being my own person. I'm not ungrateful, please don't think that. You've done a lot for me. But I think this is for the best.'

She picked up her laptop from the sofa and left the room.

CHAPTER NINETEEN

The following week, over an early evening drink, Leo recounted to Anthony what had happened at dinner with Natalie – leaving out the part about recording Sian on his mobile.

'So what happens now?' asked Anthony.

'She had the weekend to think it over. On Monday she came to see me, and said she accepted that it would undermine her standing in chambers if people were to learn that she manipulated the pupillage selection process, and that she would prefer for it not to come out. She's already putting out feelers to other chambers.'

Anthony grimaced. 'Sounds like you effectively blackmailed her into leaving.'

'Not at all. As head of chambers, I have a duty to disclose impropriety on the part of any member of chambers, particularly one that might expose us to the scrutiny of the Bar Standards Board. But now that she's leaving, I don't see that people need be told.'

'Hmm. Well, it won't take her long to find another tenancy. I can think of a number of commercial sets who would love to be seen as poaching her from us.'

'Quite. No doubt she'll find some place that will welcome her transformative ideas.'

'Her departure will leave a bit of a hole in chambers' finances.'

'I'm happy to fill it myself just to see the back of her.'

'What about Sian Attwood?'

Leo had spent some time considering the position with Sian. He liked her. If and when she came to 5 Caper Court, he had no intention of acknowledging what happened between them in France, and he suspected that, ambitious young woman that she was, she would be clever enough to do the same. He also suspected that, in the light of recent events, her relationship with Natalie didn't have long to last, if it wasn't already over.

'We offered her the pupillage. She showed herself to be entirely deserving of it. You sat on the committee.'

Anthony shrugged. 'I suppose that's true. We chose her on merit.'

'There you are, then. What Natalie did reflects badly on her, but not necessarily on Sian. I don't see why we should rescind the offer.' He finished his drink and gestured to Anthony's empty glass. 'Got time for another?'

'Just a quick one. I'm seeing Gabrielle in half an hour.'

Leo went to the bar and bought two more beers. 'So,' he said, as he sat down again, 'things are getting serious between you and Gabrielle?'

Anthony shot Leo a glance. 'Has she said something?'

'No. It was a genuine question. I don't see a great deal of

her these days. I mean, when I do, it's good, we enjoy one another's company, but she doesn't talk about you, and I don't ask.' He paused. 'Our relationship has changed. I think that finding me possessed a certain starry-eyed excitement for her, at first. But these days the romance has subsided. We get on well, but she's realised I'm not such a special person. Daniel is much more her father than I am. She's the product of his upbringing. She lives in the world he made for her. I'm not saying we have nothing in common – we like seeing one another, we have good conversations – but as people we come from very different backgrounds, with different values.'

'I sometimes feel the same way,' admitted Anthony. 'I mean, the world she inhabits, all that middle-class privilege, half the time I feel I don't really belong to it. I'm not sure I want to.' He thought back to the drunken conversation with Piers at Edward's wedding. It was something he often brought to mind. 'It's confusing. Look at the other people in chambers. Most of them went to the best private schools, and to Oxbridge, and they come from professional, comfortably off families. You and I don't fit that template. But working alongside them, earning the same money, makes us part of that elite, doesn't it? Whether we like it or not.'

'Ostensibly, yes. But that's on a professional level. Just because you understand the rules doesn't mean you have to live by them. Socially, I only buy into their world to the extent I want to.'

'I wish I could be like you,' said Anthony. 'You're your own person. I can't be that strong. That feeling of needing to belong is too powerful. And to belong you *have* to follow the rules, do the things you're expected to do, the same things all your friends are doing. Otherwise life's just lonely, isn't it? Everyone needs something to give sense and shape to their existence.'

'And that something is Gabrielle?'

'I don't know. Sometimes I want her to be. She has this easy, happy vision of what our future should be, the same one all her friends have. Marriage, a home, a few children, a comfortable life just like the one her parents have led. Conventional, closed off. It would be quite easy to surrender to it.'

'It's powerfully seductive. So, if you're contemplating doing all that with her, you must be in love with her.' He felt his heart tighten as he waited for Anthony's answer.

After a brief silence Anthony replied, 'Must I? Looking back on the times I've been in love, I'm not sure that state of mind is the best one in which to plan one's future.' He thought of Julia, with whom he'd once been so in love, throwing her silly shoes into the lake, then turning to be kissed, hoping to be taken back to the girl she had once been. 'I mean, I love Gabrielle. She's easy to love. That should be enough.'

'Yes, very often it is. As long as it doesn't mean denying your true self.'

Their gazes met, and Leo realised he had brushed too close. Anthony wasn't ready for that kind of self-examination.

'My true self. I don't think I have a clue what that is. Sometimes I think that everything I've become over the past fifteen years is down to you. The things you've taught me. Shown me. Perhaps I'm nothing more than an aspirational middle-class construct.'

'You do yourself too little credit.'

Anthony rubbed a hand across his jaw. 'I'm probably overthinking the whole thing.' He glanced at his watch. 'I should get going.' He drank some of his beer, then stood up. 'Sorry, I don't think I can finish that.'

'Don't worry. Have a good evening.'

The abruptness of his departure told Leo that Anthony felt he had given too much away. Or perhaps the honesty of the conversation had been too great a reminder of the intimacy they had once shared. The things he had said about aspiration, about wanting to belong, had been revealing. *You don't know your own mind*, thought Leo, *and I can't make it up for you.* He would just have to wait, and hope.

Anthony stood outside the pub in Fleet Street, waiting for his Uber, berating himself for letting the conversation about Gabrielle go that far. It was as though Leo had a way of tapping into his heart and mind, making him say the things he really felt, even if he didn't want to. All of it had been true, especially the part about being utterly confused.

Gabrielle was already at the sushi bar where they'd arranged to meet. He kissed her and took a stool next to her at the counter. She looked, as usual, very lovely, like an excited, happy kitten. They ordered, and she launched into an enthusiastic account of the engagement party she'd been to the night before.

'You should have come. Everyone was there. Edith and James make such a sweet couple.'

'Yes, well, I had to work late. I have this big hearing coming up next week.'

She contemplated him. 'You seem in a bit of a mood.'

'Sorry. Anyway, I don't particularly like engagement parties. I don't see that they're necessary. Just more middle-class showing off, spending money needlessly.' He knew he was sucking the oxygen out of the conversation, dampening her cheerfulness, but he couldn't help it.

'God, Anthony, why do you have to be so chippy?'

'I'm not being chippy. I just don't happen to buy into that kind of thing.'

'You seem to have real hang-ups about my friends, and the stuff they do.'

'I wasn't talking specifically about your friends. Anyway, a lot of them are my friends, too.'

'Are they? You may not realise it, but sometimes when we're with them, it's like you're so aloof, like you don't want to be part of things. People notice, you know.'

'It isn't intentional. Why are we arguing about this, all of a sudden?'

Their food arrived, and they ate in silence for a few moments. Then Gabrielle said, as though it was something she'd been thinking long and hard about, and only now had the courage to put into words, 'The thing is, it's part of something bigger, isn't it, Anthony?'

'How do you mean?'

'The way you hold back. It's like you want certain things, but you just can't bring yourself to—'

'To what?'

'—to make a commitment. Take me, for example. You say you love me, you behave like you want us to be together, to have a future, but it's like your heart's not in it.' He said nothing. 'I love you, but I'd rather you didn't pretend.'

243

'I'm not pretending.' He put out a hand to touch her face. 'I do love you.'

'Maybe, but not enough.'

He dropped his hand. 'You seem to have been giving this a lot of thought.'

'I have. If you meant everything you say, we'd be living together by now.'

There was a long silence, then Anthony said, 'I suppose that's true. Maybe we've been getting ahead of ourselves. I mean, maybe it would be easier if we just carried on as we are, without plans or expectations. Just see how things turn out.'

She looked sadly at her plate. 'If that's what you want. It sounds like you're having second thoughts about us.'

'That's not what I'm saying. I just—' He broke off, exasperated. 'Look, I didn't come here to argue with you.'

'No, well – it wasn't what I came here for, either. But maybe it's inevitable, when things haven't really been right for some time now.'

'Is that what you think?'

'Don't you? Days go by and I don't hear from you. I'm always the one suggesting meeting up, arranging things to do. It feels like I make all the running.'

'Come on, you know work's really full on—'

'Everyone's busy, Anthony. But most of us can find time for the people we care about.' She pushed her plate away. 'It's making me unhappy, feeling like I'm the one who's trying all the time. Maybe we need a bit of a break while you work out exactly what it is you want. Because from where I'm sitting, it doesn't feel like me.'

He met her gaze. 'I'm sorry. My head's been a bit messed

up since my father died. The last thing I want is to make you unhappy.'

'Most of the time you don't. But whatever it is that's troubling you – and there is something, I know there is – you need to sort it out. Then maybe we can try again.' She signalled for the bill, tapped her card for her share, and got down from the bar stool. 'Don't look like that. We're not splitting up. Just having a break, till you work things out. Let me know when you do.' She kissed him lightly, and left.

CHAPTER TWENTY

A few days later, Anthony had a phone call from Jocasta.

'I don't like the way we left things,' she told him. 'Chay wouldn't want there to be bad feeling between us.'

'Is that why you said you were changing the locks?'

'I was wrong to say that. Of course I won't – though I hope you'll respect the fact that the house is my property now. But I don't want you and Barry to feel that you have no stake in all of this. There must be personal items of Chay's that you'd like.' She hesitated, and added with evident difficulty, 'Maybe in return you could give me a hand with sorting his estate out. I'm having a few problems.'

In truth, dealing with Chay's estate was putting Jocasta to more trouble and expense than she had anticipated. There was a catch-22 in accessing the money in Chay's accounts – she couldn't do it until she had obtained letters of administration enabling her to deal with his affairs, and this involved legal fees, for which she simply didn't have ready money, and the bill for the legal advice she'd already taken was still unpaid. She'd come back into Chay's life at a time when her own small business was flagging, and money was tight. Her credit history was bad, so borrowing was out of the question. She'd had no idea the properties were so heavily mortgaged, and she was beset with nagging worries about what the banks might do. She was an inexperienced novice in uncharted territory, with no funds.

Anthony could hardly believe what she was asking. The woman certainly had a bloody nerve.

'What kind of problems?'

'Oh, you know' – she gave a small helpless laugh – 'dealing with officialdom really isn't my bag. As a lawyer you have a much better handle on these things. Would you mind terribly?'

There was a moment's silence. Anthony divined, correctly, that she was hard up and overwhelmed by the administrative and legal obstacles. A part of him wanted to tell her to get lost, to sort it out herself, but perhaps there was a bargain to be struck.

'All right. I'll come round at the weekend. Saturday morning?'

'Perfect. I really am grateful, you know. I want us to stay friends.'

Anthony decided not to mention any of this to Barry, to avoid the incendiary outrage it would provoke. He went round as promised, and drew up a list of everything that needed to be done to gain access to the bank accounts and investments, and arrange for the sale of the houses.

'Unless you intend to carry on living here?' he asked.

'I can't afford the mortgage payments,' replied Jocasta shortly.

Anthony was sitting at Chay's desk, checking the items he'd listed so far. He glanced up at her. 'I suppose you expected Chay to be worth more.'

'That's a desperately unkind thing to say. I'm not some kind of gold-digger, Anthony.'

He made no reply to this, but merely said, 'I'll settle the fees for the letters of administration. They'll take a few weeks to come through. You can pay me back once you have access to the bank accounts. Have you enough money till then?'

'Not really.' It was humiliating to have to admit this. 'My business rather dried up while I was looking after Chay. I don't have any income.'

'I can help you till the money comes through. Give me your bank details and I'll put through a couple of thousand.'

She told him the sort code and account details, and he tapped them into his phone.

'Thank you,' said Jocasta. After a pause she added, 'Anthony, don't think badly of me. I can't help what's happened. Chay wanted to marry me. He wanted whatever sense of security it gave him.'

'I'm glad you were there for him. Barry and I are grateful for everything you did. But I haven't come here to help you today out of the goodness of my heart. I need something in return.'

Her gaze sharpened.

'I want the folder of drawings of my mother, to give to her. And I want the charcoal sketches of Spitalfields. I was there when Chay told Barry he could have them.'

She drew a breath. 'I'm sorry. That's asking too much. I know how valuable those are, potentially. I told you you're welcome to personal items. But that's all.'

Anthony shrugged. 'Fine. If that's the way you want it, I'll leave it to you to get the letters of administration. And to sort out the sale of the houses.' He pulled out his phone again. 'I'll just delete these bank details, since I won't be needing them.'

She thought quickly. 'No, wait.' There was a pause. 'Look, I'm grateful to you for helping me, but what you're asking is too much. I have my future to think of.'

He contemplated her thoughtfully. She was standing, framed in light from one of the big studio windows, the sunshine haloing her cropped hair, and filtering through the gauzy layers of her dress, looking as wide-eyed and guileless as when he'd first met her years ago. Was she really as unscrupulous as she seemed?

'You know,' he said, 'Chay left my mother money in his will, because he felt bad about the way he'd treated her. He promised Barry those drawings because Barry liked them, and Dad wanted him to have them. I don't believe he had any idea that marrying you was going to change those things. Just how much do you think you deserve for coming into my father's life a few months before he died, and showing him kindness? Anything? Everything?'

Jocasta's blue eyes seemed to darken. After a moment's silence she said, 'You don't have any idea what happened after Chay and I went out to California – you know, years ago, when he was just becoming successful.'

Anthony shook his head. He had a fleeting recollection of Jocasta calling him from California at the time, happy, buoyed up by Chay's success. Beyond that, he knew only that they'd split up a few months later.

She sank down into a chair opposite him. 'We were fine for a while. He was becoming a big name, and we were both enjoying the ride, I suppose. I'd believed in him when no one else did, so I felt I was a part of what was happening to him. I loved him. I thought he loved me. I became pregnant, and he persuaded me to have a termination. He said it wasn't the right time for children, and in a way it was true. It would have complicated our lives. A baby could come later, he said. Then about a month after that I found out he was sleeping with other women. Plural.' She shrugged. 'It was inevitable. Being the toast of the West Coast artistic community was like being a rock star. Women went after him, and you know the weak kind of man he was. Anyway, I got displaced. After a little while he moved someone else into our house. A girl called Grace. Just moved her in. Maybe he would have been happy for me to stay, to carry on some kind of *ménage à trois*. In fact, I think he somehow assumed I would. But I was devastated. Heartbroken. Lost. So I left. My visa was going to run out, anyway. I had to come back to England. I had virtually no money.'

'You must have hated him.'

'I blamed myself. For not being enough. For not being more broad-minded, the kind of woman who could make allowances for the great artist. I think he expected that. Saw himself as a kind of Augustus John figure. I'm quite a conventional creature, really. I wanted him to myself, and I couldn't have that. So I simply couldn't stay. Then last year, when I heard through friends of friends about his cancer, I got in touch. I found him living alone, and it was as though

I'd been given my chance again. It would just be me. Me and him. And I was determined that this time, whatever I gave him – time, attention, comfort, love – it would be repaid properly, honestly.'

'I don't understand why you carried on loving him. My father wasn't a lovable man. You knew that.'

'No, he wasn't. He was selfish and petty, and he hurt people without thinking twice. He hurt me, horribly. But you don't have a choice where love is concerned, do you? It's not rational. If you love someone, you just do.'

Anthony found himself thinking fleetingly of Leo, and his heart tightened. Why, he wondered an instant later, had her words not prompted him to think of Gabrielle? He said nothing.

'So,' she went on, 'I feel I'm owed. I feel I'm owed for then and now.'

'Can I ask you,' said Anthony, 'did you know what marrying him would do, in terms of the will?'

'Of course not. I didn't even know there was a will. I wasn't thinking about anything like that.' She remembered the time she'd hidden Chay's mobile, and her petty attempts to bring about an estrangement between Anthony and Barry and their father. She couldn't admit those things to Anthony. He'd ascribe motives she'd never had. She'd only done it to keep Chay to herself, afraid that if his sons took over his care she'd become redundant, excess to requirements, the way she'd once been in California.

'Oh, take them,' she said suddenly. She rose and crossed the room to a cupboard, and took out the two folders of drawings. 'We're all owed something by him.' She handed them to Anthony.

'Thank you.'

'It doesn't feel like they belong to me, anyway.' She glanced at the portrait still on the easel. 'This does, though.'

'It should guarantee you a comfortable retirement.'

'I might not sell it.' But they both knew she would.

It was the fourth day of the collision hearing, and the case was grinding relentlessly on. Nothing new had been said or presented in evidence that was improving Leo and Anthony's chances of making the case for their clients, the owners of the cargo ship that had collided with the oil tanker. The other side's contention was that the tanker had given its warning, but that in making its change of direction the cargo ship had miscalculated. It seemed unassailable.

Anthony was coming to the end of his cross-examination of the second officer on duty on board the tanker at the time of the collision.

'You say you gave a warning to the *Pasanto* fifteen minutes before the collision occurred?'

The officer, a lanky Australian, nodded. 'As the smaller, more manoeuvrable vessel, the evasive action was hers to take.'

'Was there no corresponding action that the *Sancharez*, your ship, could have taken as well? Especially when you saw that the *Pasanto* was moving ahead in the collision course.'

'Changing the course of a huge oil tanker isn't easy. It can't be done quickly.'

'I appreciate that. More than fifteen minutes?'

'It depends.'

'On what?'

252

The officer hesitated. 'It's not something I've ever had to do. I mean, try to make a change to the course of a vessel that size in such a short space of time.'

Anthony seized on this. 'It's not within your range of competence?'

'Like I say, it's just not something I've ever had to do.'

'But you're suggesting that it might be possible?'

The officer glanced at the judge. 'I'm saying I wouldn't be confident of doing it. And besides—'

'We've established that you might not feel able to do it. But what you say suggests that someone with greater experience might?' A pause. 'The master, perhaps?'

'He'd gone back to his cabin.'

Anthony glanced at his notes. 'Yes, the chief officer mentioned that. Twenty minutes before you came onto the bridge, I believe.'

The officer shrugged. 'I don't know. If you say so. He came and went quite a lot. He has a bad back. All I know is, he wasn't there when the warning was given.'

'But if he had been, his judgement and experience might have enabled him to take action to avoid the collision?'

'Possibly.'

'Thank you, Mr Field. My Lord, I have no more questions.'

'In that case,' said Mr Justice Cafferty, 'this seems like an appropriate juncture at which to retire for lunch. We will reconvene at two.'

Over lunch Leo and Anthony weighed up the position. 'I don't know where we go with this,' sighed Anthony. 'There probably wasn't any evasive action the second officer could have taken in the time he had. No one's going to fault him for that.'

Leo was studying his notes. 'That thing he said about the master coming and going. The deputy watch officer mentioned something similar.' He flipped through his papers. 'Here we are. *He went back to his cabin a few times that afternoon. He would be up on the bridge for a while then he would disappear. It happened a lot.*'

'And?'

'Ask yourself why.'

'Could be any number of reasons.'

There was a long moment of silence, then Leo said, 'I'm going to take an entirely different line with my cross-examination, not the one we discussed.'

'Why would you abandon a carefully worked-out strategy at the last moment? That's an incredible risk.'

'Yes. But sometimes when you have a hunch, you have to go with it.' He flashed a smile. 'As Harvey would say – don't play the odds, play the man.'

The master of the *Sancharez* was Korean, in his mid-fifties, a watchful, slightly restless man, who spoke good but halting English. Opposing counsel took him carefully through his statement and evidence, and it was mid-afternoon by the time Leo began his cross-examination. He opened with a series of innocuous questions about the day of the collision, the weather, the routine of the watch, but after a few minutes the line of questioning became more personal.

'You told the court earlier that you've held a master's ticket for – what? – ten years, Captain Lee?'

'Nine years and eleven months.'

'And remind us how many years you've been at sea?'

'Thirty-eight years.'

'With all your years of seafaring, would you agree with

me that despite the huge technological advances in ships' navigational aids, the best way to avoid a collision is to have on the bridge and in the engine room people with high levels of skill, judgement and human competence?'

'I would agree. You want your ship to be safe? You have to be professional navigator, and be responsible enough not to lose all contacts with reality by looking on screens only.'

'Quite. There's really no substitute for experience and the human touch, is there?'

For fifteen minutes or so Leo quizzed the master on his opinion of the importance of human skills over technology, letting him expand his views on how too much reliance was placed nowadays on electronic navigation tools.

'You've been a master for almost ten years, so your experience would count for a lot in the situation that arose on October the tenth two years ago.' It wasn't a question, and Leo gave the master no room to respond. 'It's a big responsibility, isn't it, being a tanker master? Psychologically quite stressful, would you say?'

To Anthony's surprise, Captain Lee pounced on the question, eyes alight. 'It can be terrible! Nobody knows how bad. Owners can give you these rubbish crews. You finish up doing everything. You don't sleep, you worry all time. It's a big job. A bad job, sometimes.' For the next couple of minutes Captain Lee gave vent to his feelings about the stresses of his job, the incompetence of crews, and how generally underappreciated he felt.

'It's all very tiring, I imagine?'

Captain Lee nodded. 'Exhausting. Terrible.'

'And you suffer with your back, I believe?'

'I had a bad fall on the bridge a year ago, in heavy seas. It gives me pain, yes.'

'You take painkillers?' Leo's tone was still sympathetic.

Captain Lee hesitated. 'Sometimes.'

Leo's tone grew suddenly firmer. 'More than sometimes, Captain Lee. How many times a day do you take your medication?'

'I don't know. A few times.'

'A few times. Tell the court what medication it is that you take.'

'OxyContin. It's routine. Just a routine painkiller.' Captain Lee's eyes flickered back and forth between Leo and the judge.

'OxyContin is more than routine, Captain Lee. It's very powerful. So powerful it can affect one's cognitive, motor and decision-making skills, and visual-spatial abilities. And you don't just take the OxyContin, do you, Captain Lee? You were topping the medication up with alcohol, weren't you?'

Anthony couldn't believe what Leo had done. He had asked a question entirely without any basis, and with no clue as to what the answer might be. He was going blindly down a road, not knowing where it led.

'We've heard that you went back to your cabin a lot,' Leo went on, 'and there's only one explanation, to my mind, why you were doing so. The job you have, the responsibilities are so great that—'

Suddenly Captain Lee exploded. 'Nobody knows what it is like! I am in pain all the time! I can't sleep!' He carried on in this vein, railing against the owners and the crew, tearfully describing the unbearable stress he was under. Leo gave him rein for a full five minutes, then began to interject gentle, sympathetic questions, each landing one top of the other with gentle but deadly accuracy, unravelling Captain Lee's emotional and psychological problems, exposing the extent of his perpetual self-medication, his use of painkillers and alcohol to fortify himself against the demands of the job.

'The long and short of it is, Captain Lee, that you were incapable that day of taking command of the vessel in circumstances where your experience and judgement could and should have permitted evasive action to be taken, which might have avoided, or at least mitigated, the accident that occurred. You should have been on that bridge. You were the master of that vessel. But because of your abuse of medication and alcohol, you weren't up to the job that day. Were you?'

Anthony remembered the first time, as a star-struck pupil, that he had watched Leo in court, in some run-of-the-mill piece of litigation, effortlessly demolishing the other side's arguments. He had been captivated by his incisiveness, his ease of manner, his lack of theatricality, the charm of his light Welsh accent, the way he handled witnesses, opposing counsel, the judge, everyone. He remembered wondering if he could ever hope to be that good himself. *I fell in love with you that day*, he thought, *and I am in love with you still*. The forcefulness of the realisation shook him, went straight to his heart, and he saw what he had been squandering for so long. He thought about what Jocasta had said the last time they met – loving someone wasn't something you could help, however much you wanted it to be otherwise. He understood in that moment what Leo had said about betraying one's true self. If he carried on with Gabrielle, if he went down that road, the rest of his life would become a lie.

Captain Lee was wiping away tears.

'I have no further questions, My Lord,' said Leo, and took his seat. The glance he gave Anthony was brief and impassive, but behind it Anthony read the desperate relief of one who had taken a leap of faith, and made it to the other side. Only he was capable of reading Leo in that way. Suddenly everything seemed clear and obvious – and so difficult.

CHAPTER TWENTY-ONE

'I don't intend to do that again in a hurry,' remarked Leo, as they went into the robing room at the end of the afternoon. 'Still, it got the job done.' He gave Anthony a glance as he unfastened his collar. 'You're very quiet.'

'Sorry. Still getting over what you did in there. Was there something you knew that I didn't?'

'Far from it. Guesswork.' Leo folded his gown and stuffed it into his robing bag along with his wig. 'How about dinner later to celebrate the fact that I managed, through extraordinary luck, not to humiliate myself today? Giovanni's at seven?'

Anthony hesitated. It had become something of a tradition between them to go for dinner after a successful case. In his present state of emotional turmoil he wasn't sure how he would handle himself. But he nodded. 'Yes, that would be nice.'

'Right.' Leo slung his robing bag over his shoulder.

'I'm just going to have a word with our friend on the other side. I've got a few things to sort out, so I'll see you at the restaurant.'

Anthony went back to chambers and spent the next two hours trying unsuccessfully to lose himself in work. His thoughts kept winding back to the heart-stopping moment of self-realisation earlier that afternoon. He kept doing it over and over, just to relive the exquisite, expansive feeling of happiness bound up with pain. Love. Acceptance should be easy. Surrender should be easy. But nothing was that simple. He didn't know what to think. Above all, he didn't know what to do.

Leo was already at the restaurant when he arrived, scrolling through messages on his phone. He glanced up and smiled, and for Anthony it was as though some soft flame leapt through him. He had never felt so vulnerable in his life, as though the skin of his emotions had been peeled away, leaving every nerve and feeling raw and exposed. He wondered, fleetingly, how it had been that he had buried the truth of his feelings so deep for so long, and why, and the question answered itself in the same moment. It was because he was afraid.

'Hi,' he said, as he sat down.

'Hi.' Leo put his phone away. He poured Anthony a glass of wine. 'I've treated us to an exceptionally good bottle.' He kept his hand over the label. 'What's your guess?'

The wine was round and delicious. Anthony knew it had to be very expensive. He knew because Leo had spent some time educating him about wine, as about so much else.

'Barbaresco?' He eyed the wine's depth of colour. 'Ninety-six?'

'Barolo, but you got Piedmont, so not far off.' said Leo, revealing the label. 'Ninety-nine.'

They scanned the menu, the waiter came to take their orders, and Leo chatted to him for a moment in Italian. Anthony watched Leo, studying his face, the blue eyes, the tilt of his smile, as if to engrave every aspect on his heart, as though tonight something might be taken away, never to return.

When the waiter had gone, Anthony said, 'I often wonder how you came to be the person you are.'

Leo looked surprised. 'You say that like I'm a mystery. I'm just a Welsh grammar school boy made good.'

'Made good. It's an interesting phrase. Like that expression "a self-made man". I guess that's what you are. You made yourself.'

'Well, I don't want to talk about me. I'm an old story.'

But I want to, thought Anthony. *I want to talk about you, look at you, be with you, be part of you, for it never to stop. For you never to stop. Us never to stop.*

'I remember the first time you brought me here,' said Anthony. 'The things you talked about. I thought you were the most extraordinary man I'd ever met.' He was groping towards what he wanted to say, with the helpless sense that he wouldn't manage to do it. It seemed impossible.

'And I thought you were the most beautiful young man I'd ever met,' replied Leo. 'In the most remarkably bad suit.' He indicated Anthony's glass. 'You're fairly knocking that back. We're going to need another bottle at this rate.'

Leo began to talk about the wine, about a trip he'd made to Piedmont a few years ago, and from there, as they ate, the discussion moved to Italy, to economics, European

261

politics, Brexit. Anthony let Leo do most of the talking. A part of him remained detached, tense, terrified of what he might eventually say, or not say. He kept drinking, either to help himself say what he needed to, or to stop himself saying it, whichever. He was glad when the second bottle came, letting the alcohol blanket his thoughts.

Despite the flow of conversation, Leo could detect Anthony's tension, as though he was suppressing some thought or emotion that he was terrified to articulate. Something was coming, presumably when he had enough wine inside him. With a plunging sense of foreboding, Leo thought he knew what it was. His mind leapt ahead to the moment when Anthony would tell him he and Gabrielle were getting married, tasting the pain in advance, testing himself.

The conversation moved on. Anthony asked how Oliver was, and Leo began to talk about him, about the impending move, and his concerns about the new school and how often he would see him. Anthony only half listened. All he could think about was the last time he and Leo had made love. The memory was charged, overwhelming in its sensuality. Without meaning to, in a kind of blind panic, he interrupted what Leo was saying. 'There's something I have to tell you.'

Leo stopped mid-sentence. He gazed at Anthony. 'You're going to marry Gabrielle.'

Anthony laughed a little drunkenly. 'No.' He shook his head, then laughed again. 'No, I'm not going to marry Gabrielle. God, no. She and I have broken up.' He stared at the tablecloth, then looked up at Leo. 'You remember the last time you kissed me?'

Leo felt his insides dissolve. The moment felt like some fragile piece of porcelain that must be handled with the utmost delicacy, otherwise it might drop and shiver into irretrievable pieces.

'Yes.' He uttered the word faintly, absorbed in sudden recollection of the moment, a night some years ago, standing in a dark street, the last time they had held one another, before Anthony's defensive drift to conventionality had ended that aspect of their relationship.

Anthony's voice, low and intense, broke a little. 'I fucking want you to kiss me again. So badly.'

'That's what you wanted to tell me?'

'Yes. It's part of it. This afternoon, I was watching you, and I realised—' He stopped, gazing at Leo with a baffled look. 'I just want to be with you. That's all.' He closed his eyes with a sigh. 'Take me home with you. Please.'

Leo nodded. He lifted his hand to a passing waitress, and asked for the bill.

'I'm the one who should be afraid. Not you.' They were lying in Leo's bed, the curtains undrawn, the dusk deepening outside, painting the early September sky with streaks of red, turning the trees in the garden into dark silhouettes.

Anthony kissed Leo's shoulder, then his mouth. 'You know that's not true.'

'Isn't it?' he turned his head on the pillow to look into Anthony's eyes. 'I remember what you said after the last time we slept together. You said you didn't want it to turn into some grand passion. You said you wanted your freedom.'

'I said those things because I was afraid. The way I'm afraid now.'

'I still don't understand. God, I'm here, with you. Whatever you want this to be, you only have to say.'

'I'm afraid of the mess I've become.' He sighed, looked away. 'After the first time you took me to bed, I was terrified. How could I be gay, I thought, and not realise? But then – well, you know better than anyone what happened. Camilla, all that stuff. So it turned out I wasn't gay. I hadn't a clue what I was. I still don't. I mean, Gabrielle, now you – what's going on with me?'

Leo propped himself up on one elbow. 'You're not anything. You're just you. I've spent the better part of forty years thinking about this, you know. Using words – calling people straight, gay, bi, whatever – creates categories. But people don't fall neatly into them. It's like splitting sunlight into bands of colour. Sex is just another way of loving someone. It's something people do, not who they are. I've had lovers, men, who now happily lead so-called straight lives, with wives and children. I had a wife. I have a child. None of it defines me, sexually.'

'The people you love are what defines you.'

'Yes.'

'You define me. At this moment, you make me what I am. I think you have for years now.'

Leo ran his fingers lightly over Anthony's dark, curling hair. 'What do you want from this? Last time I asked you, you said we should carry on as we always have, that it didn't need to be any more than that.'

'I remember that conversation. I was frightened of being hurt. I still am. I've watched what you do to people. I can't let that happen to me, to be hurt in that way. So I don't know what I want. Maybe just this moment.'

'It can't be enough. It's never been enough, for either of us. I'm tired of the person I've been for the past however many years. Maybe it's time I stopped, just let myself love one person. Love you.'

Anthony gazed at him, and gave a sad smile. 'Ah, Leo, don't make promises you can't keep.'

'I wish you could learn to trust me. I think we could make this work. Make us work. The time, the way the world is, has never been better. No one would care, or judge.'

'I'd have to leave chambers.'

'That's absurd.'

'One of us would.'

'I don't see why.'

Anthony rolled away, closing his eyes, aware that the effects of the wine were ebbing. 'I need a drink.'

Leo got up and slipped on a robe. 'Come downstairs and I'll go down and pour us both a brandy.' He was sufficiently attuned to Anthony's confused and anxious state of mind to realise that an hour or more of tortured conversation lay ahead. 'There's another robe behind the bathroom door.'

In the kitchen Leo opened wide the folding doors to the garden. The heat of recent days, the spent end of summer, still lingered, and the night air was warm and soft, with the barest edge of chill. He poured a measure of brandy into two glasses. Anthony appeared in the spare robe, lean, young, and unselfconsciously beautiful, his hair tousled, his dark eyes smudged with fatigue, and Leo's heart turned over. Whatever it took, he had to make this work, to ensure it endured. He handed a glass to Anthony and switched on an outdoor light.

'We can sit on the terrace. It's just about warm enough.'

They talked, as Leo had anticipated, for well over an hour. A second glass of brandy was drunk. They explored every aspect of their feelings and the situation it had led them to, with Anthony anxious to examine every potential difficulty, seeking reassurances and exacting promises. In the end Leo grew more than a little exasperated.

'You seem to think that the only way this could go wrong is through me. What about you?'

'What about me?'

'For God's sake, you're twenty years younger than me. And look at you. How much resistance do you think you'll be able to put up the next time some beautiful girl decides she wants you? I know you. You're susceptible. The word could have been invented for you.'

'That's a bit harsh.' Anthony was finding something delicious about the argumentative turn the conversation had taken. He wanted the intimacy of this moment, the two of them together in the dark night air, both a little drunk, with the prospect of more lovemaking to come, to last and last. But he could tell Leo was tired. 'We just have to trust one another.'

'Yes. Fine. But you have to stop implying that I'm the only one who has to change their ways. You have a track record, too, you know.'

Anthony drained the remnants of his brandy. He stretched out a hand and folded Leo's fingers in his. 'OK. But I know how I feel. I can't ever imagine betraying you.'

Leo gripped Anthony's hand. *You can say that now*, he thought, *and mean it, but you have no idea how things will be in a year's time, ten years' time, a week's time, what temptations will come your way. I know, I've been there*. But all he said was, 'God, I'm exhausted. And cold.'

'Not too exhausted to want me, I hope.'

Leo yawned and laughed at the same time. 'Either way, let's go to bed.'

In the morning they had a full-blown argument.

'I thought about it half the night,' Anthony told Leo over coffee. They were both hungover, mildly fractious with one another. 'If we do this, I have to leave chambers. You can't, you've been there too long. It means a lot to you.'

'That's bloody silly. No one has to go anywhere. Why do you care so much about what people think?'

'We have to work with those people, with David and the others, and Henry and Felicity, and they—'

'What?'

'I won't be able to bear seeing it on their faces, whatever they're thinking. About us. Knowing about us.'

'Don't be so fucking middle class.'

'I can't just stop being what I am! I can't just stop caring about that kind of thing just because you tell me not to. The great Leo Davies, who doesn't care what people think of him. I'm not you.'

They argued for another ten minutes, heatedly, but Anthony stuck to his position, that if they were to try and make something of their relationship, he would leave 5 Caper Court.

In the end, Leo put his hands on Anthony's shoulders. 'Let's stop this. I hate arguing with you. Nothing needs to happen yet. Ostensibly, nothing has changed for either of us. If you come and live here, we can think about all of that kind of thing then. By which time you may have decided you don't care as much as you think you do, what other people think.'

'I won't change my mind. We have our practices to consider. People aren't as broad-minded as you imagine.'

'Fine. OK. Come on, I need to get to work.'

Leo sighed as he put the coffee cups in the dishwasher. The way the relationship was developing couldn't have made him happier, but it was promising to be an emotionally exhausting ride.

Natalie stepped out of the lift and headed to her room. Now that news of the fact she had secured a tenancy in another set of chambers every bit as prestigious as 5 Caper Court was about to be made public, she felt happier and more mentally robust. This place had never been right for her. Let it go on creaking at the seams. It was no longer her problem. As she tapped in her security code she heard someone say her name, and turned to see Sian in the corridor. It was the first time she'd seen her since she'd left. Natalie went into her room without a word, and Sian followed and closed the door.

'When did you start?' Natalie asked woodenly.

'On Monday. I thought I should say hello, see how you are.'

'I'm fine. I'm leaving next week, so we won't have the embarrassment of running into one another.'

'I hear it's a marvellous set of chambers you're going to. I'm glad things worked out.'

'That's an odd way of putting it.' There was a pause, then Natalie said impatiently, 'Anyway, I don't think there's much we have to say to one another. And I really have to get on.'

'Yes, of course.' Sian shrugged and smiled. 'Well, good luck. We had fun, didn't we?'

Natalie said nothing. When the door closed she sat down at her desk. It had been painful seeing Sian, but not as bad as she'd imagined it would be. Perhaps there were other new beginnings to be made. She took out her phone and scrolled to Abby's number.

In the corridor outside, Sian let out a deep breath. Good, that was done and dusted. Now there was another visit to be paid. She went downstairs to Leo's room, wondering how it would feel to see him again. France seemed a world away. The anger she had once felt about the fact he had taped her had melted eventually into amused cynicism. She almost admired what he'd done. She raised her hand, hesitated, then knocked. When she heard Leo's voice, she opened the door and went in.

Leo looked up, and when he saw who it was, he smiled. She smiled in return. It was strange. Meeting him again in this professional setting, she a lowly pupil and he the lofty head of chambers, seemed to strip away all the potent sexuality of their previous encounter. It was hard to believe it had happened.

'Ms Attwood, our new pupil. Good to see you. How are you settling in?'

'Very well, thanks. I thought I'd stop by and say hello.'

It was a dry, friendly exchange, with only the faintest undercurrent of knowingness.

'I'm glad you did.'

'I just want to say—' She hesitated, and Leo observed her thoughtfully, waiting. Surely she must realise that what had happened in France must stay in the past? 'I just want you to know that I'm grateful you didn't let my relationship with Natalie affect my place here.'

'We take people on talent, Sian. And you have' – there was a hint of mischief in his smile – 'quite remarkable talents.' He paused. 'Natalie is leaving us, as you may have heard.'

'Yes, well – we're not together any more, anyway.'

That, thought Leo, was hardly surprising. At that moment there was a light knock on the door, and Anthony looked in. 'Oh, sorry,' he said. 'You're busy. I can come back.'

'No, no,' said Leo. 'Come in. Sian just came to introduce herself. You two have already met, of course.'

'Yes,' said Anthony. 'Good to see you again. Welcome.' He and Sian shook hands.

'Right, well, I'll be off,' said Sian, who knew when to make her exit.

When the door had closed behind her Anthony said, 'I know you said there was no need to rescind her pupillage offer, but isn't it going to be a bit odd, with Natalie still here?'

'Natalie's leaving,' replied Leo. 'Found another tenancy. Hardly surprising, given her ability. Anyway, she and Sian have parted ways.'

'Let's hope things can go back to normal. Have Henry and Felicity heard?'

'Not yet. I'll let you be the bearer of that good news.'

Ten minutes later Anthony was informing Henry of Natalie's imminent departure from 5 Caper Court.

'Where's she off to?'

'Blackstone chambers.'

Henry nodded. 'She'll be better off there. Their way of doing things is more to her taste. She was never the right fit here. I'm not saying we're set in our ways, but' – he shrugged – 'Ms King had some good ideas, but she went about things the wrong way.' He tapped his keyboard and brought up some figures on the screen. 'Freshfields have paid up on that shipbuilding case, by the way.'

'About time. My bank account could do with an injection.'

As Anthony left the clerks' room, Henry glanced over to where Felicity and Dee were engaged in conversation with Stephanie about nail varnish.

'No, you really could work that colour,' Dee was saying. 'Teal's a lovely shade.'

'She's right,' said Felicity. 'You don't have to stick to reds and pinks. You could definitely get away with that.'

Stephanie frowned judiciously at her nails. The discussion continued.

Henry smiled. Since his confrontation with Natalie back in June, he had been working under a cloud of anxiety, but when Leo had hinted a couple of weeks ago that Natalie was on the move, the cloud had begun to lift. The impetus behind making radical organisational changes seemed to have evaporated, the talk about bringing in a chambers' director to oversee a shake-up in the clerks' room had begun to melt away, and Felicity had stopped having tearful discussions with him about moving elsewhere. The junior tenants had subsided, too, more interested in work and fees and their busy social lives than with the management of chambers. Now that it was confirmed she was actually going, he could feel complete relief. Peace and harmony would reign once more. He had an inkling that Leo might have had something to do with her departure, but he would rather not know the whys and wherefores. Mr Davies moved in mysterious ways, sometimes best not enquired about. It was enough that she was off. Ms King had been a good performer, bringing in the fees, always in demand, but money wasn't everything. For the first time in many months, Henry felt the chambers' vessel was again under his benign command, his to steer through whatever waters lay ahead, choppy or calm.

CHAPTER TWENTY-TWO

Since the evening at Giovanni's, and the beginning of their tentative commitment to one another, Leo and Anthony had spent only a couple of nights together. Leo knew from experience how corrosive too much intensity could be, and apart from anything else, he wanted Anthony to maintain the social balance in his life that any thirty-something should. He knew that Anthony, in his passionate way, would have preferred them to be together on a grander scale, but Leo felt that if this relationship was to endure, and become everything he wanted it to be, it had to be treated cautiously. There were certain other elements that threatened to destabilise things, and Anthony's question, as he looked round the door, was Leo's opportunity to deal with one of them.

'Any chance I might see you tonight?' asked Anthony.

'I'm having dinner with Gabrielle. She called and said she wants to talk to me.' There was a pause, in which

Leo tried to read Anthony's expression. 'Have you said anything to her?'

'Me? God, no.' Anthony came into the room, closing the door behind him. He sat down, rubbing his face thoughtfully. 'Do you think I should have?'

'The state of your relationship isn't mine to judge. But if you haven't told her, someone has to.'

'I'm sorry. That's going to be difficult.'

'Yes. She's probably still expecting you to get back together.'

Anthony nodded, then sighed. 'What a mess.'

'Don't worry. I'll deal with it.'

'Will you come by afterwards?'

Leo hesitated before replying. Anthony would want a full debrief of his conversation with Gabrielle, a minute dissection of what was said, and he had an interlocutory hearing tomorrow morning. He would rather go home and get a good night's sleep. But this was a crucial stage in their relationship, one in which Anthony would need as much reassurance as possible. 'Yes,' he said. 'I'll text you when I'm leaving the restaurant.'

Gabrielle had suggested a tapas bar in Borough Market, and when Leo arrived he found her in a queue outside, gazing at her phone.

'Hi. What are you doing out here? Didn't you book a table?'

She put her phone away. 'They don't take reservations. But it's a really good place. You'll like it.'

'I don't usually do queues. How long do we have to wait?'

'I don't know. Fifteen minutes?'

'Dear God.' He sighed, and neither of them said anything for a moment. Then Leo asked, 'How are you? Work OK?'

'Yes, it's fine. I'm very busy.'

'Good.' Another pause. 'So, you said you wanted to talk.'

She gave him a quizzical look. 'Leo, are you all right? You seem really tense.'

He suddenly realised that he had to tell her. Whatever it was she wanted to talk about, this was more important, and had to be said, now. 'Let's get out of this.' He took her hand, moving her out of the queue, and led her round the corner and into the first pub he could find.

'You've just wasted ten minutes of my queuing time!' she exclaimed.

He ignored this, sat her at a table, went to the bar, and returned with two gin and tonics. He handed her one, sat down and said, 'There's something you have to know.' He took a deep breath. 'Anthony and I, we're' – he hesitated, looking for words – 'we're together. It happened a couple of weeks ago, and—' He stopped. 'No, it happened years ago. It's been going on for years. Years. He just hadn't accepted it properly. What he felt, I mean. Until now.'

She stared at him miserably. 'You and he . . . ?'

He nodded.

'You bastard.' Her eyes grew hard and angry. 'You hated me being with him, didn't you?'

'No. Maybe I was jealous, a bit, but whatever he wanted, whatever and whoever made him happy, I was fine with.'

'You broke us up with your lies, and when we got back together, you couldn't stand it.'

'That isn't what happened.'

'You worked on him, you didn't want me to have him, and you took him.'

275

'I did nothing. He just told me one night.'

'One night. One night that you no doubt set up.'

'Gabrielle—' He put out a hand and gripped hers. 'No one can make another person love them. I can't do that, and neither can you. Things just happen. You and he had broken up. I would never have—'

She pulled her hand away. 'We hadn't! We were giving one another space. We just needed some time . . .' Her eyes were bright with angry tears. 'We talked about the future, did you know that? He wanted us to be together. We would have been fine.'

'No,' said Leo, 'you wouldn't have been. Believe me, it's better that this has happened now, rather than in two or three years. He and I have mattered to one another for a long time. It started long before either of us even knew you.'

She shook her head, gazing at him. 'I can't believe you're my father. I used to hope, when I was trying to get to meet you, to know you, that I might be like you. Now that idea frightens me.' She stood up. 'You know what? I hope he hurts you. I hope he does to you what you do to other people. I hope he lies to you, and screws you over, and leaves you.'

'Maybe he will,' replied Leo quietly. 'I have to take that chance.'

'And you know this means I really don't ever want to see you again? But I suppose that won't bother you. He must matter to you far more than I ever did.'

To this he said nothing. But as he watched her leave the pub he thought, yes, it was probably true.

* * *

276

A few days later Rachel rang. 'Can you help me out? I need you to have Oliver for a few days.'

'Of course. When?'

'The baby's two weeks overdue, and they want to induce me on Friday. I was hoping you could pick him up on Friday morning and have him for the weekend. He'll miss a day's school, but it can't be helped.'

Leo brought up his diary on the screen. It would mean shifting a couple of meetings around, but Felicity could sort it out. 'No problem. Is it safe? I mean, the inducing thing?'

'Routine. I'm actually glad they're doing it. The last couple of weeks have been a real drag.'

'Yes, I can imagine.' He remembered Oliver's birth, how he had moved from a state of emotionally detached confusion beforehand to an unexpected and inexpressible state of amazement and love when his baby son had been given to him to hold. It was good that Oliver would have a brother or sister. But it would be the start of a new phase in his relationship with his son, one in which he would see him less often, and perhaps become less important to him as years went by. That was what he feared most. 'I'll drive down and pick him up. I have no big cases coming up. Everything can be managed.'

What, he wondered, as the call ended, might life have been like if he hadn't had that fling with the nanny years ago? Might he and Rachel still be together, with perhaps more children? No, his infidelities would have ruined everything sooner or later. But maybe he would have been happier, on some deeper level. Might Anthony not have been better off, in the same way, with Gabrielle?

He told himself that things were as they were, and he had nothing to feel guilty about where Anthony was concerned, but he wasn't entirely convinced.

Leo drove to Tunbridge Wells on Friday morning.

'How is he?' he asked Rachel, when Oliver was safely in the car. 'With his new school, I mean?'

Rachel sighed and shrugged. 'Not so great. But it's early days. He'll settle in.'

'Let's hope so.' Leo opened the driver's door. 'Good luck for today. I hope all goes well.'

'Thanks.' She smiled, and Leo got into the car. The last he saw was her lifting a hand to wave as they pulled away.

On the drive back to London Leo probed Oliver gently about his new school, but Oliver's replies were terse and non-committal. After a spell of silence he said, 'Dad can we go to the new X-Men movie tonight?'

'I don't think so. Simon's going to ring at some point to tell you whether you've got a new baby brother or sister. You won't want to miss that.'

'Oh, yeah.' Oliver looked fairly indifferent.

'How do you feel about the new baby?' asked Leo. He had a vague idea that it was his responsibility, as much as Rachel's, to deal with any feelings of sibling rivalry.

'Dad, I'm not going to get all jealous, if that's what you're thinking.' He sighed, and glanced out of the car window. 'I just really, really want to see the X-Men film.'

'Tomorrow,' promised Leo.

Simon's call came a little after six. Leo could tell instantly from his tone that something was wrong. He was in the living room, watching television with Oliver, and he got up from the sofa and went to the kitchen and closed the door.

'It's very bad,' said Simon. His voice was broken, almost incoherent. 'Rachel – she died. She had some kind of embolism. Something to do with amniotic fluid getting into her bloodstream. She was in intensive care until just fifteen minutes ago—' His voice broke completely, and he couldn't speak.

'Simon . . .' Leo had no idea what to say. There was a hellish silence, then he said, 'The baby?'

'The baby's fine. She's going to be fine.'

They talked for another five minutes, Simon stumbling, distraught, Leo casting around for things to say, trying to make sense of the nightmare, and of what he would tell Oliver. When the call ended he stood for a moment, assembling his bleak thoughts. It didn't seem possible. She had everything to look forward to – the baby, her new house . . . Random recollections from a few years ago, when he had married her for the most cynical of reasons, yet had loved her nonetheless, in his way, came crowding into his mind. He pushed them aside. Later. He would think about that later. Right now, his priority was Oliver.

At that moment Oliver ambled into the kitchen. 'Can I have a biscuit?' Mechanically Leo reached into the cupboard and handed Oliver the tin of biscuits. 'Was that Simon?'

'Yes.' Leo did his best to look normal, even cheerful. 'You have a baby sister.'

'Oh, OK.' Oliver took a handful of chocolate fingers from the tin. 'I sort of hoped it would be a boy.'

* * *

279

Leo told Oliver the next day, after another phone call with Simon, about this mother. The miserable incomprehension on his son's face tore at his heart as few emotions ever had.

'She can't be dead,' said Oliver, 'because she has to look after the baby. Who's going to look after the baby?'

It was the strangest of questions, a childish blend of disbelief and denial. Leo had no answer. Oliver, seated next to him on the sofa, searched his father's face for reassurance. Then suddenly some element of understanding seemed to fall into place, and he began to cry.

'Come here,' said Leo, taking Oliver into his arms. He held him tight, as tight as he could, and let him weep.

The two weeks that followed were a mess of misery, of dislocation. Oliver remained with Leo while Simon dealt with all that he had to at his end, which included the funeral. Leo and Simon had numbly pragmatic conversations, in which eventually it was agreed that Oliver would go to live with his father on a full-time basis, and return to his old school.

'It's for the best, in some ways,' Simon said. 'He was pretty bloody outraged at having to change schools this autumn, leaving all his mates. At least that won't be happening now.'

Leo and Oliver drove to Tunbridge Wells to see Simon and the baby, now named Lily. Simon's mother had moved in to take temporary domestic charge.

'How are you coping?' asked Leo. He gazed down at the tiny infant in the Moses basket. Such hair as he could see beneath the little cap she wore was silky and black, like Rachel's. Oliver, having inspected his sister with grave interest, had gone to his room to sort out his belongings.

'It's been insane,' said Simon. 'I don't know what I'm doing. Thank God for my mother. But she has to go back at the weekend. I've got my parental leave, so . . . it's going to be just me and Lily from now on. I can do the feeds and the nappy changes, but looking ahead, it's like a fog. I know – I know Oliver has to be with you. It couldn't be any other way. But losing Rachel – and now him. It's going to be strange, just me and the baby.'

'Oliver and I will come as often as you like. You know, keep you sane. Help out. Crack a beer or two.'

'On that note' – Simon went to the fridge, took out two beers, opened them and handed one to Leo – 'thank you. I think it's important that Oliver and Lily see as much of each other as possible, don't you?'

'We can make that happen,' said Leo.

'I'm sorry I've neglected you,' said Leo. 'Us.'

Anthony had come to Leo's room. It was late on a Friday afternoon, the first time he'd seen him in two weeks, during which time they had communicated only by text and the occasional phone call. 'I've missed you. I really need to see you. I kept tonight free on purpose. We haven't been together in weeks.'

'I know. It's just – it's going to be tricky. I have Oliver now. He's just lost his mother. He and I have had a difficult time of it, lately.'

'You talk as though I never knew Rachel. She and I were close once, you know.'

281

'Yes. I remember. I'm sorry. It's hard for everyone.' He paused. 'The thing is, it's made a dramatic change in my life. Nothing is as easy as it was.'

'So, what – we're on hold?'

'I don't know. Anthony, I haven't a clue. I miss you just as much. But certain things just aren't possible at the moment.'

Anthony left without a word. As he did so he heard Leo call his name, but he closed the door behind him and went back to his room. There was no place for him at the centre of Leo's life. Well, wasn't that the way it had always been? There was always someone, or something to displace him. It was probably the way Leo preferred it. That night at Giovanni's a month ago, when Leo had made him feel desired and loved, it had probably suited him then to take him to bed, enjoy him for a week or two, then back off when he wanted to, as he was doing now. He'd had no intention of it lasting. No wonder he'd been so set against him leaving chambers. It would have been a serious step, paving the way to a lasting commitment between them. The pattern that had started ten years ago was repeating itself. He would be loved, used, tormented, loved again, in an endless cycle that would destroy his own happiness. But he was helpless in the face of his feelings. Angry, frustrated, he saw Leo for everything that he was, but he was utterly under his spell. The best he could do was to show Leo that pain worked both ways. Because he knew in his heart that he, Leo, loved him, too. His game, his rules. Fine.

It was past six, so he gathered his things together and left his room. On the way downstairs he met Sian, coming up. He hadn't seen her since the day he'd met her in Leo's room.

'Hi,' he said. 'How's it going?'

'Fine, thanks. I'm working for David Liphook at the moment.'

'Right. Well, he's a lovely guy.'

'He is. But being in chambers is a big change, after academic life. Quite a steep learning curve. There are still so many things I'm trying to get my head around.' She gave another smile. He was quite extraordinarily good-looking. She remembered during the interview how she'd had to force herself not to glance at him too often. Such a sweet, serious face, but not, she liked to think, as innocent as he looked. 'Maybe we could go for a drink and I could pick your brains? It'd be nice to get to know some of the younger people in chambers.' She caught his hesitation. 'Though I imagine you're incredibly busy, so perhaps it's not—'

'No. Let's do that. We could go now, if you like.' It would be a way of filling the evening he had left blank in the hope of seeing Leo, if nothing else.

'Great. I just have to get my things.'

'I'll wait for you downstairs.'

After Anthony had gone, Leo sat reflecting. Emotional volatility was the last thing he needed in his life right now. He had enough to contend with. Anthony had every right to feel as he did, but it was impossible, with things as they were, to find time to be together. He had Oliver now, twenty-four hours a day, and even though he had set up an arrangement with the mother of Oliver's friend, Rory, whereby she picked them both up from school every day and kept him until seven, the logistics of maintaining his practice and looking after a twelve-year-old were already becoming difficult. Trying to factor Anthony into it all was too complicated.

He paused his thoughts. *Detachment, Davies. Consider this the way you would any legal problem.* This was a critical juncture. If he didn't find a solution, he would lose one of the most important people in his life for good. *I want too much*, he thought. *I want Anthony, and want my son.* But were the two necessarily incompatible? Would it be so unthinkable for the three of them to live together? He reflected wryly that it would probably be harder for Anthony than for Oliver, living with a prepubescent teenager. But they knew one another pretty well, and the more he thought about it, the better the idea seemed. Life would be richer for all of them. What was so novel these days about a child living with his father and his partner? It would have to be taken slowly, of course. Oliver was in a precarious emotional state, and didn't need more trauma. But in the long run, it would work. In that moment, he made his decision. If Anthony was prepared to do it, then it would happen. He'd never cared what other people thought about the way he lived his life, and he wasn't about to start now.

The buzz of his phone startled him from his thoughts. It was Rory's mother, suggesting that as the boys were playing so happily together, maybe Oliver could sleep over.

Providence, thought Leo, as the call ended. He would give Anthony a couple of hours to calm down, and then he would go over. They would have the evening and the night together. They could talk and plan. For the first time in a long time, Leo felt he was making sense of his life.

Anthony and Sian were sharing a tiny table in a wine bar. The noise on a Friday night meant they had to sit close to talk. They'd made the most of happy hour, and after three cocktails Anthony realised Sian was flirting in a way that suggested she wanted more than just to pick his brains. And why not? he thought. The alcohol was doing more than drowning his unhappiness over Leo. It made him alive to what Sian was doing. He was enjoying being close to her, the way she dipped her head when she laughed, her dark, silky hair brushing her cheek, the way she touched his arm lightly now and again. He couldn't get out of his head the thought that she had been Natalie's lover. So what was she doing here, coming on to him like this? But look at him and Leo. In a messed-up way, maybe he and Sian deserved one another this evening. He felt drunk and a little reckless. Leo needed to understand that there was a price to pay for marginalising him.

'Why don't we go somewhere else?' said Sian. 'It's getting noisy in here. Mine, perhaps?' She suddenly leant forward and kissed him. Her mouth was soft, sweet from the cocktails, and it was impossible not to return the kiss, not to indulge himself in the sheer pleasure and sensuality of it. It lasted only a few seconds. But in those seconds Anthony found he could think only of Leo, filled with longing for him, and the realisation that he was treating the person he loved with utter selfishness, making petulant demands, ignoring all the problems he was facing. He had even been thinking of punishing him by sleeping with this girl, just because he could.

'What do you say?' murmured Sian.

Anthony drained his drink and picked up his jacket. He gave her a smile. 'Thanks, but I think I'm going home.'

CARO FRASER is the daughter of George MacDonald Fraser, author of the Flashman novels. She attended art school and worked as an advertising copywriter before deciding to pursue a career in law. Fraser began to write full-time while bringing up the third of her four children, and published her first novel, *The Pupil*, in 1993. Since then she has written several novels, including the critically acclaimed Caper Court series.

caro-fraser.co.uk   *@carofraser*